'Chris Mc...   ...ig-
gest of mysteries   ...nd
claustrophobic in all the right p...   ...gg

'An ingenious twisty mystery in a totally unique setting'
Claire McGowan

'Phenomenal. An utterly compelling and fiendishly
clever read – it blew my mind ten times over'
Fran Dorricott

'Boils with claustrophobic intensity. Packed with grip-
ping twists and turns . . . an inventive, entertaining
locked-room mystery that kept me utterly hooked'
Adam Hamdy

'An impressive debut and a sign of great things to come'
James Oswald

'*Guess Who* is a fresh take on the locked-room murder
mystery. The plotting is intricate, the characters well
drawn, and the pace never lets up as it drives headlong
to the surprising end'   **David C. Taylor**

'One hotel room. Six strangers. One corpse. Good fun'
Cavan Scott

Praise for Chris McGeorge

Chris McGeorge studied MA Creative Writing (Crime/Thriller) at City University London, where he wrote his first novel as his thesis. His interests are broad – spanning film, books, theatre and video games. He is a member of the Northern Crime Syndicate, a supergroup of writers from Northern England. He lives in County Durham with his partner and many, many animals.

Chris can be found on Twitter at: @crmcgeorge

Also by Chris McGeorge

Guess Who
Now You See Me
Inside Out
Half-Past Tomorrow

A Murder at the Castle

CHRIS McGEORGE

ORION

An Orion paperback
First published in Great Britain in 2022 by Orion Fiction
an imprint of The Orion Publishing Group Ltd
Carmelite House, 50 Victoria Embankment
London EC4Y 0DZ

An Hachette UK Company

1 3 5 7 9 10 8 6 4 2

Copyright © Chris McGeorge 2022

A CIP catalogue record for this book is
available from the British Library.

ISBN (Mass Market Paperback) 978 1 3987 0783 2
ISBN (eBook) 978 1 3987 0784 9

Printed   p.A.

for my grandfather

Table of Contents

A Note on Lineage

In 1936, King Edward VIII brought to the establishment his intentions to marry a young American divorcee. This request would be rejected, and this rejection would lead to Edward VIII's abdication of the throne. But what if this never happened? What if Edward allowed the establishment to find him a wife that suited their purposes? While this present Royal Family carry the name Windsor and occupy the same residences, they are born of this divergent timeline.

A List of Those Present at the Castle on the Fateful 25 December

H.R.H. King Eric Windsor

Eighty-five. Eric has been a popular king among his subjects, bringing a youthful vigour and whimsical cadence to the role. Eric has been a king for almost as long as he remembers, having inherited the title when he was ten and rising to the throne (as custom dictates) on his eighteenth birthday. Rather partial to a fiendish puzzle, as 'one must strive to occupy the mind even when kingliness offers no such relief'. Loves Christmas.

Princess Royal Marjorie Windsor-Nueberner

Seventy-two. A strong and powerful force of nature in her youth, Marjorie has tried to cling to that power in her waning years with mixed success. She has become jaded, cold and calculating, leaving many to wonder if time has not merely shown what was always there. She should be referred to as queen but the title was never bestowed upon her – just the tip of the proverbial iceberg of her venom.

Princess Emeline Windsor

Thirty-nine. First-born daughter of Eric Windsor and Marjorie Windsor-Neuberner. Born ten minutes before her twin sister, Emeline has always enjoyed a quiet superiority over her command of the line of succession. Emeline is currently courting a man by the name of Anton Blake, and the fact he is not present at the castle is a matter of contention.

Princess Maud Windsor

Thirty-nine. Second-born daughter of Eric Windsor and Marjorie Windsor-Neuberner. Born ten minutes after her twin sister, Maud is quite happy with her place in the royal line. She is the nation's sweetheart, a title that is often more coveted than anything official, even if it is sometimes a more dangerous title.

Prince David Windsor

Seventy-three. The king's younger brother, David has always skulked about in his brother's shadow. No stranger to scandal, David's bizarre and occasionally abhorrent behaviour can be attributed to many different stimuli. David has just been allowed to return from a ten-year exile while the allegations against him were quelled.

Thomas Crockley

Forty-five. Husband to Princess Maud Windsor and father to their two children, Thomas Crockley is a self-confessed 'rags to riches' story. Starting from a fish market in Wolverhampton, he has created an admittedly impressive life for himself and has never lost his working-class cadence. Crockley has just launched an Uber-like service aimed at the upper classes. Moves in many circles (some of which are even slightly important).

Prince Matthew Windsor

Eighteen. First-born son of Princess Maud Windsor and Thomas Crockley. Prince Matthew is now a man and has not quite come to terms with what that means as of yet. He follows his grandfather's example as much as possible, trying to forge a true and honest path in the world. Of course, he is also incredibly young, and often feels a regret at a childhood missed. Matthew is King Eric's favourite family member and everyone is aware of that fact, not least Matthew himself.

Prince Martin Windsor

Thirteen. Second-born son of Princess Maud Windsor and Thomas Crockley, and currently the youngest member of the Royal Family, Prince Martin is at an age where he is considering the validity of the world and whether he would desire to engage with it. Unfortunately, he is finding that the Windsor name carries all manner of caveats. Advanced for his age in some aspects and painfully behind in others, Prince Martin is a perfect example of growing up in the royal household.

Tony Speck

Forty. The only security detail on site, despite his

arguments, Tony Speck has the safety of the Crown solely on his shoulders. However, Speck is the kind of man who thinks it is always down to him and him alone. An ex-SAS operative, Speck meets the world with respect, and expects nothing less in return.

Miss Darcy Tharigold

Twenty-two. The king's private secretary, Miss Darcy is the youngest ever person who has assumed the role. A deeply loyal patriot, Miss Darcy takes her career with the utmost seriousness. Critics (and whispers in the dark corners of the establishment) have been quick to point out that her position may have not been obtained from her ability and more her family name. Her father is an important figure in the government, and Miss Darcy herself is constantly running from that criticism.

Jonathan Alleyne

Fifty-five. Private chef to the Royal Family. Of Barbadian descent. Jonathan Alleyne has often found it hard to pinpoint his destiny. When he joined the establishment, his life started to make a certain kind of sense. He harbours a deep love for the Royal Family, but specifically King Eric, who he considers a friend (and this is echoed). His cuisine is Caribbean-focused, although a distinct Britishness has crept in (for obvious reasons).

(It is important to note that all other staff have been sent away to spend Christmas with their families, as per the king's request. The notice proclaimed that they were to

enjoy a 'normal' Christmas – a desire of the king himself. It is unfortunate that a 'normal' Christmas will not be achieved.)

Prologue

King Eric used to tell us a fable about a common family who went to see the lions at London Zoo. It was a narrative of his own creation and he was always very proud to share it. He shared it often. It was a fable crafted to inspire, to encourage deep thought, to allude and tantalise a hidden deeper well of meaning, as many fables were. We came to fear the fable whenever it was regaled, but not for any reason that King Eric intended. The fable was chiselled into all of us, as commandments into stone, but still it would come to assault our ears and prod at our hearts. Every time, the king's delivery would become grander – a simple recounting becoming an unfurling parchment, turning into costumes to be worn, transforming into a show, of which we increasingly had to be a part. He meant it to inspire, but the truth was that whenever it revealed itself, we just desired it to be over – any 'deeper well of meaning' circumvented, any emotions ignored, any inspiration usurped by boredom and apathy.

However, we let the king tell it.

He did like it so.

The fable was thus – a common family one day decided to go to London Zoo, with a particular desire to see the lions residing there. They woke up early. They rode the train into the city — all morning it took them. When they finally arrived at the great gates of the zoo, they rushed to the lion exhibit, along with all the other patrons, to find a great enclosure encased in a thick layer of protective glass. Inside, the lions were woken from their slumber and paraded out in front of the expectant crowd. The children of this hypothetical family squealed with glee at seeing these great beasts. The crowd of people clapped and cheered as these majestic creatures feasted upon whatever was on the menu that day.

There the narrative would end, revealing itself to be not much of a narrative at all. We were not masters of the craft ourselves, but we knew that there should have been some kind of denouement, some kind of rise and fall and rise again until the inevitable full stop. But no, for this was a fable, and once it was done, Eric would ask a question: Which is the most important part of the story?

Some of us would say the lions, seeing as they were the entities inspiring joy and offering some respite from the family's oh-so-dull life. Some of us would say the family, as they were making the world go round, and really, if the lions had any sense, they would understand that they were merely passengers in this existence and they should delight in offering others enjoyment. Some of us would try to be smart, seeing other options — the zoo workers, for instance, who prodded the lions from sleep so the family could view them? Or, more further afield, the explorers who brought the lions to London in the first place? How about the manufacturers of the train that carried the family to London to enjoy such a spectacle? But no matter how hard we tried, *not even one of us got the right answer. King Eric would shake his head time and time again, resolving to tell the fable once more another day.*

The story has not been told today – his favourite day of the year. Christmas Day. We are all in the drawing room, after our dinner, and the time for the tale may have passed, but Eric will still find a way to fill our ears with his words. His famous post-dinner speech is looming – but this speech brings promise. A promise of change.

The king will say a name.

Just one.

I wonder what happens if my name leaves his lips. Although I know it won't. A life of even more restriction, but a life as a god. Yes, I would be a monarch – the most important person in the country. But to be royal is to be seen. We are the lions, after all. Maybe one cannot know the answer to King Eric's fable until it is too late.

Eric takes a long drink of whisky. He starts talking. 'It is an honour to be able to spend time with this family of mine on . . .' But his voice starts to crack, his face starts to go an odd shade of puce, and his hands go to his throat – the glass of whisky bouncing off the lush shag. Eric collapses violently over the table in front of him as we freeze in confusion, wondering if this is part of the speech.

The chef rushes over in a breathy panic to confirm what we all, deep down, already know.

King Eric is dead.

Hardly surprising considering I poisoned the whisky.

Now I just have to get away with it.

Ten Hours Earlier . . .

I

A Modest Breakfast

Whenever one desires the attention of those beyond a door, one cannot go wrong with three sharp knocks. No more, no less. Two knocks possess the possibility of being misconstrued, while four knocks seem needlessly excessive. This was the mantra of Jonathan Alleyne, the king's private chef, and it did not change even at five o'clock in the morning in the echoey halls of Balmoral Castle.

Balmoral Castle, an illustrious fortress of a country residence standing in the remote Highlands of Scotland, came into the possession of the monarchy when it was purchased by Prince Albert for Queen Victoria in the mid-eighteenth century. Queen Victoria loved cold, wet weather and Balmoral stood as maybe the coldest and wettest locale on the British Isles. Conditions were positively dreary at most times of the year, with whipping winds and constant rain. Locals would refer to the rain as 'rude' whenever it came, so ferocious that it would often feel as though it were piercing them through. It hardly seemed like a place for a royal, but Victoria and Albert were happy with their purchase. When the original castle was deemed too small, it was entirely rebuilt to their specifications – further proving they bought mostly for the location.

Balmoral now stood as the summer home of the current monarch, King Eric, and his family – summer being the only time of year where the sun would grace the land with its presence. However, if one were to look outside the castle windows at that moment, one might have been forgiven for thinking the concept of summer was a figment of some collective imagination. A tremendous blizzard was laying waste to the greater part of the United Kingdom, surprising meteorologists somewhat and grinding the gears of a semi-functional society to a halt. The castle, much like the country, was under siege, and Jon could hear the wind whistling around them, threatening to break in and bring the snow with it. It would never happen – Balmoral had stood against worse and would once again. The weather was often ferocious. The River Dee, which ran through the grounds, regularly burst its banks, and the castle had faced hurricanes, world wars and the destructive passage of time. Balmoral was still standing, and it was hard to imagine a world where one day it would not be.

The blizzard had started almost exactly one hour after everyone had left. The mass exodus of staff from Balmoral was truly something to behold, as if most all the workers of the castle had seen what was to come and fled. Jon's army of chefs, having stayed until the bitter end helping him prepare, had filed out of the kitchens, trying to mask the apprehension that their commander may not be able to complete his mammoth task alone. Jon

8

could not blame them – he hardly believed it possible himself.

These doubts now resided in the bags under Jon's eyes, and in his shortness of breath, and on the slick layer of cold sweat resting upon his skin, like dew on a morning lawn. As it always seemed to on important nights, sleep had eluded him. He had tossed and turned, involuntarily reciting the list of completed chores in his mind, plagued by some phantom worry that he had forgotten something terribly important. Finally, he had found a pocket of that desired thing one usually found in scenarios such as this – something akin to rest, but never akin enough. It did not last long. He was up before his alarm had roused him, instead prodding it awake. The day had begun. Time always had a pesky habit of raging on.

Jonathan Alleyne was far too well acquainted with the pitfalls and follies of time, stuck in the chasm of feeling both that he had lived too long and not long enough. He was a wistful man of fifty-five years, of which thirty-three had been spent in the service of the Crown. As the king's private chef, he regularly followed the Royal Family among their various residences, doting upon them with whatever they desired. His food had been served to prime ministers, presidents, delegates and dignitaries – and some even complimented him on it. He walked in the corridors of power, lining the stomachs of the powerful. How he loved his job – to be an important cog in this goliath of a machine.

To prepare the king on Christmas morning was a

single piece of lightly toasted wheat bread, with a layer of low-fat butter and lavish coating of raspberry jam. To accompany this was a coffee – two teaspoons of premium instant Kenco (upon strict request – 'instant coffee is often more potent, in my opinion – as if it has something to prove') and a dash of semi-skimmed milk. Jon had carried this, under a small cloche, all the way from the kitchens to the most important of the fifty-two bedrooms.

It was a journey he knew so well, he could do it blindfolded. His years of service had carved maps, calendars, menus, birth charts and all manner of other things into his brain – all to do with a family that wasn't his and would never be. Sometimes, on cold nights, Jon wondered what he would do when it was all over, when he was relieved of his duty and told to go home for the final time. The vast amounts of information he had amassed declared redundant, he would step out onto the cold, cobbled street, free to do as he wished, only to realise that his own life had passed him by. It had been forfeited so that he might be a mere footnote in somebody else's.

Would it be worth it? Many times, the answer was yes – about nine times out of ten. It was unfortunate that the world seemed to reside in the tenth. Jon had a secret. Not a nice one – like the knowledge of where the Christmas presents were hidden or that Santa Claus was indeed real – but a dark personal secret that burned his heart merely to think about and manifested a throbbing pain in his gut. Then again, maybe the pain was not just the withholding.

Before Jon had time to think on his burden, the strong call of 'Enter,' came from inside. Three knocks had done the trick. Jon did as commanded.

The fire was roaring in the large bedroom and the four-poster bed was empty, the bed made perfectly as though the maids were still present. Churchill, one of the king's calico cats, was lying on one of the plump pillows, purring away to no one. King Eric was sitting at his desk, matching a pile of Christmas cards with their corresponding scarlet paper sheaves. At intervals, he peered up through the window into the blizzard, smiled and continued his work. Upon seeing Jon, he rose – as if the chef were the royalty and vice versa. 'Jon. Happy Christmas.'

'Happy Christmas, Your Majesty. I have brought you your breakfast.'

Jon was not surprised that the king had already woken and started his Christmas morning. Standing in front of Jon, the king still cut an imposing figure, even at eighty-five years of age and dressed in a slightly unfortunate fuzzy purple dressing gown. He was a man with the weight of the country on his shoulders, and they were shoulders that could bear the burden. However, especially of late, it was impossible not to notice that the years were starting to take their toll. Jon could look at the old man and see the Eric Windsor of old – full of a (dare he say) cheeky energy and a righteous indignation that somehow coupled perfectly with a desire to uphold the foundations of the monarchy. He was still that man now behind it all – it was the body that was betraying

11

him. Eric Windsor was crumbling, decaying, unable to portray any of the qualities that made him him. The saddest part was that the man saw it himself. The good king was a picture of how time always won in the end, even against a god. If the king had to bend the knee to Time, what chance did Jon have?

Jon went to the table in front of the fire and put down his tray, knowing that the king would not get to his toast for some time yet. He knew that it would be stone cold by this point anyway, but also knew that anyone who partook in toast had to always accept this as a possibility. Jon gave the king his coffee, coming to stand at his side with a brief detour to scratch Churchill behind the ears.

Jon gazed out of the window with his king. The window presented a positively glowing scene. The grounds were under a deep layer of snow, with more whipping down on the ferocious wind. The sky was filled with clouds, promising no respite in the immediate future.

The king took a sip of coffee, raising it to his lips with a shaky hand. It had gotten worse. When he was done, Jon took the coffee again and placed it on the desk. It was an entirely wordless interaction, but one the king appreciated.

'I daresay you've come just in time to see the end of the show.'

The king nodded downwards, and Jon traced his gaze. Far below them, through the icy fug, Jon spied the slightly obscured lights of a vehicle slowly moving away from the castle. It wasn't long before the lights ceased their journey, and a small figure came into view carrying a snow shovel. Jon could not see who it was through the falling snow, but he didn't have to. 'Miss Darcy is still here?'

'She stayed for as long as she could. And then she gave me my big red box and went on her way.' The king nodded to the despatch box on the table next to the cloche. Jon had failed to note it.

'But it's Christmas Day.' The king was only allowed two days off a year – one being Easter Sunday and the other being Christmas Day. The box contained missives from the government to the monarch – dealings and events that the government thought he should know about.

'Merely an excuse to come back to the 'Moral. She's paying for her choice now, though.' A fresh bout of wind buffeted the window as if even the elements answered to him. Below, the king's private secretary, Miss Darcy Tharigold, dug out her wheels, only for the snow to whip back into the holes. 'Dear God, please let her get away. I really would not fancy having to feed another at the table. I do not desire to know what Miss Darcy considers party chit-chat.'

'I can go and help her, if you like, sir,' said Jon, although he really couldn't. He had to get back to the kitchen as quickly as he could and resume his 135-point list for the dinner.

Thankfully, the king laughed. 'And spoil my fun? No, friend, thank you. But you could answer me one question – do you think they have really obeyed the orders?'

Jon thought about this. The decree had come to them

sometime in early December – 'The king wants a family Christmas'. They did not know exactly what that meant until it was revealed that everyone was to leave the castle by the twenty-fifth. Jon had his own thoughts on whether that was likely. He did not think himself a man of high intellect (far from it), but he knew how to talk to the king. 'I believe they will obey your orders to the letter, sir. And within those letters, they will somehow find a way to do as they wish.'

The king seemed to understand but still said, 'Elaborate, please, old friend.'

Jon's eyes drifted downwards. Darcy Tharigold was back in her car, and she may have even made some progress since last viewing. But where was she going? Home for Christmas – he hardly thought so. 'This is just a theory but I believe that, at some distance, there are two dozen or so members of the Security Service funnelled into a Scottish hotel, awaiting any signal from Tony Speck that they are needed, and then they will come running.'

The king combined a smile with a sigh in an odd display of resigned dismay. It was one of his specialties. 'Yes. I rather thought the same. Blast, why can't they just go and enjoy their holidays for once? Balmoral used to be our little slice of freedom. But now it's exactly the opposite – it's the very sign we are not free. Even the wild hills of Scotland contain us. The new fences across our property lines, the security, the signs of the times. The wilds where even my private secretary will just pop up for a visit. Queen Victoria would perish all over again for the injustice of it all. Even the weather has turned against us.'

Jon did not know what to say. He had spent a lot of time at the king's side. The two of them had struck up an unlikely friendship throughout the years, ever since Jon had walked in on the king having trouble with a crossword clue, one which Jon had the answer to. After that, the king had made a point to keep the crossword for when Jon was present. They spent more time together than one would think for a king and his chef, and it was because of this that Jon could see that the old man was genuinely troubled by his soliloquy. The vines of royalty had gripped him for his entire life, but never – it seemed – more tightly than now.

The moment passed, the dark cloud banished, and the king became cheery again. 'Ah, before I forget.' He almost skipped around Jon to his desk and plucked the card from the top of the pile.

'Sir? I'm afraid I didn't get you one,' Jon said, taking it.

'Pish posh, you're making us a grand dinner all by your own hand. I daresay I can forgive you a card.'

'Then thank you very much, sir. I must get back to this dinner then, and make it as grand as can be.'

'And I must get back to this ongoing Miss Darcy situation. I wonder when she is going to retrieve the horses to pull her car like a sleigh. You are dismissed.'

They separated there – the king going back to his joyous voyeurism and Jon heading for the door, believing the exchange to be done. Before Jon could open the door, however, the king said, 'Thank you for being here with me. It's a big day, old friend.'

Jon nodded. 'It's my honour, sir,' before leaving the king to his observation.

For the rest of his life, Jonathan Alleyne would forever come back to that last thing the king said to him in the early morn of Christmas Day.

It's a big day, old friend.

A common enough sentiment, especially when factored with the decorum of the occasion. But when applied retrospectively, Jon had to wonder – did the king somehow know what was about to happen?

And if so – why did he not find some way to run as far and as fast as he could?

II

An Immodest Dinner

Jonathan Alleyne had never felt at home anywhere in his life until he found himself in the kitchens of the king.

Born in 1967, of a Bajan mother and a British father he never knew, in a minute box room in an attic in Soho, he regularly found himself torn between two worlds – the bright sunny beaches of Barbados and the grey rainy streets of London. He spent most of his youth in the former, for, when it was clear his father was never planning on making another appearance, his mother whisked him off across the sea to live with her extended family.

Jon was quite happy in Barbados for the early years of his life, having never known anything different. He started to see less of his mother as she lost interest in her child in order to explore the other thing that his father had burdened her with – a dependence on illicit substances. Sometimes, she would disappear for weeks at a time.

The Alleynes were not a wealthy family. The Alleyne house was small, cramped and packed with four generations, so, often, her absence went unnoticed to the wider family. Jon was frequently overwhelmed by how many bodies were in the house, and the number seemed to constantly change. At one time, he counted three aunts, three uncles, six cousins, one niece, four grandparents and one ancient great-grandfather, but all that mattered to him was that there was no mother.

Jon's grandmother, his mother's mother, saw his pain and most likely linked it with some of her own. She took him under her wing and raised him almost as if he were her own. She kept him with her as she pottered around the kitchen making sure everyone was fed. Cooking was taught to him vicariously, while she actively taught him the ways of the world, his need for manners, how to conduct himself. She was good to him in a way he'd never known.

Jon shared a bedroom with his grandma, but when he was old enough, he had to move into a room with the six cousins and only three bunk beds. They made him sleep on the floor. He was different to them – he knew it, they knew it, it was plain to see. As children always did, they seized upon that, weaponised it. They used to break into a chant whenever Jon entered the room – 'Is he white? Is he black? Dunno where he came from but send him back!' Jon's light skin would always mean he did not fit in in the Alleyne house.

It was not until his mother's funeral in 1983 when he really felt his tremendous displacement. He did not cry as his mother was lowered into the ground, surrounded by a town full of mourners who seemed far more interested in her now she was dead than when she was alive. After it was done, he sat on the church steps with Grandma and he told her that he had to leave.

Grandma did not stop him – she spent a month's income from her cleaning business to buy him a plane ticket to England and give him enough to get settled. She was the only one who went to the airport to see him off. 'You do this for you, dear child. You go out there, and you find what you're looking for. Because the Lord isn't going to bring it to you. And your momma isn't either. It weren't the drugs that killed her, Little Jon. It was the fact she didn't know what she was doing here. So you go. See the world. And, more important than that, you let the world see you.'

Jon, only sixteen years old, did cry while watching Grandma disappear as his plane rolled onto the runway. He found his tears then, because he understood somehow that he would never be back and that he would never see her again and she had known this all along. He reached into his pocket for a handkerchief and instead out fell a folded piece of paper. He unfolded it. It was full of Grandma's swirly scrawl, indecipherable to the untrained eye. But Jon understood – it was her recipe for flying fish, her most prized possession. And that gave Little Jon a place to start.

Jon's early days in London were defined by exhaustion, loneliness and a dwindling motivation. He was able to use Grandma's money to rent a small room in Islington, but not to furnish it. He slept on the floor for a year, spending his days trying to get a job at any restaurant that would take him. He got lucky a few months in as a new establishment was opening up in the West End.

Caribbean Plaza was purportedly a high-end Caribbean fusion restaurant, just around the corner from the

Lyceum Theatre and poised to take full advantage of the theatrical crowd. Jon was taken on as a dogsbody – chopping vegetables and washing dishes. He was just happy to earn a wage.

As the years went by, Jon had the chance to step up into a junior chef role and become part of the team in the kitchen. He was content with how his life was going, finally finding somewhere he thought he could belong – until one night changed his life.

On an unassuming Wednesday in 1989, the restaurant was to be closed to the public for a very exclusive party of guests. The head chef and part owner, Jason Heartland, would not tell any of his team of the guests this party consisted of, just that they had to give their all for the service and this was one of the biggest nights for the restaurant in its history.

Jon saw this as a chance to prove himself even further. He was assigned a dish, the duck, and he would be expected to deliver the highest quality all night. As service began, the duck was in high demand, until the worst happened. They ran out just as another order came in. Heartland swore loudly as he saw the number of the table that had just ordered, but his eyes lit up as he told Jon that he would have to go out and personally apologise to the table. Jon knew what that meant – he was being used as the scapegoat, even though he was not in charge of stock.

Jon tentatively stepped out into the dining room to a sea of black-suited white men. The sight made him pause at its oddity. The man, the woman and the two daughters

20

of his destination table seemed to be the only average, if slightly overdressed, diners. As he approached the table, he started to have the strangest feeling that he knew the young family. He had seen them somewhere before – maybe on the street, or on television, or in the newspaper.

It didn't really matter who they were, though. What mattered was he could not serve them what they had ordered. It turned out that one of the daughters, both looking to be about six or seven, had ordered the duck. Jon apologised profusely as he said that they could order from the menu again or he could make her something personally. The glamorous woman tutted into her wine, but the man was amicable. He said that he would much prefer something personalised too.

Back in the kitchen, Jon kept his head down and talked to no one, even when asked what was happening. If this were a fable, Jon may have made the man and his daughter Grandma's flying fish recipe, but, alas, it was not. He rustled up a simple goat pelau, adding flourishes to elevate it to restaurant standard, and took it out to the table. The man thanked him and that was that.

Heartland pulled Jon into his office after service when everyone else had left and started to berate him. Jon had many rebuttals – he was not in charge of ordering produce and if that was the most important table, then why were ingredients not held back for the order? – but he knew where this was going. He was getting sacked.

Until there was a knock at the office door. The man from the table appeared from nowhere and Heartland

21

became very flustered. The man apologised and let him continue, so Heartland did. Jon found himself without a job, in two simple words.

The man at the door frowned and turned his attention to Jon. To his (and to Heartland's) surprise, the man offered him a job. Jon accepted, even before he realised the man was the King of England.

So, no, Jon Alleyne had never truly had a home. But the kitchens of the various castles he attended as the king's chef were the closest he had ever come. These were now the places that inspired homesickness if away from them for too long. This was where his team, not unlike a family, resided.

But today, Christmas Day, it was just himself, in a room that was built to function with twenty, thirty people, all working in tandem. Jon was meant to be a link in the chain, and now he was the whole chain itself. Self-pitying did not cook a meal, though. So he began, quickly organising himself at one singular station. His mission was a simple one – provide a Christmas dinner of the highest quality that felt as though it were prepared by the usual number of staff.

His chefs had done what they could. Late last night, this kitchen was filled with personnel, carving carrots, parboiling potatoes, unsheathing sprouts and boiling beef skin and bones for the gravy, among other activities – all working in tandem. It was the standard nightly ritual before a big event, but this time was slightly different. The actual work the next day would have to be undertaken by a sole chef.

Him.

It had seemed insurmountable at the time – now faced directly with it, it was even worse. He took a deep breath and put on his white double-breasted jacket (pristine white now, but for how long?) as he got back to the kitchen – his mind swimming with tasks that needed to be done. Almost absent-mindedly, he slipped the Christmas card from the king in the small gap above one of the waist high fridges and under a preparation table. He didn't even have time to open it.

He got to work. The turkey needed prepping, stuffing and seasoning. The slow-roast duck needed a reduced temperature in twenty minutes as it had been in since he'd risen. The gammon was ready to go in, but that had to be timed right. The potatoes were the key – Jon's speciality – and would have to be carefully monitored. The vegetables needed checking. The bread sauce needed finishing. The starter – a British Christmas soup of Jon's own concoction – and one of the desserts – a traditional trifle – needed to be conjured up in their entirety as all but the Christmas pudding needed to be fresh. Those were just the major jobs. So Jon began.

There were to be eight members of the Royal Family present at the Christmas banquet: King Eric and Princess Marjorie were joined by their twin daughters, Princesses Emeline and Maud. The latter was joined by her partner, Thomas Crockley, and their two children, Princes Matthew and Martin. Princess Emeline was courting, but her partner, Anton Blake, had not been invited to the castle, which was likely to come up at some point. Rounding out the party was Prince David, the king's younger (although, at a certain age, that distinction seemed moot) brother, whose presence was likely to be the looming shadow over the day. It was not Jon's place to speculate, but he was sure that no one actually wanted him there. There was an ugliness prevailing around the king's brother, but the government was keen to move past it and must have appealed to the king for David's place at the table.

Jon had observed that the entire family seemed to be on rough ground, or, at the very least, rougher than usual. Not one for eavesdropping, it was still impossible for Jon not to hear the short, snippy conversations and the curt, untoward remarks to one another, coupled with the fact that the Windsor family had not all been in the same room for quite some time.

Princess Emeline had arrived just two days ago from her home in Yorkshire, more than a week after she had been due to come, which was likely due to the fact that she would understandably rather be spending Christmas with her beloved. On the opposite end of the spectrum, Princess Maud's family unit had been at Balmoral for nearly a month and never usually stayed in one place for so long. They were positively bouncing off the walls, with only Maud leaving for the odd engagement.

The king and Princess Marjorie always avoided each other, and Jon was not unaware of the disdain they shared, set against the backdrop of a love that they couldn't quite remember but which must have been nice at the time. Marjorie had become something of a blizzard herself the last decade, and although Eric's true feelings were often hidden behind rhetoric, Marjorie frequently attempted to tell anyone and everyone exactly what she thought about her family when she had had a tipple – and tipples were becoming a startlingly regular occurrence.

Analysts reported Princess Marjorie's change in demeanour towards the king, as well as his (and officials') consistent refusal to allow her the title of queen. Jon had not known this to be a part of legislation until it had become relevant, but while a queen's husband was not the king, a king's wife was usually the queen, so in that context, it was slightly odd that Marjorie was still a princess. The princess royal, but a princess nonetheless.

A timer buzzed as if the universe were reminding him of what he should concern himself with. He thought on what that particular timer had been for, and then checked the duck and turned the oven down, setting a new timer for when he had to check it again. He used egg timers, and colour-coded them with miniscule Post-it notes. He coded the timer red. Now he just had to remember what red meant. He put it on the side.

Next, Jon prepped the turkey. The bird had been seasoned two days ago so it would be as succulent as possible. Firstly, he carefully pierced the skin and lifted it, spreading a homemade garlic butter underneath. Then, he wrapped the turkey in the finest Scottish pancetta that money could buy. He prepped the shallots, garlic and carrots that would be cooked in the tin with the bird and then put inside it partway through cooking. Finally, he arranged the roasting tin and put the turkey in the oven. He spun a timer to the desired length of time, coded it yellow and put it next to the other one.

The bread sauce was a major component – King Eric's favourite. As a chef, Jon saw the value in all different types of dishes, ingredients, condiments and components. He knew that, although he had preferences, everything had its place in world cuisine. There was one exception, however – Jon could not understand how anyone could even tolerate bread sauce. The mere name, bread sauce, made Jon feel queasy, but the king practically begged Jon to make it every Christmas.

Jon continued to do what he could for his other tasks – the other components of the dinner. The gammon had a green timer. The soup had a purple timer. The pudding had an orange one. When Jon was done, there were six egg timers on the prep table.

He stopped for a moment to update his list of jobs, using the towel tucked into his waistband to dab at his brow. He knew that he was overdoing it, but what else was to be done?

He sat down for a moment to catch his breath. Out of the corner of his eye, he spied a figure standing in the archway at the entrance to the kitchens. There was only one person it could possibly be – who had a habit of popping up at the worst times.

Tony Speck announced his arrival, unnecessarily, with a severe clearing of the throat. His mountainous frame had been pressed into a crisp black suit – happily denoting his role as head of security – and he was currently zipping up a blue parka that was somehow even smaller for him than the suit. 'Taking a break, Alleyne?' He was an odd specimen – an ex-SAS powerhouse who was now being house-trained with a newly acquired pencil moustache. Jon didn't like the fellow, but even he had to concede that it was hard not to feel safe around him. 'I trust everyone has had their breakfast.' His voice was devoid of anything denoting character, which, in a way, was all one needed to know about him.

'I took the king his breakfast personally. I highly doubt Princess Marjorie will rise until dinner. Prince David requested no breakfast last night. And the princesses were quite adamant that they wanted to prepare their own.'

Speck sighed, forcing Jon to meet his gaze. It involved peering upwards, even though Jon was quite far away. Speck seemed positively repulsed. 'Princesses getting their own breakfasts? Jesus. And you let them get it, did you?'

'I wouldn't know. Breakfast is usually served in the kitchens closer to the bedrooms. Are they even awake yet?' Jon inspected the clock. It was 8 a.m. Where had the time gone? He couldn't be sitting here making idle chit-chat.

'Princesses going to the kitchens?' The exact same diction and tone. It was really rather impressive. 'They'll be popping to the shops next.'

'Well, let it be known that the royal revolution started with a bowl of cornflakes,' Jon sniped. 'Is there anything else you need?'

'Yes, Alleyne, I need you to go down to the drawing

room and make sure everything is well for the rest of the day.'

Jon could not quite believe what he was hearing. 'Sir, I am rather busy here. Could you not do it? Or ask—' He stopped there. There was no one else, no other name to finish that sentence. It was quite the adjustment to realise this.

'No, Alleyne, I am going to patrol the grounds. Hence the parka. A blizzard such as this would make a perfect cover for some kind of assassination attempt, don't you think? Look, I know this situation is not ideal, but it is what it is. So, be a sport and do as you are told.'

Jon's eyes fell on his list. There was too much to do, but Speck was of a higher rank and Jon did indeed have to do what he was told. He looked back up to see that Tony Speck was already gone, fleeing to a less chaotic place – a blizzard.

Jon let out a long and steady breath before ripping off his jacket and stuffing the timers into his pockets.

III

The Knack to Stoking a Fire

Jon would not let Tony Speck know, but going to the drawing room at that point did have its advantages. He took the service lift up (so early in the day to fear the stairs, but there it was) and stopped off at the pantry to retrieve the king's favourite brand of whisky – Anchor Haven Single Malt. Jon always made sure that they had a brand-new bottle for the occasion, as the king made a tradition out of everyone having a glass of whisky to raise a toast before his after-dinner speech.

The king hated to watch himself on television so, instead, at 3 p.m., as the rest of the country sat down to hear his address, he wrote a special address for his own family. It was often long, humorous, somewhat risqué and best enjoyed slightly tipsy.

Jon carried the Anchor Haven bottle to the drawing room, moving slowly to conserve his energy. The pain was already starting. He ignored it and quietly slipped inside. If one had any confusion over what time of year it was, the grand drawing room of Balmoral would very quickly set them straight. Colour and joy assaulted the brain on entrance and did not relent for one's entire stay. The large room had been decadently draped in lavish Christmas decorations that had been in the royal household for decades, from ancient hanging adornments dangling from the ceiling to faded tinsel around the fireplace, to cracked baubles littered on the imposing Christmas tree by the window. Even the two chaises longues in the centre of the room had been adorned with Christmas cushions, and there was a smaller version of the tree on the coffee table between them.

Tony Speck would probably remark that this room represented how they got to this point. Christmas was always Eric Windsor's favourite holiday, and he seemed to revel in his authority over it. The family had decorated this room, using the decorations they wanted, meaning that the place was dressed as a traditional family Christmas instead of a Clintons card. Eric often said that Christmas was the only time of year he felt like a normal person.

Outside of the trip to church on Christmas morning, which was a moral duty but also a royal one, the family could be left alone. This Christmas, for obvious blizzard-related reasons, the church trip had to be called off, which no doubt Eric secretly enjoyed. The entire day was to be their own – and this year especially, due to his startling recommendation.

It wasn't hard to understand that King Eric would eventually ask to be left alone at Christmas, dismissing the staff. Jon wasn't expecting anyone to actually agree to this, but a planning committee had been liaising with the royals, and eventually they had all come to an agreement. The Royal Family would celebrate Christmas alone with Tony Speck their only protection – well, and the high walls and gates of Balmoral – and Jon to serve them dinner.

Jon was not privy to the government's stipulations, although he had been exposed to one the night before, when Speck had been tasked with gathering up the family's mobile devices. He even took Jon's, although he never had it while on duty anyway. 'We can't have anyone know that the United Kingdom's most important asset is up here in the Scottish wilderness alone. I am not risking this family's lives for the sake of Twitter.' Many were relinquished willingly, but it had taken a long time to get young Prince Martin to part with his iPad. The devices had gone into a lockbox and Speck had taken them away, to a location that only he was aware of. The only communication devices left on any personage in Balmoral Castle were Jon and Speck's analogue walkie-talkies.

Jon placed the Anchor Haven on the sideboard by the door and made his way around the room, carefully avoiding the towering Christmas tree branches and the empty loungers. A smattering of wrapped boxes lay underneath the tree, although the pile was not particularly uniform. Had Speck sent him down here just to reorder some boxes, while the duck burnt and the soup spoiled?

'Oh, there you are, Butler.'

The sound jolted him. Prince David's old and decrepit figure was crouched down in front of the fireplace, almost betraying his modesty in his traditional Scottish kilt. The Windsor family crest, a tradition for each of the family to wear on special occasions, was clipped to the top of the kilt like a belt buckle. He was fiddling with the logs and kindling of the fire, placing and re-placing items with an incompetent confidence that was almost admirable. David got up and dusted his hands, as if he had been doing God's work. 'I've been trying to get this blasted thing to light for the last hour. I'm rather afraid I'll overly succeed and burst into flames, and give the rest of my family their deepest wish.'

'Your Royal Highness,' Jon said, forcing a smile. David had called him the butler ever since he had arrived – it didn't bear correcting. The timers in his pockets were weighing him down, and he had bigger worries. 'I often find that particular fire to be somewhat temperamental.' He advanced and tried to light it himself, as the prince stood back. Within three tries, the fire slowly flickered to life.

'Ah,' David laughed, 'success. Well done, Butler. It seems to be all in the wrist. There is a knack to stoking a fire. I would take note, but I hope to never need to reach into the sooty depths again.' He sank down into the armchair facing the fire and picked up a newspaper that was three days old. 'How is the weather out there?'

'Rampant, sir. A true blizzard.' Jon made sure the fire was not instantly going to go out, before making his way back to the whisky bottle. He put it onto a tray, along with the king's favourite square serving decanter, and took it to the coffee table. The king liked the whisky to air for a few hours before drinking, so Jon cracked the bottle open, hearing the seal break, and poured the entire thing into the holding vessel.

'By God, it really is primordial, isn't it?' David slid his glasses down his nose, spying the window, while wafting the broadsheet. He seemed to note what Jon was up to, already thirsty no doubt. 'We really are all alone here. Anything could happen.'

'Sir?' Jon asked, more than a little thrown by the foreboding comment.

Before David could explain, two melodic laughs came from the corridor beyond, and the door flew open as two elegant women glided in. The twin princesses were by no means identical, but were very much alike. It appeared that both Princess Emeline and Princess Maud had grasped their freedom with both hands as they seemed in high spirits. They were truly beautiful, even at this early hour. The nation's sweethearts around the clock.

'Isn't this a scream, Jon?' Maud remarked gleefully upon seeing Jon, and it took a moment for him to realise that she was referring to the pile of dirty plates in her arms.

'May I take those, Your Royal Highness?' Jon said.

'If you must,' Maud said, almost sadly. 'It would save me trying to find the kitchen again.'

'We've just been having a leisurely stroll without any aides snapping at our heels,' Emeline explained. 'The place is quite peaceful, really.'

'I hope you didn't set foot outside,' David's voice called, and this time (much as Jon had), the sisters jumped. David's form was now masked by the high chairback, making him invisible to his nieces.

33

Their moods soured almost instantly, turning the air in the room into a thick soup of distaste and revulsion.

'Didn't see you there, Uncle,' Emeline said, using an inherited royal civility that was often a wonder to behold. 'Happy Christmas.'

'And Happy Christmas to you too, Emeline. And to you, Maud.'

Maud's mouth twisted into a small smile of recognition – that civility fighting through – before turning. 'I have to get back to my family. I left Thomas and the boys watching the latest episode of *The Monarch*. I want to be there when Matthew finds out that Evan Peters is playing him. He does enjoy him.'

'Oh, that blasted television programme,' David moaned. 'I'd warn them off that, if I were you. A load of sensationalist nonsense used to sell advertising space.'

Maud stopped her retreat at this. 'Oh, I'm sorry, Uncle. Are you so distressed by the manner of the production? Or are you worried that they're just about to get to the bit with the assault allegations?'

'I didn't punch anyone!' David huffed.

'It's on film, Uncle. And why did you punch her anyway? Maybe they'll include that too.'

'Maud!' A harsh hiss that signalled the arrival of their matriarch. Princess Royal Marjorie Windsor-Nueberner stood in the doorway, in a pink suit with a long skirt. Marjorie was the very image of an elderly stateswoman, but was really anything but. Among the royals, she was known to be the most problematic in recent years. Servants could barely hide their discomfort when they learned that they were assigned to her. Marjorie was a woman who had the pleasure of living like a queen but also the curse of knowing she would never be one. 'Please, don't talk about that codswallop on Christmas, and apologise to your uncle.'

Maud rolled her eyes and mumbled, 'I'm sorry, Uncle.' She left, but not before seeing the whisky on the coffee table and turning her nose up at it. Princess Maud did not like whisky and always found a way not to drink it.

'Thank you, Margey,' David said, after Maud had left.

'Oh, shut up.' Marjorie staggered into the room, and Jon saw with horror that she may still be slightly inebriated, or (possibly worse) already inebriated again. Maybe breaking out the whisky so early was not a good idea – it was not to be touched until 3 p.m.

Emeline saw her mother's state too, and went to her, linking her arm with her mother's and guiding her to the chair next to David's. Once she was done, Emeline went over to the Christmas tree and started sorting the presents, thankfully relieving him of a job.

'May I get you any breakfast, Your Royal Highness?' Jon said, already making mental calculations in his head about what he could make in the time he had.

'No, no,' Marjorie fussed. 'Unless a liquid breakfast is on the cards.' She had noted the whisky.

'I'm sure I could easily procure some orange juice, ma'am.'

Marjorie glared at him icily. 'You know what I mean. Don't be smart, Jon. It's not becoming of someone of your background.' Jon would give Marjorie the benefit of the doubt and assume she was referring to his profession and not the colour of his skin. Concessions had to be made, and tongues were forever bitten. 'We should be getting ready for Church now. All this tradition gone – opening presents on Christmas Day and not Christmas Eve, no church . . . we don't even weigh ourselves any more! My husband is really making his mark.'

'I hardly think us not going to church is Eric's doing, Margey,' David said.

'No, I suppose not. How is the weather?'

'Rampant. It's a true blizzard,' David parroted Jon's words.

'A white Christmas, all alone at the 'Moral. Anything could happen, eh, David?' Marjorie cackled.

There that phrase was again. An odd sensation was forming itself in Jon's gut, besides the pain. It was a sensation that everything was not quite right. A sort of vibration – a sixth sense, Jon thought, until he realised that the vibrating was real, and Marjorie and David were looking at him with perplexed expressions on their faces.

'Jon, dear, I surmise from your buzzing trousers, you may have somewhere to be.'

One of the egg timers had gone off.

IV

In Search of a Light

The rest of the morning fell away, no matter how much Jon tried to grasp at it. At every hurried glance at the clock, hours seemed to have gone by, so he tried to do it as little as possible. Jon experienced the strange ethereal sensation of not being in charge of his own body, as a force (equal parts habit and survival) channelled through him to thunder him towards his goal. The vegetables were done, the meat would be done, the Christmas pudding was ready to be put on to boil in the wake of the main courses. Jon was busy doing the ancillary things – the gravy, the garnishes and the bread sauce – as he finally realised that he had used every egg timer in Balmoral.

At one point, he spied Tony Speck returning from his morning rounds, trying and failing not to bring half of the 'Moral's snow inside with him. The man did not come in and offer a hand or any words of encouragement, and Jon was almost glad of the fact.

His other visitor was far more interesting. A mousy man in his mid-forties strode into the kitchen in a light-brown suit, tightly cut trousers and a novelty Christmas tie depicting a fuzzy reindeer. His family crest was clipped to his breast pocket like a badge of honour. Jon didn't notice the man at first, so when he looked up to see Thomas Crockley standing there, he almost dropped the jug of bread sauce.

'Sorry, old bean,' Crockley said in his odd manner. Crockley had the air of an old transatlantic movie star out of time, crossed with an East End market trader. If that sounded incredibly bizarre, it was precisely because it was. Crockley was always hard to place, to pin down, and that was why most found him incredibly uncomfortable to entertain. There was always the creeping notion that one was not meeting the real Thomas Crockley, and maybe no one ever had.

'Good morning, sir.' Jon smiled, hoping that he would rather quickly get to the point of his interruption. Even though the main players of the dinner were sorted, the chorus still needed to be prepped.

'I was just in search of a light. Thought the kitchens might be the best place to come for an open flame.' Crockley glanced around. 'You really are all alone down here. I mean, I heard of the command to send all the servants away, but I didn't actually think that the old man would be obeyed.'

Jon set down the sauce while he could and went into a drawer to bring out a firelighter.

Crockley took it with thanks. Jon hoped he would leave, but instead he lit his cigar there in the archway. 'Credit to you, Alleyne. Always need a smoke when I get up from a snooze. Even if it's the middle of the afternoon.'

Jon smiled. 'Well, if you ever need a light, there's means in the drawing room. And if you can't get there, there's a box of firelighters in the pantry.'

'Thank you, old boy. Thank you,' Crockley chuckled, faltering in the archway. 'It smells gorgeous in here.'

Jon had been so busy that he hadn't had time to acknowledge the beautiful aroma of Christmas dinner wafting from every corner of the kitchen. He thought that maybe if he had had time to stop, he would have had to also acknowledge how impossibly famished he was himself.

A small smoke pyre was drifting from Crockley's cigar and assaulting the mouth-watering aroma. 'Can't possibly be as good as last year's though, can it? I mean, no offence to your abilities, but you are just one man.'

Jon recalled a similar sentiment crossing his mind when he'd heard of the plan for 25 December. But Thomas was stalling and, what was more, he was in the way. 'Is there something else I can help you with, sir?'

Crockley grinned, his teeth a gleaming white barricade. 'Sharp, aren't you? Yes, I just figured it good to get away from it a bit, you know. The children and the in-laws – there's something brewing up there. Maud's disposed, and the boys are off doing God knows what. I have always thought of us more as a parenting team, anyhow.'

'Where is Princess Maud?' Jon knew that it was not his business, but with Speck the only security present, maybe it was.

'Oh, she is in her father's private study. He's calling them all in there, one by one. It has the air of some kind of Draconian march. They come out much less happy than when they went in. Her Uncle David just came out looking like a flamin' radish.' Crockley stopped himself then. He had just realised that his mask had slipped. Thomas Crockley was not as eloquent as he liked to portray himself to be. Jon could relate — it was almost as if the royals spoke their own language, a language that was infectious. Crockley's East End accent came through occasionally, as did Jon's Bajan one, but all too often everyone sounded like everyone else.

This was an interesting development. King Eric was having private counsel with his family individually. Jon wondered what could possibly have been said to David, a man who, even when accused of the most heinous things, had consistently kept his natural pigment throughout. He really would have liked to have known, but, as always, he came back to the fact that speculation did not cook dinner.

'Stupid old sod. Why is he even here?' Thomas was talking of David, and not the king, and not Jon. 'It brings the mood down. Puts everyone on edge. It doesn't matter if he's blood, at least it doesn't where I come from. You know, I think I may take a walk. Enjoy this on the move.'

'The weather is rampant out there, sir,' Jon said, reclaiming the word from Prince David.

'Yes. Rather less rampant than upstairs though, I assure you.'

'If you must, take my coat, sir. The red anorak. It's on the rack down the hall.'

'The anorak on the rack. Thank you, Alleyne. One of the best ones, you are.'

One of the best ones. Jon was unsure what that meant, but before he could summon the energy to inquire, Thomas Crockley had disappeared.

Jon went back to his work with thoughts of what the king and his brother could possibly have discussed. And then there were the other members of the family too. It was as if the king were tying up loose ends – having the final say – but there was no reason to believe he was intending to step down today, was there?

Not for the first time, Jon had the intense feeling that the real story was happening elsewhere and that he was a small part of something bigger. A singular piece of the puzzle. And he was far from the most important piece.

V

To Be Young

Dinner was set for twelve thirty, and as it came to twelve fifteen, Jon got to the end of his long list of tasks and could hardly believe he was finally done. One may have thought that everything being ready fifteen minutes ahead of time was actually too much of a victory – so much so that everything would be ruined by serving time, but Jon had factored in that he would have to transport everything halfway across the castle to assemble it in the smaller kitchens near the dining room. He had once envisioned trying to do everything in that kitchen, so this very journey would not have been necessary, but the kitchen upstairs was woefully inadequate for grandeur such as this. It was entirely intended for day-to-day use, with only two small ovens (barely big enough to cook a quail, let alone a gorged turkey!), limited counter space and (although not strictly relevant) a rather depressing lookout into a forgotten courtyard. There was only one thing that made that kitchen better than this, and it was the two large steam tables that Jon himself had fought to acquire. These tables would be key in keeping the dinner warm.

So it was that Jon commenced his pilgrimage of the

food trolley with the entirety of the Christmas dinner packed onto it and left his valiant kitchen for pastures new. The thing was incredibly heavy, and by the time he got to the old service lift at the end of the servants' quarters, he wondered if he had factored in enough time. He often forgot what an old specimen he was nowadays, with bones starting to creak, the pain in his gut throbbing at him to remember his secret and an altogether slower mind. What a curse getting old was. The trolley creaked in agreement.

He pushed the trolley into the lift and as the doors closed, making the exact same sound as his joints after a hard day, he spied Thomas Crockley at the other end of the corridor returning from his walk and hanging up a snow-covered red coat on the hooks next to the entrance door. This was an action that Jon thought to be of no importance, and indeed, at that moment, it was not.

As the lift ascended, the creaking stopped. Jon found that even the staff were like this – rickety and common and crass below stairs but transformed above. Today, he would have to transform a little more than usual – he willed that he had the strength to finish this day and live to tell the tale. He had noticed himself decline, and thought it incredible that no one else had. Of course, it helped that no one was ever looking at him. He used the lift ride to take a breather, leaning on the trolley. The deep ball inside his gut was pulsing, shooting pain throughout the rest of his body. The doctor said that was mostly psychosomatic, but it didn't make it hurt any less.

He wondered where on earth Tony Speck was – their jobs never intersected on a usual day, but today was not that. Jon had expected something in the form of assistance, but maybe Speck was correct. The family's safety was of the utmost importance and, although it belittled Jon, that mattered more than a potentially spoiled bread sauce.

Upstairs, Jon took the trolley down the grand corridors, with the lush maroon carpet fighting him at every step. He checked his watch to see that he had fallen slightly behind, and resolved to quicken his pace. As he looked back up, however, he was horrified to see someone race out of the door directly ahead of him, and stray into the path of the oncoming trolley. Wilson, another of the Windsors' cats, was being chased and dashed off to parts unknown. Rather than following, the figure seemed frozen in the trolley's wake.

Jon had to halt immediately and pull against the forward momentum he had amassed. His breath caught in his throat as everything on the trolley shifted forward. Luckily, however, it seemed that all the food kept in its proper place, if a few millimetres to the north.

Jon tried not to gasp in relief as his eyes fell on the roadblock in front of him. The young boy seemed nonplussed at the culinary genocide he had almost caused and was more intent on plunging his hands deep into his pockets and employing a faux-genial facial expression.

Prince Martin was Princess Maud and Thomas Crockley's youngest son. At thirteen years old, he was a slim and wide-eyed child, who always had the air of constant

44

confusion at the state of the life he was thrust into. Outwardly, his confusion translated to his manner. He always seemed mightily uncomfortable in the suits he was placed in, the hairstyles he was forced to adopt – now a simple short cut with a slightly longer fringe brushed to the right side – and the halls he was supposed to inhabit. Whenever Jon encountered him, he often wondered how the child would be if he were allowed to choose. It was perhaps the saddest fact that no one would ever know.

At this moment, Martin considered Jon much like an animal would before being hit by a car – contemplating life and the sudden fact that it would not last for very much longer. The young boy fiddled with his crest awkwardly, pinned to his lapel in much the same place as his father's. Jon would have seen the guilt on his face more clearly if he still wasn't worried about the meal.

'I'm sorry, Your Royal Highness,' Jon remarked, referencing the near-collision – not that Martin seemed as fazed by it as he was by being seen.

'Martin,' the young prince said, almost inaudibly. He had that quality that many young people tend to possess. He hadn't fully understood that one had to constantly justify their place in the world, and that included speaking up.

'Martin, I mean. I'm sorry.'

'It smells good.'

'Thank you, sir.'

Martin did not move as one might when faced with such a sight. Jon held his hand to the cart, trying to suppress the compulsion to check his watch.

45

'I was just . . . Sometimes I like to look around, you know. And Wilson wanted to play, so . . .' Martin continued, his eyes growing ever wider. It was very clear that he assumed he was in trouble, and was trying to mitigate it. Unfortunately, it had the exact opposite effect. 'Mummy calls me a snooper sometimes. She told me to stop. You won't tell anyone you saw me, will you? Please.'

'Of course not, sir.' Jon's eyes rose to the plaque on the still-open door. He was exactly where he thought he was, of course. The upstairs pantry.

'Martin.' Matthew, Martin's brother, strode out from the turn in the corridor. Matthew was eighteen and looked very much like Martin, and his parents, except for his sandy blond hair. He was a well-put-together young gent, beloved by the public and often touted to one day wear the crown. However, there was a more complex side to him that those outside of the castle didn't see – a boy constantly wrestling with the order of the family, together with the chaos one of his age should be engaging in. 'There you are. What're you doing in there? The dinner is starting soon.' Matthew's eyes fell on the pantry door, on Jon and, lastly, on the cart packed with the aforementioned dinner. 'Oh, Jon. Should I take Martin to the drawing room or bring everyone else out here?' He laughed, but there was an undeniable cold edge to the cackle. Something was troubling him.

Jon really had to get moving, decorum be damned. 'It is lovely to see you, Your Royal Highness, as well as yourself, young sir. And Happy Christmas to you both. But I really must be going.'

Matthew interpreted this. 'Get out of the way, Martin. Bloody hell. Can't you see you're blocking the man?'

Martin stepped aside.

As Jon continued his journey, he heard Matthew and Martin talking. Matthew had just come back from his private audience with the king, and Martin wished to know what was said. Matthew denied him, however, saying, 'I guess you'll just have to wait and see. You'll all know soon enough.'

Jon did not have the sufficient brainpower to even wonder what that meant. As he left earshot of them, Martin was reprimanding Matthew for not wearing his family crest. Matthew let out a very uncharacteristic expletive before finding it in his pocket.

Jon got to the kitchen at twelve twenty, relieved to see that the steam tables had indeed clicked on when he had set them to. After loading in the main-course dishes and Christmas pudding, he left again, rolling the starters to the grand dining room, adjacent to the drawing room. He set down the soups upon each available mat and gently plopped three Camembert croutons into each. He poured wine for each place, and with a final look of confirmation, he saw that it was good. He went over to the door that joined the rooms and knocked.

It was exactly 12.29 as Jon entered the drawing room. The young royals gave nothing away as they crossed the room to join their peers. King Eric had joined Princess Marjorie and Prince David. The king seemed to be quietly contemplating something by the fire as his brother and wife laughed together. David and Marjorie were in

47

high spirits, in more ways than one, it seemed, as the empty glasses by their sides illustrated.

Princess Maud had assembled her family, with Matthew and Martin having obviously just arrived at her side, and Thomas Crockley still red-faced from the whipping winds of the outdoors. Princess Emeline stood with them as she had no one of her own at the castle. Both twins had changed into very similar light-pink dresses, with gold sashes fashioned around their waists. They both wore their crests around their necks as fashionable necklaces.

At Jon's entrance, the family din quickly died. The Royal Family were now the Royal Stomachs to be filled, and Jon was honoured to be the one to do it. 'Your Majesty. Your Royal Highnesses. Happy Christmas to you all. I am proud to announce that dinner is served.'

VI

A Christmas Dinner, in Three Movements

Windsor Christmas dinners were often long affairs, as was the case with most of the world's families. The dinner could be adequately split into three main movements – a ravenous, hopeful start, where all participants were looking forward to what they were about to consume; a contented, jovial middle, where everyone was happy with their tablemates and their light conversation as their stomachs still left room for more; and a full and irritable end, where everyone was well and truly fed up with everything happening around them – conversation drying up and still more food lying there, less a delicious sustenance and more a vile challenge. All of these cavernous movements felt feature-length, especially for the man who had to stand outside the dining room door, forever ready to leap to action at the sound of a bell.

Thus it was that Jon listened to the family tuck into chicken and parsnip soup with crisp Camembert croutons and realised that he would be in it for the long haul. He had to go back to the small kitchen to switch the dishes in the steam tables. But the rest of the time would be spent here, just outside the dining-room doors, in case he was needed within.

'This looks positively scrumptious,' Maud said as the door closed behind Jon. He was glad that the first thing uttered when he was not present was a compliment and not a slight. Compliments were far more impressive when not made under duress.

'What are those things?' Martin said. 'They look like cheese.'

'I think they may be cheese, oddly enough,' Matthew replied.

It is important to note that Jon did not wish to eavesdrop on the dinner. If he were called for within, it would be by a small bell alerting him. However, the doors to the dining room, which were directly behind him, were thin, and Jon could hear everything said, whether he wanted to or not. He might as well have been in the room, but he could understand the need for the illusion of privacy. The illusion of privacy was something that the Royal Family had gotten used to.

For the starter, as custom dictated, the conversation (much like the soup) was light. Presented by Maud, the topic was the television programme *The Monarch*. *The Monarch*, as no doubt already surmised, was a television programme on ITV1, unofficially dramatising the events of the reign of King Eric. It was currently in its fourth series and was getting closer and closer to being up to date.

'. . . I for one think it's just what the country needs. An impartial look into our lives. Thomas, darling, tell them about your encounter.'

Crockley launched into a long story about how he was approached by one of the researchers for the programme in an upmarket London bar called The Gentlemen. 'He wanted to pay me to liaise with him about the family. Tried to give me his card. Of course, I told him to sling his hook.'

'It does open the question of whether we should be liaising, though,' Maud said. 'We could help them to get some of the details right. Emeline, you were saying how they got your courtship with Anton wrong.'

'Oh for heaven's sake. Anton this. Anton that.' Marjorie sniped, so quietly Jon almost did not hear.

'I'm just saying that they are getting things wrong, and omitting other things entirely,' Maud said. 'They didn't even mention Poppy.'

'Poppy?' Marjorie scoffed. 'Poppy? Who is . . . Do you mean that golden retriever you wanted to adopt once? Wasn't that it? What a startling omission.'

Maud said nothing to this.

'We do not concern ourselves with television dramatists, Maud,' the king said, cutting in with the vindictiveness of one who had recently spent ten hours recording a seven-minute Christmas speech. He had told Jon afterwards that he performed the speech in one take perfectly, but the damn director wanted to get 'artsy' with it. 'I would have you remember that if these researchers ever come knocking at your door.'

'I hasten to agree,' David said.

'And why would that be, Uncle?' Maud said rapidly.

The aged prince changed the subject. 'The lack of

seasoning really is apparent, isn't it? Maybe time to lay the old boy out to pasture, eh?'

'Nonsense,' Eric said.

Horrifyingly, the conversation moved to Jon's ability to cook. Therefore, he was mightily glad that his timer started vibrating, and he had to move off to the upper kitchen. Once there, he loaded up the trolley with the finest Christmas dinner in all of England, and wheeled it to its final destination.

As he got back to the dining room, he knocked before pushing the trolley inside. Despite the comments, David and Marjorie were the only ones to whoop and cheer. This was most likely attributed to the fact that there were somehow already two empty wine bottles between them. Jon replaced them with full ones from the trolley after clearing the soup bowls and placing fresh plates in front of the family. Lastly, Jon placed all of the food in the centre of the table – he started to serve meats, advancing on the turkey with a skewer, but the king waved him away with a smile. With that Jon left the room, and went to prepare the desserts. As the desserts were finished and were largely cold, Jon put them on the trolley and started wheeling it through the castle.

When he returned to his place outside of the dining room, it was not long before he was joined by another. As the Royal Family feasted upon sumptuous turkey, duck, gammon, bacon-wrapped pork sausages, honeyed carrots and parsnips, Brussels sprouts tossed with walnuts and pancetta, mashed potatoes, roast potatoes and all manner of condiments and garnishes including three different types of homemade gravy, Jon had to stand there with a growling belly and try to maintain conversation with Tony Speck, who appeared from the opposite direction to the drawing room and the kitchen. He must have been outside, as there was still snow sticking to the ends of his moustache.

It did not begin well. Inside the room, the family were talking of their interpersonal relationships, and outside the room, Jon could only think of his lack of one with the oaf standing next to him.

'Is everything in order?' Speck said, eyeing up the desserts.

Before he could stop himself, Jon snapped, 'Where have you been?'

Speck frowned. 'Protecting the monarchy. Where have you been?'

Jon ignored the flagrant bullheadedness of the question. 'The last I checked, the monarchy was in here, and not in the apocalypse outside.'

'You do not have a head for threats, Alleyne. You are no tactician.'

Jon would have argued that every single action in the kitchen today had proved him a brilliant tactician, but there really was no talking to Speck. It was easier to just shut up and take his mockery.

'Assassins stalk this world, Alleyne. I must think like them. And I am.' He sounded like he rather enjoyed it. 'Really, one of the best things about today is it gave me licence to requisition that new Balmoral security system I've been wanting. I now have sensors everywhere on the grounds. All kinds – thermal, auditory, movement. If anything triggers them, I am notified immediately. If anyone strays onto the grounds, if there's a soul here besides the two of us and the Royal Family, I will know.' Speck fumbled in his jacket and brought out a tablet. 'Look here.'

He held the screen up to Jon like an excited toddler showing off his Christmas present. The screen showed a topographical wireframe map of the surrounding area. Ten small red dots pulsed inside a lined facsimile of the building – like something out a science-fiction film.

'The red dots are us.'

'This is thermal imaging?' Jon asked.

Speck nodded proudly.

'But there are other heat sources in the castle besides us?'

'That's what makes this system so good. It can weed out the cats and the microwaves, and just show me the humans that are on the property. Assassins, Alleyne. They don't stand a chance now.'

'How does that work?' Jon asked, genuinely curious but, of course, Speck shrugged. He didn't understand the equipment, he just used it.

'All that matters is the Royal Family is the safest it has ever been.'

Jon was a little thankful for that – Speck's new system was indeed comprehensive. His men had spent the entirety of the last week installing it. It did offer some sort of feeling of safety, even if it was in Speck's hands. But the impressiveness of the system did beg a question. 'If the Royal Family is so safe, why do you need to be out patrolling all day?'

'This is why you are the chef, and I am the protector, Alleyne. You would simply not understand.'

Speck was absolutely correct – Jon did not understand one bit. 'I assumed that when the two of us were assigned today, there would be a trifle more . . . give and take.'

'Give and take? Christ, Alleyne. You wanted me to help you whisk something, and then what? How are you of any use to me? Just because you're old doesn't mean you get to lord over me.'

'That's not what I meant and you . . .' But Jon could not complete what he started. He knew it to be fruitless. The two servants, standing to attention like the beefeaters outside the Tower of London, fell into an uncomfortable silence. If not for the sound of far more interesting interactions happening within the dining room, Jon would have found it hard to stay where he was.

Inside, it seemed that Prince Martin was regaling the family with random facts. 'Did you know that there is a fruit that tastes like chocolate pudding?'

No one appeared to be paying attention to him, however. 'I am just saying that I would have preferred my private scolding to have been separated from Christmas,' David was remarking.

'I'm sorry, dear brother. I truly am. I simply had to air a few things out before—'

'And while we are at it—' David interrupted, before he himself suffered the same fate.

'Before?' Emeline said. 'Before what, Father?'

55

'Hmm?'

'Did you know that hot water freezes faster than cold water?' Martin said.

'You said "before", as if we were quickly hurtling towards something only you are privy to.'

The king seemed to pause. Jon knew he would be scratching his chin in the way he always did – usually when stuck on a particularly fiendish puzzle. 'Well, yes. There is always a before, and always an after. We are currently in the in-between. So why don't we just enjoy the moment, hmm?'

This was clearly not the answer anyone wanted to hear from the sighs coming from the room, and Jon had to admit that he would have liked to know himself what the king really meant by his use of the word 'before'. He stole a sideways glance at Speck, who was adjusting a cufflink with a look of extreme apathy on his face. He wasn't listening.

The room inside was silent, and Jon bet that someone was going to speak up about this more, but Prince Martin broke the spell. 'Did you know that there's a place where you can shoot a man in the gut and it'll go straight through, and he'll survive?'

'There's many of those places, Martin,' Matthew said.

A familiar tutting, loud enough to hear anywhere in the castle. 'You have to do something about these children, Maud.'

The conversation became about Maud and Crockley's parenting, which Jon found about as painful as they did. He felt his interest waning, and stopped listening. He was just about to try small talk with Speck, but realised it would not be appreciated by either party so didn't. He just stood there, until the bell signalled they were ready for dessert.

Jon sprang into action. The desserts were set in front of the family, and Jon was back outside the dining room door in such a well-oiled manner, he was almost strangely annoyed that this was the last time he would have to do it. Tony Speck, in a display of great goodwill, even kept the door open for him as he served the family, watching him every step of the way.

'Not bad, Alleyne.'

It must be Christmas.

Squeals of joy came from the dining room as the Christmas pudding raged.

'Look at that,' the king marvelled. 'A real pyre.'

As desserts were consumed, it became apparent to Jon that they had arrived at the final stage of Christmas dinner – the deepest and darkest of the lot. The stage where a family realised that the small talk was all burned up, and there was a reason that they did not sit together like this more often, and that they were bound by blood and not much else. Luckily or unluckily, the Windsors were bound by something else: royalty, and here was where civil conversation ran dry.

'I was saying, before the interruption,' David scoffed, 'about my scolding—'

'Yes, yes, Uncle,' Maud said, her words as soaked in sarcasm as the pudding was in alcohol, 'we all understand your terrible plight.'

'I do believe we were talking about me, Uncle,' Emeline said.

'Ah, yes. Emeline and Anton, you have my full support,' the king said earnestly, 'and I think, although you may have to search a little deeper inside some people, you have the full support of everyone at this table.'

'If that were so,' Emeline countered, 'why is he not *at this table*?'

Silence.

'And that, my dear darling daughter,' Marjorie slurred, 'is the greatest answer you can get from a king. Silence.'

'Marjorie, when you are quite through weaving your webs, would you pass the Christmas pudding?' Eric snapped.

'For once, she is not entirely wrong, Father,' Emeline said.

Jon felt for King Eric there. He was sure that Anton's absence was not entirely his decision in the slightest, and any prejudices it might have implied were completely placed at the wrong door. The government still had power here, within these walls, even if they weren't physically here. The king did not have as much power as the common man thought. The government's influence had gotten even stricter of late – Jon had a feeling that this day was to appease the king for another year and make him more lenient to other manipulations.

The king was silent, and the room was too.

'Let me cut in here to address the elephant in the room as we are all talking around the subject with words marinated in others entirely,' David said. 'Why not just tell us what we all want to hear, Eric? Hmm? So this guessing game can come to an end. Your shake-up of the succession rules leaves us all in contention, yes?'

The new succession rules were elusive to Jon, as he tried as hard as he could to not concern himself with such matters. However, from what he had heard, the new rules abolished the idea of a traditional line of succession, and when it came to naming a new monarch, the retiring one would have more power in choosing a suitable candidate from the royal roster.

'What is he talking about, Daddy?' Maud said.

The king said nothing.

'Martin, do you have any more facts?' Matthew asked, showing himself wise beyond his years and jumping to his grandfather's defence.

No facts came, however, but a mumble from Speck did, meaning the conversation from within moved on without Jon.

'Do I have a dinner?'

'Excuse me?'

'Do I have a dinner, Alleyne?'

Jon knew exactly what Speck was getting at, of course, but he thought it would take him only a few seconds to think of hundreds of ways to phrase it more politely. Give him the whole afternoon, and he could have come up with thousands. 'The leftovers are in the residential kitchens. You can choose what you like from there. Do not eat much of the turkey though – the king likes it in his sandwiches on Boxing Day and I would like to make a pie.'

A few minutes went by, with Jon so furious that he could not focus on anything happening in the dining room, or indeed out. What a nerve! Unfortunately, it was only to get worse – 'Be a dear and plate me up some, would you? That way, I don't overstep my turkey allowance.'

Jon saw a violent red but tried his best to exude a serene blue. 'I'm sorry, sir, but I don't have the time. I have to clear the table, load up the trolley, see the family from the dining room, then go and wash up.' As if on cue, the bell rang that indicated the family were finished.

'Very well, Alleyne,' Speck snarled. 'I'll throw you a bone and settle the family in the drawing room myself. But I must do another perimeter sweep in twenty-six minutes, and I would like a full stomach by then. Be a chap and give me extra sprouts, yes. You could give me yours for being such a good sport.'

Jon bit the inside of his cheek as both of them went inside the dining room.

VII

Contented Retirement

The compliments about the dinner more than justified the manpower of making it. As Speck went to see the Royal Family away to the drawing room, draped over the various furniture as though they had just fought some tremendous battle, Jon went back to the upper kitchen and made himself up a small dinner from the leftovers, eating it while rinsing the plates and admitting that it was rather good – no matter the strange manner in which it was assembled. He also made a dinner up for Speck, and he did indeed give the security man his sprouts. He supposed that that was the kind of man he was, and he wasn't sure if that was a good or bad thing.

He remembered that there had been a period, when he'd first arrived under the king's rule, where it did not look as though his new employment would pan out. The king, although pinching him from Caribbean Plaza, enjoyed British cuisine more than he had first conveyed and Jon had had an intense period of adjustment, learning aspects of cooking he had never even considered before. He was aware that he was losing the root of himself, but it was a root that had never felt that strong anyhow. These days, he sometimes wondered what his grandma would think, but he would never know – she had passed years ago in her sleep. It was months after her funeral that one of his cousins had thought to look him up on the internet and inform him.

After his hunger was sated, Jon made his way back to the drawing room – slipping inside without any of the Royal Family noting his arrival. Tony Speck noted it gleefully, however, dashing off to parts unknown before the door had time to close. Jon decided at that moment to cease to be amazed by Speck's rejection of his plight. He hoped he enjoyed his sprouts though – Jon had given him the overboiled ones.

The family had seemed to collectively recover from their food-induced fatigue and were far too busy embroiled in distributing Christmas presents to note anything around them. The king was sitting in his high-backed chair by the fireplace (the very same one David had resided in that morning) and the others seemed to radiate from him. Marjorie and David were sitting in chairs of their own. Maud, Matthew and Martin were squashed onto the small chaise, while Thomas Crockley was stood behind it. The small coffee table in front of them was the home of an ever-building stack of presents, and Emeline was retrieving them one by one and placing them on the larger chaise, with the air that this was an important royal duty – which, in the very purest sense, it was.

So many years he had seen similar scenes – watching this family gleam in front of his very eyes. Jon experienced such a wide gamut of emotions at these sights: honour at the privilege of being a part of them, pride at how far they had come, and in the deepest, darkest corners of his heart, he felt a seething jealousy at being so much of a part of them but having to stand to attention and hold a silver tray of drinks, as they went on without him.

As the presents were opened, and the usual cavalcade of expensive knitwear, novelty items and appliances destined for a single use (if they were lucky) were laid to rest on the table, Jon started to think of his family in Barbados. He was unsure whether they would think of him at all, or what they would be up to at this moment – as he so rarely thought of them, he could not blame them. He barely remembered Bajan Christmases, he only remembered glimpses – dancing colours, his grandma's laugh, platters of food.

If not for the king, Jon's Christmas would now have been spent alone in his house in Camden. He barely spent any time there as it was, so had no need for friends, or family, or even pets. His life was consumed by his career, and it was forever true that Christmas was the time of the chef. He had not had a Christmas Day off in all of his time working for the king, and would not wish for it to be any other way.

He surfaced from his roaming thoughts to see the last present being plucked. David unsheathed a Blu-ray box set of *The Monarch*. ('Is this some kind of joke?' David murmured. 'Well,' Maud laboriously explained, 'we knew you'd surely be watching a certain episode coming up, and we would hate for you to be lost.') Marjorie laughed, a reaction fuelled by alcohol, while everyone else in the

63

room assessed whether the exchange was actually funny, deeply sad, drearily dark, or some morose combination of all three, and by the time they had found an answer, the time for a response was well and truly gone.

David thrust himself upwards, throwing the box set onto his modest pile of gifts with a tremendous clatter. His face was thunder, and for a moment Jon thought that the aged prince might actually launch himself at his niece. In the face of a threat, albeit from within, Jon cast his eye around the room.

He was saddened to see that there was no salvation to be found. He imagined that Speck had started another circuit of the castle grounds in his precocious parka – trudging along in search of assailants who, in all likelihood, were not there. They definitely had not been on his thermal security read-out when Jon had viewed it. Maximum effort at doing minimum work – or at least that was the way Jon saw it.

Thomas Crockley stood in in Speck's stead. 'Now, come on. Just a bit of jest, you understand.' Crockley's accent was fluctuating wildly in a sea of wine and was completely undermining his point. He caught David's shoulders with the ease of a leaf being caught on the autumn wind.

'There is nothing jestful about this, Maud. These heinous lies will be the undoing of me, the undoing of us all.'

'David,' the king commanded. He still had the power to silence a room. 'Please, not at Christmas.'

David rounded on his brother. 'You had no trouble

speaking of it earlier. Raking me over the coals and then presenting me with your foul question.'

'That was in private, and it shall remain as such. Jon, I believe we are all in need of a top-up.'

Jon was just grateful he could put down the tray as he served everyone their tipple of choice. David's spirits seemed to lighten once he had a fresh drink in his hand, and it seemed that the scene had concluded. That was until Eric sidled over to the Christmas tree.

'And what is this?' Eric said, reaching down with surprising nimbleness to pull out a neatly wrapped box. The label – a garish thing in the shape of a Christmas tree – had 'Eric' written in non-descript capitals. 'One last present, and for me, eh?'

Jon looked around at the other members of the family to see who the giver was, but he couldn't tell. No one was giving anything away.

'No sender. I do love a mystery.' Eric was checking the label, and greedily pierced the paper with his nails. His excitement at every present was infectious – a true high point of the season. In no time at all, the paper had been ripped from its prize beneath and Eric sat holding a wooden box. 'Curiouser and curiouser. What do you think of this, eh, Martin?'

Martin goggled at whatever was inscribed on the front of the box. 'What does that mean?'

Eric placed the box down on the table, so the others could view the title. Jon tried to appear as though he was not interested, but really he was as curious as every other set of eyes in the room.

The front of the box gave little away. It was a puzzle box – one of Eric's favourite pastimes. Puzzle boxes at their simplest only had one mechanism to work out, but the boxes that Eric fascinated himself with often had upwards of one hundred components to figure through. This box appeared misshapen, with mechanisms piercing the sides, gears lining the face, and even a smaller box jutting out of it, much like the towers of Balmoral. When placed, as it was, among the other presents of the day, there was no comparison – this was the winner.

It was the name of the puzzle box that seemed to be drawing most of the attention, however. Carved into the face of the box in uniform letters was the foreboding title:

INTERREGNUM.

VIII

The Mystery Gift

The grooved lacquered letters glinted in the firelight. The king picked up the box and moved it back and forth, making the letters look like they were dancing. 'And who do I have to thank for this work of majesty?' Eric asked an audience of confused faces.

'What does it mean?' Martin piped up, his attention drawn to the box when the intrigue of his own pile of presents had been exhausted. He was asking the question the rest of the party was wondering as well, Jon also.

Eric peered at the smallest royal and laughed. 'Come, Martin, what do you think it means?'

Martin came to stand next to his grandfather, rather unimpressed with the attention he was receiving. 'Interregnum. I don't know.'

Eric did not hold the youngster's lack of knowledge against him. 'Interregnum is a very important word. It refers to a particular time period. The term is comprised of two Latin words. The first, "*inter*", means "between" and the second, "*regnum*", means "reign". So when placed together the title of this puzzle, in its very literal sense, is "between reign".'

'Between reign?' Emeline said. 'What an odd name for a puzzle.' She seemed so genuinely curious that Jon thought he could erase her name from the suspect list of who had given Eric the gift, but then he remembered Emeline had a cunning side. He recalled hearing of a certain time when she was five and she had let loose on the walls of Windsor Castle with a felt-tip pen. She had everyone somehow convinced, for the longest time, that the perpetrator was one of the cats, who had clutched the marker in its teeth. When Eric regaled the tale to Jon, he couldn't hide how impressed he was that she had had everyone fooled.

Eric traced the letters with a finger. 'A royal puzzle. I would question what this meant if only I knew who to direct the question to.' The clear call to action was not met with a name. For a second, it seemed that Eric, scrutinising them all in turn, would not get past this point and would spend the rest of the day getting to the bottom of it. In a mere second, however, all was forgotten and Eric's face stretched into a boyish smile – the likes of which Jon had not seen in a long while. 'Well, no matter. I will have this open in a jiffy. Do feel free to talk amongst yourselves.'

Over the next hour, King Eric poked and prodded the box, turning it over in his hands, attempting to break into it, with an intense look of determination on his face. Jon watched him for a while, before even he became fatigued by the fact that the king seemed to be making little progress. He had gotten the front side open slightly, but it seemed that the entire mechanism was hinged on three separate puzzles around all but one side.

Jon decided it best to leave the king to his work, and made a circuit of the room, handing out drinks and topping up glasses. He had not been watching the other royals, so it was interesting to see how they had progressed.

David and Marjorie, the familiar duo, were now standing as far from the king as they could, by the far wall. They almost seemed as if they were contemplating leaving the scene altogether, hovering by the door. They were in intense discussion, with Marjorie swaying slightly and steadying herself by touching the wall, and David still in high emotion.

'They need some discipline, Marjorie.'

'I know, I know. You try to talk to a king. I've said ever since they were babies that they would need a firm hand. I had it, my mother had it, my mother's mother had it, my mother's mother's mother had it, my . . .' She was silent for a moment, breaking from her cycle. 'But he never listened. I used to be naughty, be disciplined and then not be able to sit down for days for the spankings. But every time I did try to sit, I'd recall why I couldn't. And I wouldn't do what incited them again.'

'Exactly, Margey. But seeing as they have not had that, they are now set in their ways. And their ill manners cannot be undone. Maybe I could have a word with him?'

Marjorie was in the same conversation but on her own path, eyeing her youngest daughter with suspicion. 'I only hope that she is not imprinting on Martin. I think Matthew may be a lost cause already, but . . .' Marjorie lurched, and her eyes met Jon's. 'Alleyne, do you often eavesdrop like that?'

'I'm sorry, ma'am. I was just waiting for the best time to cut in. Would you like a drink?'

Marjorie snorted. 'Does the king leave the seat up? That means yes, Alleyne.'

Jon filled Marjorie's glass with a smile that he hoped seemed genuine. 'Prince David?'

'Yes, I suppose I ought. How long until the speech, do you think, Margey?'

'Not long, I hope.'

'It better not be about that common family at the zoo again. I fear I could recite that in my sleep as it is.'

Jon took his leave, moving on to Emeline, Maud and Martin, who were standing around the Christmas tree, and laughing together. Well, the sisters were – Martin seemed to be the odd one in this gathering, glancing around as if to find a way out.

'What do you think Daddy will talk about in his speech to us?' Emeline was saying as Jon entered earshot.

'Hard to know, really,' Maud mused. 'He always pulls something rather funny out of his hat though, doesn't he? I think he could have been a comedian if he wasn't . . . well . . . king.'

'Have you seen his Christmas message for the BBC?'

'No. He sent over a copy, but I didn't have a chance. I was opening a RSPCA cattery in Plymouth at the weekend. The pair of scissors they gave me to cut the garland were blunt – that's really all I remember from the experience.'

'He said that the Beeb cut out all of his jokes.'

Maud laughed – a glorious sound, much like a song-bird. 'See – a comedian. But it doesn't surprise me. You have to leave room for the Military Wives after all.'

'No, this year it's some choir of orphans or something. I wonder who taught them to sing? Jonathan,' Emeline said, startling all others in attendance. She was the only one who had noticed him hovering in the periphery. 'Have you come to fill our cups?'

The two princesses shared matching smiles and it was impossible for him not to smile too. 'I have, ma'am.' They offered up their glasses, which Jon filled.

Martin looked expectant. 'Can I have some more?'

'I suppose so, as it's Christmas,' Maud conceded, nodding her consent to Jon. 'But don't drink it too quickly, and don't tell your father. Or the *Daily Mail*.'

Thomas Crockley was standing alone on the other side of the tree, drinking and playing with a particularly shiny bauble. He seemed happy to see Jon approach, and before Jon could offer up a tipple, Crockley had embroiled him in conversation.

Ten minutes later and it was still happening – 'We have a fleet of cars out there on the streets twenty-four-seven. Uber cannot touch us – and believe me, they've tried.' Crockley had made his money kickstarting a taxi-like app for the upper class. Jon had never used it himself – was hardly in the pay bracket to qualify – but it was meant to be the lap of luxury. From Crockley's sales pitch, it did indeed sound splendid.

Jon filled his glass without Crockley even breaking a

stanza of self-congratulatory smugness. He moved away from Crockley as soon as he could, seeing that he realised he had missed one royal entirely – and this providing ample excuse to move on.

Matthew was also alone, rolling his tumbler between his hands, lost in thoughts beyond his years and gazing at the king with admiration shimmering in his eyes. Jon came to him and asked him his question, almost sorrowful to disturb the picture.

Matthew held out his glass, with a 'Please. The brandy.'

When he was done, Jon gazed with Matthew awhile.

'How does my grandfather seem to you, Jon?'

It was not often Jon was asked his opinion, and Matthew had never inquired about it before, so he had to think a moment. 'I don't know, really. In what regard?'

'You've been with him for how long now?'

'Over three decades, sir.'

'So you've seen him slow down.'

'Yes, sir, I have a little, but I have slowed with him, as have your grandmother and your great-uncle. Time is only your friend when you are young. Soon enough, it becomes your enemy.'

Matthew watched the king, appearing to try to apply Jon's words to what was ailing him. 'There's always been something about him. King Eric Windsor, but also my grandfather. Two very different people, but somehow the same. I look up to both. And, now, seeing him fade. You're right, Alleyne – time.'

Jon almost felt the need to leap to the king's defence.

'Not fading, sir. Just not as fast as he once was.'

Matthew wanted to say something, voice some other fear – it was written on his face – but at that moment, a cry of triumph came from the king's direction.

'I think I have it. Jon, would you please refill my cup so I can toast my victory! I beat Interregnum.'

IX

A Short-Lived Victory

As Jon made his way over to King Eric with the drinks tray, the king started to laugh. 'How fabulous.' He had just managed to open the lid of the box and was sniffing at the air, almost comically.

'Sir?' Jon said, having to stifle a laugh.

'Ingenious. Someone trapped a scent in here. Roast potatoes, maybe? I can smell the goose fat and garlic. Enough to get me hungry even though I am full to bursting. Sniff?' Eric held the box up to Jon, but the smell had already dissipated. Jon shook his head, and Eric pouted like a disappointed schoolboy. 'Oh well, I promise it was glorious, and wonderfully Christmassy. This puzzle box is indeed the finest I have ever seen. The craftsmanship is unmatched. Now, let us get this thing done. There seems to be one final step.'

To Jon's horror, Eric thrust his hand into the box and started to rummage around. Whatever was happening inside the wooden marvel Jon did not know, but he had never seen such an intense expression of concentration on anyone's face, let alone the king's. Even on the nights when Jon had sat with Eric Windsor as he attempted one of these oddities, he had not seen such a famished desire to achieve as the king exuded now, struggling with the inner workings of Interregnum.

However, the struggle worked, as one final click resonated from the box and Eric withdrew his hand as an opening revealed itself in the front side of the box, and a small wooden figure rolled out onto the table. Eric tried to catch it, but it eluded him. Jon caught it and handed it to him. A small tinkle of 'God Save the King' came from somewhere within the box.

Eric held up the figure. A king chess piece. He glanced at Jon with the air of a child looking for praise. Jon was glad that he was chosen to give it. 'Well done, sir. I am always impressed by how you do these things.' It was true. Matthew had just been saying how the king had slowed, but in certain ways he had become faster. This was almost his fastest puzzle solve yet.

'There's a language to these things, old friend. Much like with anything.' He set down the miniature king next to the Interregnum box and took to examining the solved puzzle with freshly victorious eyes. 'To approach something such as this is to reconfigure one's view of the world. One must see things as the puzzle-crafter does, just as reading a Shakespearian sonnet takes you into the mind of the playwright himself. One is not solving the puzzle but solving the man.'

Not for the first time that day, Jon felt as though the king were trying to tell him something more, trying to unlock the doors of some deeper thought. The king often spoke in such riddles – it delighted and infuriated people in equal measure. 'That is a lot of secrets to place inside a small box, sir.'

'What is a man if not a box of secrets, old friend?' The king gazed upon him deeply, Jon had the feeling that he were getting solved at that very moment, and then the moment passed. 'But what a fabulous thing. It must have been commissioned just for me. I have never seen anything like it. If only I knew who to thank. Do you have any clue who it could be, Jon?'

'I'm afraid not, sir. But it is a work of art. I can only wish the answer was myself.'

Eric offered a sad smile. The king knew that Jon would indeed buy him such a present if he were able, Jon could see that. He would buy him the world, even though he already owned it.

The relationship between the king and his chef was something of a puzzle itself. At times, Jon thought of the king as a father, who was there to look out for him and had happily inducted him into the family. Other times, Eric Windsor was his saviour, who had rescued him from the tyranny of the dingy West End kitchen he had skulked about in. Other times, it seemed that Eric was his equal – two good friends who enjoyed one another's company. It may also be worth noting that Jon never thought of Eric as he actually was – the king, yes, but, more importantly to Jon's station, the client. The most astutely critical observer may think Jon was suffering a variant of Stockholm syndrome, where King Eric could be seen as the captor figure and, therefore, Jon Alleyne the captive.

'Nonsense,' King Eric said. 'You being here is enough. Dinner was exceptional, by the way. You have truly surpassed yourself – and to make it alone, too!'

Jon outwardly presented modesty: 'You are too kind, sir,' but inside he was so elated by the comment he could hardly control himself. It was Eric's opinion he always cared about the most, so even when Marjorie had turned her nose up at a beef goulash, or the young princesses had refused Jon's twist on liver and onions, the chef had remained steadfast in his ability. As long as the king enjoyed his cooking, little else mattered.

'You must be ready for a good lie-down. I'll tell you a little secret – so am I,' Eric laughed – but there was something in the sound that wasn't quite right. Jon was about to enquire about this, but the ornamental clock over the fireplace interrupted, chiming in a new hour. It was three o' clock. The country would be silent – families with full bellies and wavering sobriety sitting down in front of their televisions to hear from their king. Balmoral was no different, although this family would be treated to a live performance from a different script. 'Time always has a habit of slipping away nowadays, doesn't it? Jon, please will you make sure every member of my beloved family has a glass of whisky?'

Jon paused. It was always Eric who poured the whisky, but today the king just waited in his seat and smiled sadly at him. Seeing his chef's confusion, he gave an almost imperceptible nod. So Jon did as he was commanded, making a lap of the room with fresh glasses and the square decanter. He did not stop until every Royal

77

had a glass, even pouring Martin a little drop at Maud's quiet approval. The last glass he filled was the king's.

'Thank you, old friend.'

Jon nodded, standing back. 'An honour, Your Majesty.' He spoke no lie.

The king rose, grasping his glass – the whisky inside whirling as its owner steadied himself. Jon did not know if something was amiss, but finally Eric straightened, and became the king he knew again. The family did not seem to notice – they were simply waiting with their drinks, for the inevitable.

It seemed Marjorie was fighting every impulse to drink, David was regarding his brother with a wry smile, Emeline and Maud were standing together proudly, Thomas had paused his inspection of the tree to hear the king out, Matthew was leaning against the far wall and contemplating his glass, while Martin was sniffing at his and turning his nose up.

'Ah,' King Eric began, 'the Royal Family. Such an enigma, hmm? It is often that we spend so much time thinking of what the public thinks of us that we forget what we think of ourselves. So for now, let us not be royal. Let us be just a family.' Eric raised his glass to his lips and took a deep drink. He savoured it as he swallowed. 'Can we allow ourselves that?'

Jon looked to Eric's audience to see that the opening of the speech was somewhat falling on deaf ears. The only member of the odd congregation who seemed enraptured was Matthew, who was once again watching his grandfather's every move – proud and firm.

King Eric did indeed seem proud, surveying his family. The love he had for them all, in equal measure, spread across his face and invigorated the aged man. Momentarily, he appeared to be the man he once was – the man that Jon had served in Caribbean Plaza over thirty years before. His eyes did not move from his family, except for one singular moment that would live in Jon's life for ever. The king's eyes flitted over to him and he smiled, before they returned to his fellow Windsors.

'It is an honour to spend a Christmas alone with this family of mine . . .' Eric stopped. His eyes slid over his family and came to rest on Jon again. But this was not a face of love, pride and contentment now – it was a face of discomfort, pain and fear.

Something was deathly wrong.

Jon tried to move but found his fear had frozen him in place. He saw that the other Windsors were much the same, with somewhat gormless and almost apathetic looks painted on their faces. The room was a still-life, but for the king.

Where in the bloody hell was Tony Speck? Jon could not do this alone. He was not trained for anything like this. His place was in the kitchen, not here.

King Eric was spluttering now. He dropped the whisky glass and it clattered from the side of the table, bounced off the shag carpet and ricocheted somewhere near the fireplace – where didn't really matter. Jon's eyes never left Eric's face. All that youth gone, now Eric was what he had always been afraid to become – a scared old man. He was still spluttering – coughing and clutching his throat, but for all his attempts at dislodging this phantom obstruction, all that was coming out of his mouth was a thick, sticky foam.

With one final heave of life that shook Eric's very being, he fell forwards – crashing over the table he had been sitting at mere minutes before. A wine glass shattered as it was thrown from its place, the Interregnum puzzle box fell to the floor and the musical mechanism inside was triggered again. In a sickly comedic gesture, 'God Save the King' started playing once more. Eric's body exhaled one last long breath – his entire frame deflating.

Jon came to his senses and rushed to the king's side. Once again, the question – where in the hell was Speck? But even the answer didn't matter much any more. Jon knelt over the king's frame. 'Sir, sir.' He looked up to see the Royal Family frozen in their worry – no one had moved an inch. He would have thought them cold and callous had he not known the feeling. 'Your Majesty?'

Jon held his finger to the king's neck and found the place where the evidence of life should be. He held his own breath as if that would make some kind of a difference. He already knew – there was not one in that room who did not.

His head rose to the remaining Royal Family.

'The king is dead.'

And history began.

X

The Real Interregnum

Is it not true that one of the worst parts of a tragedy is the fact that the world so readily carries on after it? The planet continues turning. Time barely falters in its eternal march. Buses keep running. Tomorrow is to be expected no sooner or later than usual. Pain is all-consuming and is one's to carry alone. The lives shaken are the only ones out of sync.

As a matter of fact, this was exactly how Jon would have described the drawing room of Balmoral at that moment: 3.03 p.m. – the longest minute of his life. A place out of time. Less a minute and more a destination – one he never wished to visit again. He was there for years, as were the others around him. It took them all of 3.03 p.m. to realise that King Eric had ceased to be. And then the clock ticked over to 3.04 and it all continued happening. Planes did not fall from the sky. Power stations did not explode spontaneously. War was not declared. King Eric still spoke from fourteen million television sets throughout the British Isles. Posthumously – although his subjects were blissfully unaware of the fact.

The first thing that happened, in that newest period of interregnum, was that someone screamed, and the second thing that happened, curiously, was that someone laughed. It was an odd fact that it was not the first thing that finally made Jon accept the reality of the situation they found themselves in, but rather the second.

The royal who produced the scream was Emeline. 'Father? Father?' Emeline, like much of the rest of her family, was horrified by the scene in front of her, but she seemed to be emotionally ahead of everyone else. She understood, much like Jon did, that King Eric was gone – there was no question. He was dead – his soul no longer present. Jon did not know where his essence was – but it was no longer in the vessel laid before him. It was not a shock that anyone's first reaction may be to scream – let alone Emeline, who had just lost a father.

The cry seemed to jostle the other royals out of their transcendent state and understanding started to infect them all. Most exhibited feelings much the same as Emeline. But then the laugh occurred, and it was shock that Jon felt upon realising that one royal had decided it was an appropriate reaction, outwardly, to exhibit.

Jon straightened up. The world did not. He was standing over the dead body of a king. His friend. His mentor. His anchor. The sight of Eric Windsor draped over the coffee table was too much to bear. 'We have to move him.'

Marjorie was cackling like a loon and seemed to be mightily puzzled at why none of the rest of them were too. 'Well, he's not dead.' She put down her glass of whisky, and, evidently deciding that a death in the family was ample grounds for the death of decorum, picked up a wine bottle instead and upended it into her mouth.

'He's done this before. Get up, Eric. You're getting stale, doing this again.'

Maud erupted into cries, closely followed by echoes from her sister. Jon was unsure if it was Eric or Marjorie who elicited the reaction. Thomas Crockley rocked back on his heels, clicked his tongue and comforted his wife – viewing everything that was occurring as if it had nothing to do with him.

'He'll get up in a minute,' Marjorie said. 'You'll see.'

'Shut up, Marjorie,' David snapped. The king's brother had gone an almost radiant shade of white – with tears threatening the corners of his eyes. 'How could you say that? Just look at him.'

Jon seized the king's shoulders. 'Somebody help me.' There was a body next to Jon then, and Matthew was hovering over the king's form. Matthew and Jon looked at one another and nodded. They lifted the king as gently as they could and laid him on the carpet.

Matthew withdrew as quickly as possible. As Jon drew back from the king, he held in a sob as he saw the old man's face. The king's eyes were closed, his eyebrows were raised in expectation and his mouth was agape in the middle of gasping for a breath that would never come.

'Oh God, father,' Emeline wailed. The twin sisters were just that, in that moment – mirroring each other perfectly. She ripped Maud from Crockley's clutches and held her tight. 'Jonathan?'

The rest of the Royal Family were standing over him and the king. They were all looking to him for some sort of guidance, but he had no idea what to do. He was the chef, for God's sake!

He turned back to the king and knew that he would have to try to clear the man's throat. He took two fingers and stuck them inside the king's mouth, grimacing as he raked through something slimy. He scooped out three loads of brown grimy sludge – a substance that did not look like it came from this planet, let alone someone's body. In reality, it was probably a concoction made up of whisky, red wine, Christmas dinner and maybe even breakfast toast.

'Oh my God,' Maud sobbed.

'He's played dead before, believe me,' Marjorie was continuing, evidently absent from the rest of the room. 'Remember our wedding night, eh, Eric?' She made a snorting sound that seemed to be endless in its perversity – very unbecoming of a princess, much less one who would be queen.

'Please, Margey! Look at him!' David roared.

'Does anyone know CPR?' Jon said breathlessly, looking up to blank faces. He had never had CPR training himself, although he always thought he should have. Whenever he brought it up with anyone, there was always the thinly veiled insult that someone far more important would be around to save a Royal's life if the situation arose. The irony was not lost on him, even in such a dire moment.

'Wait, he does,' Emeline said, pointing to Crockley. The man looked sheepish. 'Thomas, you won't stop going on about the bloody Badgers. The St John Ambulance or something. This is not the time to tell me that was one of your bloody lies.'

Crockley was hesitant, but the accusation fuelled him. 'Now, look here, I was a Badger. But that was back in the day. Protocols have changed since then. If I do something wrong, I could really hurt the old boy.'

'Thomas, he is bloody dead.'

Crockley glanced around at his inherited family with the right amount of panic and apprehension. 'OK, point taken.' He stepped over the king and knelt down. Jon shuffled out of the way as Crockley, with a mixed amount of confidence, tipped the king's head back and stared into his mouth. Next, he traced the outline of the king's ribs, finding the right spot, and locked his right hand over his left, hovering it above. 'I don't suppose anyone could hum me the Bee Gees, could they?' It was clear it was not a joke – the man was petrified. But when no one responded, he began his chest compressions.

1, 2, 3, 4, 5. Crockley haphazardly pumped down upon the king's chest. Then he moved to the king's head and, with a little hesitation, blew into his mouth twice, lips locking down to form a seal. Jon watched him anxiously, fearing the worst – he didn't think that the king would miraculously spring back up, like the other royals were clearly hoping. And after a few minutes of Crockley switching between breathing for the king and trying to beat his heart, that hope was dwindling.

'Stop, Thomas,' Maud said, through tears. 'Please, stop.'

'You will keep going!' Emeline snapped.

'Brother!' David whispered sadly. 'Dear God in heaven.'

'Thomas, please,' Maud begged, partly to her husband and partly to her sister. 'Please just stop. He is gone.'

Jon staggered to a stand. The royals were behind him on their grief – and Marjorie was still in denial, looking as if she were holding back gales of laughter. The princess royal snorted again, a sound met with the motion of another swig of wine. The old woman was positively Roman in her shameless decadence – the shambolic paper Christmas hat nestled in her wiry hair did not help matters either. Elsewhere, even David was crying, with the twins clutching each other, and Matthew trying to comfort young Martin, who was staring wide-eyed at the whole scene.

'Keep going!' Emeline screamed.

'He's gone, Aunt,' Matthew said to her.

The king was dead. Jon's legs threatened to give way and send him back to the floor. What was this? How could this have happened? The Royal Family were the safest they had ever been – wasn't that what Speck had said? All the security systems in the world could not have predicted or prevented this. The king was dead.

Jon tore his eyes from the king and the family surrounding him to look out the window past the Christmas tree. The world was still glowing with pure white snow. He could not see outside properly as frost and snow clouded the glass. It almost seemed as if the blizzard had gotten worse – as if the weather were mourning too. Maybe the snow had known what was going to happen here today and had come to take a look.

But nobody could have known. Could they? Jon thought back to the king's final act, a simple drink from his glass and then . . .

'What do we do?' Maud said, defeated, as her husband finally gave up the battle. Crockley shuffled back from the body as though it were diseased. He clutched his stomach and barely made it over to the wastepaper basket before vomiting.

'I regularly feel that way after a kiss from the king,' Marjorie said, chuckling. 'Isn't that right, Eric?' It was clear that no one had the space in their own emotional process to accommodate her. The princess royal would have to forge her own path through grief and understanding.

'Dear brother,' David said again. He was openly weeping, a show of raw emotion that had never painted his face before, at least in these walls. He tipped his glass of whisky as if in ceremony.

Jon felt that something was very wrong, and his body acted before he even knew why. David raised the glass to his lips, and this was the motion that finally unlocked the connection in Jon's brain – so bright, he wondered why no one else had seen it also. In one swift movement, the type that he did not know himself capable of any more, he threw himself to David's side and slapped the glass out of his hand just before it touched his mouth.

The glass sailed through the air and became caught in a web of Christmas tree ornaments, becoming one itself.

David scowled at the chef in utter amazement. 'What in the great hell has gotten into you?'

Jon silently asked himself the same question, but it all became clear as he moved around to face the entire family. 'The king has been poisoned.'

The worst part of a tragedy is that the world carries on so readily after it, even when you wish it wouldn't.

XI

The Poison Chalice

The room was at once a silent tableau, every subject pointed at their purveyor. Jon's statement plagued his lips, made them burn − was this what the king had felt as he died? Could his theory be true, and if so, what did that mean − for the king, for the rest of the family, for him? He was still thinking on it when David finally broke out of his painted panic.

'What on earth are you talking about?' His hand was still outstretched, cupped, holding the glass that now lay in the Christmas tree.

Jon said again, breathlessly, 'I'm afraid I mean precisely what I say. The king. He has been poisoned.'

David snorted. 'Preposterous.'

'The whisky.'

'It once was whisky, yes. Now it's coated on the ceiling. You ought to know your place, Butler.'

Jon collected himself. 'One of the final acts His Majesty performed on this earth was to take a drink of that very whisky.' The whisky. Anchor Haven. That had to be it. That had to be why the king was now lying on the floor, cold and broken.

Jon shuddered. No. The king was not here any more.

The king had left Balmoral, left this world, left this blasted shared consciousness they called existence. The body lying on the floor of the drawing room was not the king. It looked like him, but it could not be further from him. King Eric was always full of life. Until he wasn't.

Jon's plain statement had somehow made its way through David's thick layer of vileness. The old prince was thinking intently, until he came to the same conclusion Jon had. 'Dear God – the whisky.' David's hand went to his own throat with the panic of what might have been. 'Nobody touch the whisky.'

David's command was redundant – no one else had kept hold of their glasses. The sisters had not even heard the commotion – drowned in their grief. Thomas Crockley was still recovering from his sickness, still trying to scrabble up from the floor. Marjorie was in her own world, still smiling and swaying with wine bottle in hand. It was only Matthew and Martin who seemed really to have acknowledged David's remark.

Matthew, with his hands on Martin's shoulders, guided his younger brother over to his mother and aunt, before joining the two men. It was obvious he was trying with all his might not to look downwards towards the king, but as he navigated the coffee table and the dual chaises longues, he had to. When he did, he choked back a cry that nestled so comfortably in with Maud and Emeline's constant ones.

'What did you just say?' Matthew asked, glassy-eyed.

'The whisky,' David cried. 'Poison in the whisky!'

'I don't know,' Jon conceded. 'This may be a natural

thing – not one that I've ever . . . But it could be. We also need to seriously consider the possibility that the king was assassinated. No one else is ill, so we can rule out anything in the food. It is most likely that there was something in that whisky.'

'He has been murdered? My grandfather has been murdered?' Matthew said this with a tone wavering between uncontrollable anger and rampant sorrow. 'How could something like this happen?'

'Let's not jump to conclusions. But let's be careful also,' Jon said.

A sound escaped David then – an odd wailing moan. Jon looked into the man's face to see a look of complete despair. He was shattered by this. At this vantage, David's bulbous pores were positively abhorrent. The man was indeed a vile specimen, but he was still a man. A man who had lost his brother. A single tear rolled down his rocky cheek.

Matthew put a calming hand on his grand-uncle's shoulder, just as he had with his brother. It was an odd act of kindness to bestow on the old prince, and it was clear that David was not used to it. He almost broke down at Matthew's touch.

Before he could, however, there was a fresh cry, and a new task. Princess Emeline was reprimanding Crockley, somewhat unjustly. 'Well, if you can't bloody save him, at least pick him up from the floor. He's my father. And most importantly, he's the King of bloody England.'

She was right, of course. Jon stepped forward, but Matthew held up a hand to him and did so himself.

91

He beckoned to his father for help. Crockley had just achieved a standing position, and seemed very reluctant to bend down to the floor again, let alone touch his father-in-law's body, but he did it all the same. Jon watched as they lifted the king – Crockley at the man's shoulders, Matthew at his legs – and carried him over to the left-hand chaise longue. They gently placed him down there, as though he were sleeping off a Christmas tipple. If not for his pained expression, he could have easily been mistaken for a snoozing monarch.

Both living participants in this transaction once again backed away, as the now familiar ambience of sobs and wails started up again from the princesses. This time, it seemed as though Prince Martin might start too. It was not as if Jon could blame them – if not for his station, he would be distraught himself. The only thing holding him together was his duty – to this family.

If only others would feel the same. Speck. Where in the bloody hell was he?

Jon reached to his belt and unclipped the walkie-talkie. With one final look at the king, he strode to the door of the drawing room and then stopped himself. Everything was amiss here – could the family really be left alone?

'Where is she going?' came the small question from Thomas Crockley.

Marjorie was stumbling over to the king, half sitting and half falling by his side – her rapid descent not stopping her from taking a drink of wine on the way down. 'Come now, you can get up, Eric. Enough is quite enough.'

As Jon returned to the scene, he passed the whisky on the coffee table. Poison. It sounded barbaric, idiotic, putrid. How and why would someone poison the king? Of course, it was someone outside the castle, but . . .

No.

Jon paused, towering above the cubed crystalline serving decanter. It was still half full, ready and primed for second helpings. Jon thought intensely – not only of his day, but the day of the whisky stretching out in front of him (or, more accurately, behind him). He saw things, heard things, sensed things, things that led him to one conclusion. The only conclusion. 'My God.'

David and Matthew thundered over to meet him, or maybe to meet the decanter.

'We should pour this out. Get rid of it!' David shouted.

'Eric?' Marjorie said, off in the distance. She was still at his side.

'We can't get rid of it,' Matthew said to David. 'If it's not the whisky that poisoned him, we need to know. And if it is, it's evidence.'

Jon started away. 'I must try to raise Speck,' he said, holding up his walkie-talkie.

'Eric. Get up.' It was hard to care about Marjorie's plight in that instant, but she was finally understanding.

'What is it?' Matthew asked, seemingly seeing the fresh panic in Jon's eyes.

'We have to get rid of it!' roared David. 'I will not have the thing that killed my brother in the same room as me.'

Jon looked sadly from Matthew to David. 'People kill people. Not drinks.'

He stopped himself from saying any more. They did not need to know yet – it would only make it worse – because if Jon was correct, the killer was here, at Balmoral, and what was more, they were in this very room.

From her husband's side, Marjorie finally started to cry.

XII

Where in the Bloody Hell is Tony Speck?

Jon could not delay, but he could not leave the Royal Family alone either. If he was right, one of them was capable of murder, and had demonstrated that they were quite capable of carrying it out. Only this singular individual could know if more parricide was in store.

This was how Jon came to the conclusion that it was someone in the room. He had picked up the bottle of Anchor Haven whisky this morning from the pantry on his way to stoke the drawing-room fire for David. He had unsealed the whisky in the drawing room with David present – he remembered the crack as the plastic lid ripped in two – parting so it could be unscrewed. He had poured it into the decanter and then it had sat in the drawing room all morning to air. Which family members could have slipped poison into the bottle was something that Jon would have to uncover, but the facts were there and they were plain. There was no way anyone else could have had access to the whisky. One might be able to reseal a bottle, but definitely not someone in Balmoral with limited resources to do such a thing. The bottle of Anchor Haven had sat in the pantry for months

95

– he had received the delivery himself and seen there was nothing amiss.

Jon made sure he was as far as possible from the family, stepping around the Christmas tree. Most did not even notice him slip away. The only two that did – Matthew and David – were more interested in continuing their debate over the whisky. Jon stepped towards the window, hoping that may help his connection with whom he wanted to talk to. He brought the walkie-talkie to his mouth.

'Speck, come in.' He tried to sound as composed as possible, but his words were soaked in a fiery panic that was nothing if not shockingly evident.

Of course, there was one last suspect, and Jon had thought of this himself. Tony Speck, the last resident of Balmoral on this cursed day. The more he thought, however, the more he saw it was unlikely. He could not rule it out, but he could not see an ample opportunity either. Tony Speck, as frequently noted, was obsessed with patrolling the grounds. That meant when he was travelling in and out, he had to use the door that went past Jon's kitchen. Jon would have noticed Speck's return and did once, but that was after the drawing room was occupied. He found it hard to see how Speck could have poisoned the whisky while the family was about. For one, he would likely have had to make small talk with them – an act he was utterly terrible at, and which would have aroused suspicion straight away. The whisky was alone at dinner, but Speck was with Jon then, and when he wasn't, he entered and exited from the opposite way to the drawing room.

Speck was an insufferable oaf, but that was all he was. At least, Jon hoped against hope that he was, because otherwise he was truly alone in this.

Silence. For a time, Jon thought the walkie-talkie wasn't working, and then came a burst of static.

'Speck, come in.'

Jon felt an all-encompassing loneliness then – a feeling that pounced upon him with the speed of a foul wind, whipping around him and creating an impenetrable cocoon. He was truly alone – the last line of defence between the remaining Royal Family and a merciless killer. Was he the only one who would have to ascertain the difference between the two?

'Speck, come in. Please.' He was almost pleading to the handful of plastic and wires, as though Speck would hear it. But it seemed he would not. 'Speck, we have a situation here. Something terrible has happened.' Jon was acutely aware that the family could hear his every word if they decided to, so he lowered his voice to slip under the crying of the princesses. 'The Bridlepath Causeway has flooded. Hear me, Speck – the Bridlepath Causeway has flooded.' There were special codes for the death of the royals that the staff had to memorise. 'I said – do you hear me, Speck? Bridlepath Causeway.'

The walkie-talkie choked out another set of static coughs before falling silent.

'Speck . . . Tony . . . please come back. I don't know what to do. Everyone is scared, and panicked, and confused. And they could really use the head of security right now. I could really use him too. Please, Speck.'

It would all be painted as Jon Alleyne's fault. Jon Alleyne failed to save the king – hell, Jon Alleyne practically killed the king himself. He might not have been the one to lace the whisky, but he had served it up. He may not have been the one with the murderous plot, but he had exacted it.

'I don't know what to do.'

Although this would have seemed like a message to Speck, it was more a message to himself. He had not pressed the call button – it was apparent that there was little point. Clearly, Tony Speck was not going to save them – he was not going to ride in on a wave of Scottish snow and revive the king, apprehend the one responsible and whisk the others to safety.

It was just Jon – the one who'd killed the king through his incompetence, his inaction – left to pick up the pieces. What would they do to him? What would he do to himself? Not only had he lost a king, but also a dear friend. He rarely thought of the future, as it didn't concern him – but now he did. What did a future without King Eric even look like? What did a future without this career look like?

A final burst of static brought him back to the moment. This was not about him, and it never had been. He replaced the walkie-talkie on his belt – hoping that he would not have to try again, but knowing that he would. Until Speck reappeared, it was clear what his part in proceedings had to be. For now, he had only one true purpose – to protect the remaining Royal Family at all costs. If he had to lay down his life for one of theirs, so be it. Such was the role he had been forced into. He would do it – for them, for the Crown, but most of all, for the king.

XIII

A 'Moral Quandary

'No joy?' was the question greeting Jon as he made his way back to Matthew and David. He had never really noticed before what an odd expression 'No joy?' was. No joy indeed. He felt like he might never feel joy again, and he expected that all in the room would express the same sentiment.

'Speck must be out there in the snow. He either can't hear me or the connection isn't getting through at all.'

'Well, he's deserted us, hasn't he?' David was watching Marjorie and the princesses grieve with a morose stare. They were hugging in a ball on the floor, their expensive dresses rubbing on the carpet. 'I never did like the look of him. Who's to say that he isn't the cause of this?'

'Then we cannot rely on him.' This from Matthew, who seemed to be talking about one thing and thinking about another. It was easy to forget the young man was only eighteen. The way he carried himself, it was astoundingly mature – even in such grave circumstances. 'Well, when he appears he will very quickly disappear again. He won't have a job come tomorrow; Christmas spirit be damned.'

Jon was glad that Matthew realised the importance of Speck's absence. He wasn't necessarily happy about a man losing his job, but it was the man's own fault. There was nothing to say that if Speck were here events wouldn't have transpired exactly as they had. But he simply should have been here. Unless there was a very good reason.

'Damn Speck,' David muttered.

'There are other issues with Speck's disappearance, besides safety.' Matthew was looking grave. He stared directly at Jon as he said this as if communicating silently to him. Unfortunately, Jon did indeed get the message. The young prince was right – it was hard to believe he had just come of age, and now was having to deal with this. Jon stifled an expletive as the prince continued, 'Speck collected all of our phones, as per the king's instructions.'

'Oh,' was all David could manage, he didn't seem to care for what his great-nephew had to say. Somehow, a glass of wine had materialised in his hand and he was drinking it freely.

There was something else – another roadblock Speck had, hopefully, unintentionally erected, something that only another member of staff would know. 'Speck has the keys as well.'

'The keys?' Matthew asked.

'Speck has the only set of keys on site for the lockbox at the front gates. Inside the lockbox is a number pad to open them. I know the code, but without the keys, that doesn't matter. We couldn't get in there. We could trudge out into the blizzard, to the gates, but nothing is getting past that box. The other way is the trek across the Highlands to the property lines – the fence there is not as high, and we might get over it, but then what? There is nothing that way for miles, and the jeeps won't drive in this weather.'

'So call someone with the keys,' David snapped. 'It isn't a difficult predicament.'

'My mobile is with Speck, just as yours is. And . . . the landlines went down last night in the blizzard. As did the wireless internet.'

A ripple of discomfort and distrust passed through the men. Matthew voiced it – 'Why were we not informed of this?'

Jon felt ashamed to say it but – 'Speck said it was better that you weren't aware. He said it better not to disrupt your Christmas with worry.'

'But Grandfather would have been calling the prime minister to wish him a Happy Christmas after his speech.'

'I'm assuming that Speck would have quietly mentioned the phone lines to the king then.' Jon felt as though he were making excuses for the absent man – a back foot he had no intention of staying on.

'So let me just summarise for myself,' David said. 'We have no phones, a raging blizzard outside, no way out of the gates if we even reached them and, lastly, no way to call for help. We are well and truly stuck at the 'Moral, with the dead body of a king here. Not to mention that the poisoner could still be lurking.' His voice rose for that last crescendo – the first time he seemed not completely in control of his emotions, apart from that one true tear. One might think he was feeling some genuine sorrow – Jon did think that. He failed to recognise that David may indeed be in a state of mourning, but rather a state of mourning for himself – imprisoned like a wasp in an upturned wine glass. Was David all that he appeared?

'The question remains – what do we do now?' Matthew said.

Matthew looked to Jon, as did David. They were like children, revelling in independence and then looking to an adult the moment something went wrong. 'There isn't any protocol for this kind of situation. And if there is, I don't know about it. I am just the head chef – I am not included in everything.'

'Well, that doesn't help much now, does it?'

'No, sir,' Jon said, entirely without sarcasm. David was correct.

'Grand-uncle! Please. We need to realise that we are no different. Being royal means little here and now.'

'Don't grand-uncle me, boy. And being royal is everything. That is what you new-wave royals fail to understand. Even in times such as these . . . No! Especially in times such as these, we must remain steadfast in our morals and demeanour.'

Matthew opened his mouth to respond, but Jon cut in before he could start – a disciplinary offence in any ordinary circumstance. 'We mustn't get off track.'

'Hear, hear,' Matthew said. 'The question still remains – what are we going to do?'

A fresh wail from the direction of the princesses gave them no answer, but a fresh voice did. A new participant had entered the conversation radius without their knowledge. The debate had been so heated that even his fumbling feebleness had not been noted. 'Someone should move him.'

The three men turned to see Thomas Crockley standing there, hunched over the sideboard, holding a handkerchief to his mouth. He was pale, but his voice rang true. 'I'm sorry, I don't feel quite myself.'

'No. You're right, Father,' Matthew said. 'Protocol. A monarch should be laid to rest. We need to take the king to his bed.'

'What?' This from David.

Jon knew Crockley was right. King Eric deserved to be at rest, quiet in his slumber, and that was not possible in this room. There was also no way that the princesses, or the others for that matter, would be able to focus on the tasks at hand while the king still had a presence here.

'Need I remind everyone that this is a crime scene?' David barked.

'We are the crime scene, Grand-uncle. The king has already been moved twice now. If the police were to come, which we know is impossible, I doubt anything would be gleaned from him being here. Isn't it better to give him some rest? And give them some rest?' Matthew nodded to the three women on the floor, intertwined in a tangle of bereft misery.

Jon would have quite happily joined them – fallen apart himself. The noise the table made when Eric had collapsed echoed back into Jon's mind. It was hard to think that Eric would ever be at peace – at least until this day was resolved.

'Yes,' Jon said. 'But how do we move him?'

David was shaking his head in dismay at the idea, and Matthew and Crockley did not have any answers. They didn't seem to understand the quandary, but Jon, having walked these halls thousands of times, saw it plainly.

The king's bedroom was down five corridors, up a flight of stairs and through countless doors. They could not carry him all that way while giving him the respect he deserved. Jon thought back to his journey with the dinner, hard to believe that that had happened mere hours ago, and how difficult that was.

Jon let out a disgruntled sigh, without warning – even to himself. He knew how they were to do it, but that didn't mean he approved. The other men looked to him, expectantly. 'We move him using the food trolley.'

XIV

The Body of a King

David protested until he was practically blue in the face, proclaiming, 'You cannot treat my brother like a stuffed turkey, Butler. He is a Windsor – the king!' Jon was acutely aware of this, had been for about thirty-three years and had never forgotten it, but he didn't see another way forward.

The food trolley was, as previously illustrated, not what one might think it to be – no doubt David was conjuring to mind a rickety tea trolley, pushed by an elderly woman around a bingo game. No, the trolley was professional – made to transport large quantities of food, as it had this afternoon. It closer resembled a gurney and the irony of that was now plain to see.

Jon felt some misgivings about going to get the trolley himself. He would have to leave the Royal Family alone. The alternative, however, was far worse – sending one of them to get it. For starters, it sounded absurd to him that he would boss them around, although he was sure Matthew would have done the deed with no fuss. Secondly, and more importantly, it would be isolating a member of the Royal Family, and leaving them vulnerable. No, it had to be Jon, so he went.

As Jon went to retrieve it from the upper kitchen, he was wishing, with all his heart, that he would happen upon Tony Speck. It was untrue that the nightmare would be over – it would still be very much in motion – but Jon himself would be able to step back into a role more natural to him. He had had to learn to be the leader in the kitchen – it had taken years. He could not be the leader everywhere else.

But Tony Speck was not there. The halls of Balmoral were silent, eerie and oppressive – business as usual. Tony Speck had to be outside in the cold to miss Jon's call. He hoped the blizzard hadn't claimed him.

The kitchen, unlike Speck, was still there, just as Jon had left it. The steam tables were still humming with life, still in their cooling cycle, even though they had been turned off with dessert. The place needed cleaning – a once-over with a cloth and the antibacterial scrub. The washing-up was sitting on the counter, waiting to be loaded into the dishwasher. It begged to be done – washing-up had never looking so inviting. If he finished this load, there was more to be done in the kitchen downstairs – he could make a day of it. He could pretend that the tragedy of the drawing room had never occurred – such was the promise of those dirty plates.

But no – there was no running away from this. Jon clutched the trolley and started rolling it back to disaster. Before he left the kitchen, he tried the walkie-talkie again, to make sure it was not his location that had been the issue. It was not. Still no answer from their protector.

Back in the drawing room, the royals watched Jon as he parked his steel hearse. Matthew and Crockley, still hesitant and coughing, were trying to explain to the women what was discussed earlier. It seemed like they had come to some sort of understanding, and Matthew and Crockley started moving towards the king.

Jon followed, trying to ignore the stares of David and Marjorie. The duo had reunited and were watching proceedings with glassy eyes – David with a comforting arm around his sister-in-law. Jon checked where the last inhabitants of the room were, tired of wilting under the oldest royals' gaze, and found them in the far corner. Prince Martin was sitting, constantly tugging on his tie, finally resolving to take it off entirely. The twin princesses were hovering, trying not to cry.

As Jon came to the king's side, and the three men started to plan how they were to transport his body to the trolley, a fresh shriek came from beyond them. Emeline was protesting again.

'It's better this way, Aunt,' Matthew said, as they assessed the king. 'We will put him to bed and it will be as if he is asleep – and the rest of us can see what to do to get us out of this predicament.'

This seemed to be enough (although – how could it ever be enough?) and Emeline grew silent.

Jon, Matthew and Crockley talked through the approach, until there was nothing left but to carry it out. They bent to the king – Jon taking his shoulders, Matthew his legs and Crockley tentatively hovering over events in case of emergency. The man had started to lose colour in his face and seemed like he might faint. Jon hoped an emergency would not happen, as he wasn't sure how much help Crockley could be in his current state.

Jon counted to three and they hoisted the king upwards, carrying him as quickly as possible to the trolley. One of the king's arms, which had been placed across his chest, became loose in the movement and fell, hanging in mid-air. Crockley tried to right it, but there was really nothing to be done.

As they got to the trolley, Jon saw that someone had placed a cushion at the head of the trolley for the king to rest his head. Martin was now standing at the trolley, holding a blanket ready to drape over the king. Martin nodded to Jon. Jon felt a surge of emotion for the youngest royal, who seemed to be both coping incredibly well with his grief and acting the most pragmatically of the remaining royals.

They set the king down as softly as possible, the cushion doing well to support his head. The king's face was a horrific sight – a face of a tremendous battle ending in defeat. Jon was almost thankful when Martin stepped up to give him the blanket. Matthew took it instead and, with a sense of duty, covered his grandfather.

Prince Matthew turned to his family. 'We will take him to his bed, and final words can be said later.'

There was a murmur of discomfort somewhere in the room, although Jon could not tell from where. If he were looking, he might have known, but his eyes were frozen on the king's face. Although now covered by the blanket, Jon knew that, underneath, the sight was still there. King Eric had died in confusion and pain – possibly at the hands of someone in this room. Anger and sorrow swirled in his heart, combining and coalescing into a need to find out who did this and bring them to justice. As he glanced up, with a new sense of purpose, Crockley turned back to them.

'Look, if it's all the same to everyone,' Thomas Crockley mumbled, 'I rather need a sit-down.'

Jon looked at him – really looked at him – for the first time in quite a while. The man was incredibly green around the gills and was slick with an almost slimy sweat. There was something happening with Crockley, and it was unfortunate that it was merely a footnote at this time.

'Then I am coming too.' Princess Emeline had stepped to their side.

Maud, from behind them, began, 'Emeline, I don't think . . .' Her arms were out to Emeline – her life preserver was leaving her. Without it, she might drown. She needed something, some kind of direction.

Jon suddenly had an idea. He pulled his notepad and a pen from his pocket and went to Maud. 'Princess Maud, may I ask something of you?'

The princess faltered. 'Well . . . yes . . . I suppose you may.'

Jon tried to smile. It didn't work. The events of the day hooked onto the edges of his mouth and forced them downwards. 'If you could, could you note down the movements of this room this morning? I want to know when everyone entered or exited and, specifically, if anyone was alone.'

Maud dabbed under her eyes with a handkerchief before taking the notepad. 'Of course, Jon.' She simply seemed happy to have a task to undertake, she didn't think why she was doing it. Jon was hoping that she wouldn't, and he was glad to give her something to occupy her mind.

Maud turned away with her new task.

'I'll stay then. I will try to keep morale up here,' Crockley said, having sunk into a chaise longue.

Emeline, however, was not as sympathetic. 'I honestly could not care less what you do, Thomas.'

Rather than be offended, Crockley appeared relieved.

Emeline exchanged glances with Jon and Matthew, before her gaze drifted downwards to the mass of her father beneath the blanket upon the trolley. 'Let us get this done,' she said.

With a nod between the three of them, Eric Windsor's final journey began.

XV

Eric Windsor's Final Resting Place

To describe the process of transporting the king from the drawing room to his bedroom would be an exercise in tedium and absent ceremony. The three bearers remained silent as they walked the halls, assuming familiar positions. Jon was at the head of the king, pushing the trolley, Matthew was at his feet, pulling it when needed, and Emeline, in a complete deviation from her station, was there to open doors and support where necessary.

The major obstacle was having to take the trolley up a flight of stairs (sadly the service lift only went from the servants quarters in the basement to the ground floor), but the journey was surprisingly uneventful. They used the stairs in the entrance hall, where the king often greeted his guests. The food trolley got caught on the tartan rugs of the hall, but that was the only thing of note. The head of a stag, killed by the king himself up in the wilds near the castle, watched them from the wall as they prepared themselves.

Given that the staircase was wide and carpeted, with stairs slowly ascending, and the king was light – being thin and wiry – the three of them could easily lift the trolley off the ground and manoeuvre the thing upwards. The bend in the stairs was an incredible non-issue – providing a short respite for Jon, who was out of breath, despite the veritably light load. It was hard to recall, even for him, that he had been up since the early hours, working his heart out to prepare a dinner – a dinner that had now been grimly upstaged. It almost seemed ridiculous, the amount of importance it had had in his life just this morning.

There was one thing that reminded Jon of the energy he was exuding, however. His limbs, his head and his gut were all slowly throbbing in unison, trying to get their host to slow down. Jon wondered what the doctor would say if he could see him now – having been on his feet for over twelve hours with no end in sight. It didn't matter. *He* didn't matter.

The odd procession came to the king's bedroom soon enough, and entering without the express permission of the man seemed a foreign concept. Jon almost wanted to shout, refusing Emeline entry (even a princess should knock) as the young woman opened the door. There was no exclamation from within, no raking over the coals for entry without admittance.

Matthew pulled the trolley across the shag carpet of the bedroom – a track it was never meant to be on – before stopping at the head of the four-poster bed. 'Right then,' he said grimly, and looked to his aunt, who was white with the knowledge of what they were to do. 'You don't have to do this. Jon and I can manage.'

Emeline shook her head, almost angrily, at the thought that she would suffer the journey but not partake in the main event. She was crying softly – maybe she had never stopped.

'All right,' Matthew said.

The three of them raised the king much as before, Emeline taking Crockley's place, and carried him to the bed. When it was clear that Matthew and Jon could indeed handle the king's weight on their own, Emeline went to the bed and pulled back the covers, while Jon and Matthew placed him on the bed and covered him, so when they were done it almost was as though the king had merely slipped away in his sleep – if not for his expression.

Once the job was complete, the three of them stood there, somewhat haphazardly, looking to the king, as if this act was meant to give them some clarity as to what to do next. Of course, no revelation came – the king did not reveal to them a path forward. The situation was still cloudier than the marshes and colder than the deep snow piling outside.

Emeline's sobs started to become audible – a pitter-patter of mourning softer than summer rain. 'May I have a moment alone with my father, please.'

'Of course, ma'am,' Jon said, and Matthew nodded his head, adding a sadness to the motion that should not have been possible. The two of them made their way to the door, and whereas Matthew seemed eager to leave (merely a different method of grief), Jon paused at the door and chanced a look back.

114

Emeline had silently moved to the king's side – her hand placed on his forehead as if checking him for a fever. She was openly crying now. Jon somehow knew exactly what Emeline was thinking – as it had just come to him too. In the transporting of the king, the three of them had ended Eric Windsor's story. Whatever would happen now, on this most cursed of days, Eric himself would have no part in it. He had uttered his last dialogue, performed his last action – he was done. He could rest now.

Eric Windsor's legacy would carry on for ever. The mourning of the country had not even begun. The funeral would be grand and viewed worldwide. However, that did not matter to anyone in the room. They were something more – family, a friend, a mentor. No one else's grief beyond these walls could touch any of the sorrow within.

'Goodbye, Daddy. Thank you for everything,' Emeline muttered at his side, before whispering something in his ear, filling his head with secrets and tears.

Jon left her alone to say her goodbyes as she should have been allowed. He went out into the corridor and shut the door as quietly as possible, but not before the princess came into view one last time. There was something odd in her face now that she thought she was alone. Jon did not know what it was – and grief was a complex emotion. However, if Jon were forced to describe the look on Princess Emeline's face, looking down at her dead father, he might even say it was one of relief.

XVI

The Bridlepath Causeway Has Flooded (and Other Fun Phrases)

Jon and Matthew waited in the corridor while Emeline finished her final goodbyes. The two men – one old, one young, with little in common except the heavy weight of existence – did not meet each other's gaze. After a few minutes, the sounds of soft crying came from Matthew also, and Jon found it hard not to echo him. But he had to remain steadfast and strong for those who were left. Unsurprisingly, this made it harder to keep the tears from falling. He wanted to sit down in the hallway, curl into a ball of exhaustion and never surface. His gut throbbed harder, as if agreeing with that strategy. He couldn't though – the Royal Family needed him. The king needed him – still alive in spirit, if not in form.

What would Jon have said this morning had he known? He had stood here with the king's toast and the king's coffee and his own hope for the day. What if he had known that this would be the last toast, the last coffee, the hope all spent? What would have been his last words to an old friend? – 'I'm sorry, Your Majesty. You did not deserve this. You were always good to me, better than all the others. You came along at a time in my life when I didn't have a home, when I didn't know who I was. And you gave me that – you gave me a home, you gave me an identity. And for that, I will be forever grateful.'

Was that it? Or would he have said something else? Or even if he'd known, would he have bottled it, and remained silent regardless? It was all unspoken anyway – between them. Always unspoken. He knew. They knew. But sometimes, that was not enough.

In that short interim between his mother's death and leaving for England, Jon had sat with his grandma at their kitchen table, over a crock of some delicious-smelling meal, and finally found some sorrow for his mother. Once he had started crying, he could not stop. Grandma must have sat with him for hours as he wept, so much so that he forgot what he was even crying for – his mother, his father, maybe even himself? He had found the well of self-pity, that one must always visit but never fall into, and he spent the afternoon there. At one point, between wails, he had uttered that he wished to feel like he was home, he wished to know why he was on this earth, he wished to be at peace.

Grandma shook her head, almost disgusted, and pointed a bony finger at him. 'Don't say such a thing, Jonathan Alleyne. What a thing to say!'

Jon was awestruck by this reaction, so much so that he had quietened to hear what she said next, words that would stay with him for ever.

'I do not think anyone wants to be at peace. Not really. Peace from grief is lovely in concept, yes, but when you think on it, when you really think on it, what is it? It is to be finished. Peace is to be done. And what then? We shouldn't be done. We should never ever be done with this – with what we are feeling right at this moment. Because peace is all-encompassing, peace is to put your other feelings in a box, like memories frozen in photographs, and push them to the back of a shelf, not gone but not there either. And we wouldn't desire to forget, but in time we would. Nothing resolved, nothing gained, no experience or reason. Just a box, on a shelf, with fading photographs of grief. At peace. What a horrible, horrible state to be in.

'So you hold on to your pain. You hold on fast and tight. You don't let anyone tell you anything about it. You don't let them say "I know how you feel" or "I've been through it too." It's yours – grief is different every time. No one knows how you feel. No one has ever been through exactly what you are going through now. No one should ever be sorry. Because you have something and they don't. And you keep it as long as you wish, and do what you like with it. But never ever forget. Never the box. Never wish to be at peace.'

Over time, Jon had thought on her words and seen that, although she was not completely correct (as no one ever was on matters so complex), she spoke words truer than he had known in that moment.

Princess Emeline stepped out of the king's bedroom wiping her face with a satin handkerchief that she had not long unwrapped. If Jon's memory served, it was actually a present from the king himself.

Emeline stood there, her bloodshot eyes eventually raising to meet the two men's. 'He is there, but he is not. He is just . . . He is asleep.'

Jon nodded. No words had ever been invented for a situation such as this, and if they had been, they were inadequate.

'What is happening here?' sobbed Matthew. 'I am constantly asking what next? What next? So we did this, and now this is done, but still the question remains. What next? What do we do now?'

What do we do now? Matthew was correct – the question oppressed everything. It hung there on the walls, lay thick in the air, had gotten trodden into the carpet. Everywhere Jon looked, he was confronted with the hopelessness of their situation. Matthew and Emeline were too.

Emeline went to her nephew and grasped him in a tight embrace, so hard and formal one might have thought she had never done it before. 'We work it through, as we always do. We continue. The Windsors prevail, that's just how we were built. There's nothing but tomorrow.'

'But tomorrow without him,' Matthew said.

Emeline assented, her voice cracking, 'Yes. Without him. We all now have to do this without . . .'

'It seems like if we react to this, we have to accept it,' Matthew said, with a renewed sob, shaking himself, evidently to try to collect himself. 'He's really gone.'

'Yes.' What else was there to say?

'Jonathan, have you ever seen anything quite like what happened?'

119

Jon almost forgot he was present. 'Excuse me, sir?'

'I suppose I am asking something like – is there any way that what occurred here was natural? Maybe my grandfather suffered some kind of a heart attack?' Matthew clearly did not really think this a viable avenue. He was there watching at the time, quite intently, if Jon remembered correctly. Jon had never seen a heart attack in person before, but it quite clearly didn't look like the king's fate.

'No. That was not a heart attack – at least no natural one. Maybe some kind of heart event was brought about by what killed him – which, in my working theory, is something he ingested, almost certainly the whisky.'

He did not add that his working theory meant that one of the Royal Family had killed the king. It was not only that it was not the right time. It was also because he could barely think it, let alone voice it. He had served the Royal Family for over three decades, and although some members were more hospitable than others, he found it hard to compute that any could be capable of murder.

'How long was it from his drink to his passing?' Matthew mused, checking his watch as though he may have noted the answer there. He instantly seemed slightly better at finding something else to busy himself with. He wiped his eyes, and thought aloud. 'He started his speech, took a drink of whisky, said some more, and then . . . It was maybe twenty, thirty seconds, wouldn't you say?'

'I . . . Yes, I think that is probably true, sir.'

'That is very fast-acting, no?'

'I have no experience with poisons. But I have seen allergic reactions before. I can only think they work somewhat the same. As soon as something enters the body, if it is incompatible, it can cause a reaction very quickly.' If Matthew were getting this in-depth in his thinking, it would not be long until he stumbled across the cold truth himself. Maybe Jon would not have to voice his suspicion after all, Matthew would do it for him.

That immovable question bore into the back of Jon's neck. It made the volatile lump in his gut pulse with laughter – it was laughing at him. *What now? What now? What now?*

Clearly, Emeline felt it too, as, maybe out of respect to Matthew, she tried to comfort him with possibilities of safety. 'We could wait out the blizzard, wait for Tony Speck to return, wait for rescue.' Emeline stopped, evidently having said 'wait' so many times that even she saw the problem in it.

'If there is someone dangerous in Balmoral, then waiting is not an option.' Matthew was back to some sense of himself, and he was also correct. 'Most likely, it is an intruder, one we do not know is here – and the bastard is stuck in here with us.' Matthew was going a different direction with his theory, but then he realised the other route himself. 'The other option – it was one of us. Both are equally terrifying and require immediate response.'

'I agree,' Jon said, and despite some apprehension, it was clear that Emeline did also.

They started back towards the drawing room with a renewed sense of purpose, a refreshed sense of worry.

With every step, every corner, every stair, Jon expected to run into this phantom poisoner who potentially skulked around Balmoral. It would be an almost fatal shock, but also somewhat of a relief – it would mean that no royal was capable of murder.

But this intruder theory was impossible. It was favourable, but pointless to wallow in this fantasy. Jon knew there was no intruder in Balmoral – the new security system would not allow it. Jon had seen for himself the screen that showed the little red dots of everyone in the castle – the dots that could only be humans. It was the Royal Family, and it was Speck and himself. They were the only ones.

Maud would now be creating a timeline of the drawing room that morning. If the whisky were never alone, then it wouldn't matter even if there were an intruder. And if any member of the Royal Family were alone with it, then that had to be the answer.

As they made their way back, Emeline strode ahead, her pink evening dress at odds with her almost military march. Jon fell into step with Matthew, who quietly mused, 'What was that phrase you were using when you were trying to talk to Speck? Something about a Bridlepath?'

'The Bridlepath Causeway has Flooded. It's code. It means the king is dead. Everyone on staff, and people in government positions, would instantly know what that meant and to act accordingly. It was easier than explaining the details to Speck – exactly what the code was implemented for.' Jon paused and then added, 'I don't know if I could have brought myself to say anything more anyhow.'

Matthew sighed. 'Everyone around here does like saying anything other than that which they actually mean, don't they? All these codes and not one member of the Royal Family knows about them. I often feel they're speaking a different language. Do I have a code if I suddenly keel over?'

Jon thought twice before telling him, but then he didn't see how it could hurt. Things would be different after today – almost in every way. The codes were the least of anyone's worries. 'The Abattoir Now Sells Stamps.'

Matthew snorted. 'Preposterous. What is my aunt's?'

Before Jon could say anything, 'I do not wish to hear mine,' came from in front of them.

Matthew shrugged and continued, 'So someone is supposed to say that phrase and all the king's horses and all the king's men come running, hmm? Well, I'm afraid it looks like it didn't work. Not even Speck showed his face.'

'I don't even think he heard,' Jon said. 'There was nothing on the end of the walkie.'

'Do you think something might have happened to him?'

They were currently descending the staircase mere minutes from the drawing room, but this gave them all pause. Matthew stopped in his tracks, straddling two different levels – a man lopsided. Jon, who was on the landing, turned to them – this new possibility finally revealing itself. 'What?'

'Could it be possible that whoever killed the king saw to Speck as well?' Matthew then thought better than to start down that path. Maybe he was reacting to Jon's shocked face. 'Let us deal with one thing at a time. Right now, my family is falling apart, and all that matters is Speck was not here to stop it.'

They caught up to Emeline and started onwards again and none spoke until they were faced with the doors of the drawing room. The sight was incredibly nondescript, especially when juxtaposed with the chaos that had occurred within. Jon couldn't quite believe that the sights he saw regularly were now turning to something sinister, something foreboding. The drawing room would never be a happy place again; the dining room would always be the place of Eric's last meal; the kitchens would always be where Jon prepared that meal. The 'Moral, once his favourite of the king's residences, would forever have a dark cloud hanging over it, forever be the home of a brutal murder.

Jon reached out to clutch the door handle of the drawing room – bracing himself to unleash the chaos within – but Matthew caught Jon's arm before he was able. Jon was slightly confused by the touch. 'Sir?'

Matthew looked reluctant as he said, 'I feel I have to say one thing before this goes further—'

However, it was very quickly apparent that that one thing would have to wait, as a tremendous shatter came from beyond the door, followed by a roar of anger. The three unfortunate souls glanced at each other in turn, before opening the door.

XVII

A Timetable of Sorts

Blood. Balmoral was becoming soaked in cruel intentions. This was not one of those moments, however. Jon saw blood, and panicked – but it was ill placed. It was very clear what had happened as soon as they entered – Marjorie had dropped her wine glass, and for some reason, after it had shattered, she had attempted to pick it up again, likely to finish off her drink. She had cut her palm and David was pulling her arm above her head to try to quell the stream. It was not working, as blood was trickling out of her open hand like a morbid water feature. 'Elevate, Margey, elevate.'

The roar that the travelling group had heard was a little trickier to locate, but finally Jon's eyes, which had been checking the status of everyone in the room, fell on the huddled frame of Thomas Crockley, bent down in front of the fireplace. The fire, left unchecked, must have gone out at some point in the proceedings, and Crockley, having haphazardly placed new logs on it, was trying to light it, much as David had earlier in the day.

The final two souls in the drawing room, Maud and Martin, were sitting on the sofa, son wrapped in mother, both silently transfixed by the empty table in front of them that had become their patriarch's final end. Maud was clutching Jon's notebook, having completed her task (hopefully) and reverted to her previous state. Martin was absent-mindedly fiddling with a wooden box of sorts – Jon had to take a moment to realise that it was Interregnum, the puzzle box the king had got for Christmas. At Jon's entrance, Maud untangled herself from her son and got up, but shrank back down when she realised he had more pressing matters to attend to.

David screeched, 'Butler, we need some first aid here.'

Jon had a better background in first aid than any of the royals (even if his knowledge only extended to minor scrapes and not CPR), and even though he wasn't a butler, he made his way over to the scene of the accident. David seemed to be far more panicky than even the victim herself. Marjorie was plainly looking up at her elevated arm with a morose fascination – no doubt slightly brought on by the constant shock of the day, but mostly her blood-alcohol level.

Jon leapt into action, looking for his forgotten drinks tray for a bottle of water and the red cloth draped over the tray. He found it eventually, on the sideboard – it was odd, he had no memory of placing it there! – and quickly whisked what he needed back to the injured party.

'Please, show me the wound, Your Royal Highness.'

Marjorie looked to him as if he were an extraterrestrial. It was only David guiding her hand downwards that provided them any progress. Jon could not see anything but the streaming scarlet blood, so warned the princess before dousing it with water. Marjorie hissed with pain, as though the cut was expelling air that was keeping her upright and the unveiling of it was only hastening her demise.

Slowly, the cut revealed itself and it appeared far more dramatic than it actually was. She had a long and deep gash, almost directly following the palmar crease around her thumb. Jon inspected it, making sure that there were no remnants of glass within, before binding it as tightly as he dared with the cloth. Finally, he needed something to secure the cloth – and happened upon a bag of abandoned and ripped wrapping paper, which was left over from the great present opening. He looked inside to find exactly what he needed – a loose piece of tape attached to a ripped sheet of particularly garish glittery paper. He dislodged the piece – which thankfully still had some stick to it – and attached it to Marjorie's makeshift bandage. He was somewhat pleased with himself at his quick actions, but Marjorie's glassy eyes offered no thanks. It was not unusual, so he did not let it jostle him.

Next, he went over to the fireplace and took out the firelighter that he still had in his pocket. Crockley stood back with a 'Blasted thing. So cold in here, you see,' and let Jon do his work. In barely a second, the fire was stoked. 'Magic hands, old boy. Well done!' Jon once again felt discomfort at being so praised for carrying out such a simple task. But he felt even more discomfort at seeing the state of Crockley. He was abnormally pale, and it was nowhere near as cold in here as the man thought. Crockley smiled though – alleviating some of Jon's worry. 'I'll just stay here a moment.'

127

Jon couldn't stay with him. He had other responsibilities – big ones. He stood back up, almost wishing he had taken longer with the easy problems so he could further ignore the demanding one.

The flicking flames were transfixing. Maybe he could stay here with Crockley.

'Is it done?' a familiar voice said beside him. Maud had taken her chance to talk to him, somewhat covertly.

Jon nodded.

'I did as you asked,' she said, pressing the open notepad into his hands. 'I don't quite understand why I did it.' Maud's face betrayed the fact that she did know – very clearly, in fact – but it was not what she wanted, so she simply refused it.

'Thank you, ma'am.'

'Maud. I'm Maud. I think we all need to dispense with that now, yes?'

That would be difficult for Jon. Thirty-three years of habit to overwrite. 'I will try . . . Maud.' It sounded wrong and he expected it would not stick.

Maud nodded, returning to her youngest, and leaving Jon to her notes.

Before he inspected them, he thought of what they may contain. A timetable of the comings and goings of the drawing room. Did someone have to be alone to poison the whisky? Well, no, but it would be the safest way to ensure one wasn't seen. If one was alone, it was most likely them. If one was never alone, it was least likely them. It was a start, and Jon could lay some groundwork for what was to come.

He inspected Maud's notes:

DRAWING ROOM – CHRISTMAS DAY 2022

08:00 – David
08:30 – David, Jonathan, Emeline, Maud, Marjorie (Jonathan only here for ten minutes)
09:00 – David (Emeline gone to see King, Maud gone to family, Marjorie gone back to bed)
09:30 – Thomas (David gone to see King)
09:31 – Emeline (Thomas gone to light cigarette – only in drawing room for a minute)
09:45 – Emeline, Martin (Emeline leaves for a minute to go to toilet)
10:00 – Emeline, Martin, Matthew
10:15 – Matthew (Emeline left to find Maud, Martin left for his hijinks)
10:25 – Matthew, David, Maud
10:50 – Maud (Matthew and David left to get ready for dinner)
11:05 – Maud, Matthew, Marjorie
11:30 – Marjorie, Maud (Matthew gone to find Martin, Maud goes to get cloth to mop up drink Marjorie spills (gone for about two mins))
11:45 – Marjorie, Maud, Emeline, David
12:00 – Marjorie, Maud, Emeline, David, Thomas
12:25 – Marjorie, Maud, Emeline, David, Thomas, Matthew, Martin
12:30 – Christmas Dinner

Private Audience Order
Emeline, David, Marjorie, Maud, Thomas, Matthew

Jon digested the timetable as thoroughly as he could, and it took a moment for him to realise what it meant. It hit him on the final line, and took him two more scans of the tidy writing to confirm. His heart sank. His throat grew dry. He had wanted the timetable to inspire some kind of immediate answer, but it had done the complete opposite. He observed the Royal Family quietly through new suspicious eyes – he hated having to, but now he did. He'd wanted to know who had been alone with the whisky, and he had gotten his answer.

Every single one of them.

XVIII

Cards Upon the Table

Jonathan Alleyne had experienced many events in his life that may be labelled that age-old cliched adjective 'earth-shattering'. One was when he stood in the back office of Caribbean Plaza and Eric Windsor properly introduced himself. Another was when one of his distant cousins contacted him a few years back to say that Grandma had finally passed. A big one was sitting in the doctor's office just recently as the doctor said many words he couldn't understand, and one he could only wish he didn't. As Jon studied the timetable, he felt the same shaking feeling that might resemble an earth shattering.

Every single member of the Royal Family had been alone with the whisky between the time it had been unsealed and the dinner. What was more, the drawing room had never been empty, and Tony Speck had not been present. Neither had anyone else – Matthew's phantom assassin was nowhere to be seen, although Jon already knew they wouldn't be.

It was one of them.

One member of the Royal Family was a murderer. That meant a lot of things, but perhaps the most pressing was that the other six members of the Royal Family could be in mortal danger.

Jon stepped forward. They deserved to know, even if it meant alerting the guilty party as well. What he was going to say was to be decided by the gods as he opened his mouth with no plan.

'I need everyone's attention.' Emeline had stepped forward as well. She addressed the room, in the commanding way only a daughter of the Crown could, and indicated the two other culprits of the conversation. Princess Emeline, as the firstborn (having arrived a full ten minutes before her twin sister), was first in line for the throne before the succession-rule shake-up. If Emeline had become queen, Jon knew she would have been a formidable one. 'We've been conversing while on my father's final journey. I think we all need to put our cards upon the table.'

Jon and Matthew stole a glance. This was what the princess had been stewing over as she strode ahead?

'Now, this may be difficult for some of us to accept, but times have taken the worst of turns. My father, our king, is dead. All signs appear to point to him being murdered. We only know facts. We all saw him – he began his speech, he took a sip of whisky and then he started to choke. He frothed at the mouth and clutched his throat before collapsing. I anticipate that he was dead before he hit the coffee table.' She said all of this as though she were addressing the nation – coldly, emotionlessly conveying the information. 'I think we need to discuss this and what we do now. It does not appear that the blizzard will stop any time soon, the man tasked with protecting us is missing, and we have a predicament. In the absence of any rescue, or safety, or protector, we must proceed as if none will materialise at all.'

'What are you trying to say, Daughter?' Marjorie snapped. She had resumed drinking, masterfully negotiating the glass with her bandage.

Emeline looked to Jon, which meant that everyone else did too. 'Jon, I believe you are seeing more here than any other of us can. You are on the outside looking in, tell us what you see.'

'I . . . think . . . well, I . . .' Jon had gotten over his nervousness at addressing the Royal Family quickly when he'd started working with them. Now it came flooding back. They were all looking to him expectantly – maybe even anticipating good news. 'I have reason to believe that the king was murdered by someone in this room.'

Silence. One could hear the field mice breathing in their homes under the snow. The wind whistled outside. The faces of the Royal Family were frozen in confusion, all eyes dropped to the floor. Only Emeline met Jon's gaze – she had come to the same conclusion.

Marjorie broke the horrible quiet. 'How dare you speak such nonsense, you wretch!'

'Mother,' Emeline boomed. 'You will not call him a wretch. Jon simply speaks the truth. If we do not listen, we might as well just be consumed by grief or, worse, go back to exactly what we were doing – which, in your case, is drinking yourself into an early grave, although you seem pretty happy about that.'

'There's nothing about my grave that would be early,' Marjorie said with that familiar venom. Maybe the Princess Royal had used some of that venom to kill the king, although after her layered (to say the least) reaction, Jon found that unlikely. When he thought about it, her reaction might have been the most genuine – complex in its robustness, as all human emotion was meant to be. 'In fact, I feel my grave would be incredibly timely, just as today has demonstrated.'

'Yes, Mother, but the king's death was not a natural occurrence. He was murdered – quite probably by one of us here in this room.'

A cold shiver passed through Jon, and continued through everyone else. It was so tangible that it threatened to extinguish the newly licking fire.

'You can't possibly think that to be the case,' David moaned. 'Why would any of us have cause to hurt my brother? At least within the family.' He glanced at Jon – a look of such violent malice that Jon had never quite seen in the prince.

'I wouldn't know who would hurt my father, Uncle. But I do know that only one of us here is already a criminal,' Emeline said.

'The allegations were withdrawn!' David exclaimed, and it was Marjorie's turn to hold him.

'Withdrawn?' Maud relinquished her son and stood. 'And how have they been withdrawn, Uncle, hmm? I'm sure quietly and politely and not without the promise of sizeable compensation, either by you or the British government.'

David made a sound that could only be described as a frustrated squawk. 'That is tantamount to treason, Maud. What a poor judge of anything you are, Niece – seeing shadows on the wall when none are there.'

'Please,' Emeline commanded, and the others fell quiet again. 'Jon, may you continue?'

Jon did not want to in the slightest, but he knew he must. The eyes of everyone in the room threatened to bowl him over as he spoke. 'I am not accusing anyone out of malice. I am just looking at the situation as plainly as possible. It all comes down to the whisky – which I think we can all agree is the murder weapon here. The king took a sip of whisky, and within a minute he was dead. He had shown no prior complaints of being ill, or said he was as such. In fact, he was in great spirits before his drink.

'So if we move forward with the idea that the whisky was poisoned, where does that take us? I unpacked the whisky from the Christmas shipment myself. I placed the bottles of Anchor Haven in the pantry. They were all sealed and stored in their usual place. This morning, on the way to attending to the fire for Prince David, I picked a bottle at random. They were all the same, I had no need to select a specific one. It was still sealed. Once I got to the drawing room, I cracked open the seal on the whisky. It was so loud I would venture that Prince David even heard it.'

David, now the subject of stares, reluctantly nodded that he did and then hurriedly said, 'That doesn't mean anything.'

Jon continued. 'I poured the whisky into the decanter as the king likes me to do a few hours before consumption. The decanter then sat on the table in this room until I picked it up to start serving before the king's speech. We have a window of opportunity where the whisky could have been laced with a poison.

'While myself, Prince Matthew and Princess Emeline took the king to his bedroom, I asked Princess Maud to collate a timetable of sorts – a timetable which would show the comings and goings of this room in the run-up to Christmas dinner.'

'So that's what you were doing, Maud, with your questions?' Marjorie sneered, sounding utterly betrayed.

'Silence, Mummy,' Maud said.

'This is the timetable,' Jon said, holding up the notepad. 'You may all look at it if you like. Unfortunately, it shows that every single one of you was alone at some point and had ample time to lace the Anchor Haven. Furthermore, if you have all been truthful, it absolves Tony Speck from any suspicion, as no one mentioned anything about him being anywhere near the drawing room at any point.'

'The dinner,' David said, thrusting a finger into the air in a 'Eureka' gesture. 'The whisky was alone during the dinner. We were all in the dining room. Speck, or some intruder, could have laced the whisky then.'

'I'm afraid not,' Jon said, and he was. What he would not give for an assassin right now. 'I was outside the doors, and when I was not, I was busy in the kitchens with the meal. I understand that you have to take some of that at face value, but there we are. As for the other options, Tony Speck was with me for some of the meal, outside the doors. When he appeared and departed, he went in the opposite direction to that of the drawing room. On the subject of an intruder, or anyone else in the castle who is not meant to be, that is also impossible. Speck showed me the interface for his new security system – an interactive map of all our heat signatures at the time of the dinner. We were all red dots. Ten. No more and no less. In the whole castle, and the grounds.'

Once Jon had finished, an uncomfortable quiet fell upon the room. Stolen glances and open mouths were as rampant as the snow outside.

Emeline stepped towards Jon. 'Thank you, Jon.' She did not seem as shocked as everyone else, as though Jon had merely been reporting her thoughts all along. 'I hope we all see what kind of predicament we are all in. It does seem that one of us killed King Eric Windsor, our own flesh and blood. Only one of us here has any hope for something akin to an outsider's perspective. And he has already demonstrated, just this moment, that he is up to the task.'

Jon saw where Emeline was leading everyone just before she said it. And the earth shattered again as Emeline said, 'That is why, until more qualified people appear to save us, I think Jon should lead an investigation.'

XIX

The Election

Emeline's statement was announced, and it took a while for everyone to digest, none more so than Jon himself. What was she saying? He was to lead an investigation into the king's death. Did she mean he was to act like a detective? He couldn't do that – he was just a chef, after all. There weren't many skills there that were transferable.

Jon couldn't manage to summon any response, which was just as well, as the floodgates suddenly opened and everyone else wanted to speak their opinion.

'This is utterly ridiculous,' David scoffed.

'I don't . . . I can't . . .' Marjorie said. 'Have you lost your mind, Daughter?'

'I think Emeline is right,' Maud said, nodding to Jon. She had seen, through her task, what Jon had seen. 'He is the closest thing we have to objectivity at this point.'

'Well,' David snarled, 'objectively, Maud, you are both naïve fools.'

Thomas Crockley stood up, the fire seeming to have rejuvenated him somewhat. 'Now, look here, sir, that may be your great-niece, but she is also my wife and I will not allow her to be—'

'Nobody likes you, Crockley. You only see the world in green. Maybe you killed the king for – how low would you go – a five-pound note?' David was a spinning top and even when grasped would not stop. 'Or maybe it was your decidedly weird spawn.'

'He is thirteen years of age. "Weird" is practically a requirement,' Maud said.

Martin opened his mouth to say something, but decided against it.

'But, no.' David just continued spinning. 'We are missing the most obvious suspect here. And not only that! You propose to put him in charge of the whole bloody ship. The only one of us who does not belong and, I may add, the very one who served the damn whisky.'

Jon didn't know what to say, but luckily, he didn't need to.

'Uncle, really, your aim is shoddy beyond belief.' Maud was in his corner, although at this point he thought it was less about being with him and rather more about being against David. 'Jon has been with us for decades. In fact, he has spent more time with us than you have. He loves the king and all of us as if we were his own. And what's more, he's served the Royal Family more meals than anyone could count. He chooses today of all days to exact some kind of fictitious vengeance?'

To so plainly hear Maud's passionate thoughts – whatever the intention – was almost enough to bring tears to Jon's eyes, even when David very deliberately laid out a valid counter. 'Maybe he chose "today of all days" because there was no one else here to stop him.'

'No.' This was Matthew – the young man stirred from deep thought. 'I don't think Jon had motive. And he didn't have the chance to tamper with the whisky anyway. But one of us does have motive, and we all had chance. We all know what the king was about to announce in his speech. That was why he was killed.'

A ripple of confusion from the royals.

'What was he about to announce?' Marjorie asked.

'Come now.' Matthew seemed genuinely taken aback, even chuckling a little nervously. 'It was obvious. Not to mention what he said to me in his study. I assumed he had told us all the same thing. He was going to announce his resignation from the role. He was going to step down as king and announce his recommendation for successor – a recommendation that we know would most likely have been honoured as per the new rules.' It was clear from the rest of the room that no one else had known this concretely. 'This was not what was talked about in private with you?'

The others who had received a private audience – all but young Martin – stared blankly back to him.

'He was going to announce his successor?' Maud said, a fresh coldness that Jon had never heard in her voice before – the fact that it was aimed towards her own son only lowered the temperature.

'Well . . .' It appeared Matthew was starting to realise that he might have spoken out of turn. 'Yes, he said he would.'

'And I suppose that Eric would have elected you, young prince?' David said, uniting with his niece for the first time. 'What a victory for Twitter. And what a motive for *us*.'

'Everyone please be quiet,' Emeline shouted. 'We cannot undergo a sufficient investigation into this matter with everyone on equal footing and the wolf among us. It is clear that, to go forward today, we are going to need a singular direction, a lone voice, one that stands apart from the rest. This quarrelling only proves my point.'

David was still eyeing his new prime suspect, but found time to question his favoured niece. 'What does that mean? Speak plainly.'

'We need a leader, some kind of captain to this ship, wading on the sea of mistrust.'

'I said "speak plainly!" and you talk like you're reciting *A Midsummer Night's Dream*?'

'Do not raise your voice, Uncle,' Maud interjected.

'Well, this is all just ridiculousness. And that's quite enough from you, Maud,' Marjorie said.

'Mother, can you stop him? I don't need you to leap to my defence, but a general skip in my direction wouldn't go amiss.'

'I agree with him, Maud. Now shut up, the grown-ups are talking.'

'I'm forty years old in two weeks, and anyway my age is of no consequence to this discussion. You two are too well suited to each other. Old David and Margey. Every time you are together, I feel quite unwell.'

'We need a central investigator,' Emeline rushed out.

'Like a detective!' Martin chipped in. 'Like Enola Holmes.'

'Yes, if you like,' Emeline said. 'Jonathan Alleyne. He has brought us this far along this day. I'm sure he can take us the rest of the way.'

'I'd say there's not a better man,' Matthew said.

'Hear, hear,' agreed Maud, enthusiastically.

'Sure,' Martin said, slightly less enthusiastically.

'Are you all quite mad?' David shouted. 'But he's no more than a commoner! Have you lost your minds? You would put your lives, your truths, into the hands of this peasant creature?' Jon forced himself not to react, although inwardly he recoiled. Remarks such as this were not uncommon from David – but some still managed to penetrate his armour. 'And, I may add, he is the one who I still think is most likely to have killed my brother. Why, it's absolutely preposterous – and anyone who sees this any other way is a complete buffoon.'

'I stand with my brother-in-law. We can handle this together, without resorting to such . . .' Marjorie sized Jon up and down – 'dirty measures.'

'Both of you will be the death of us all,' Maud muttered.

'Oh stop being dramatic, Maud. Drama always inflated you around the cheeks. It makes you look quite ridiculous.'

'Mummy, this is not about the Crown. This is about justice.'

Marjorie had already turned away, pulling herself from the conversation and evidently the scene in general. 'Do as you wish, Daughters. Employ this plebeian for your means. I will have no further part in this – leave me to my mourning. Let this sham only serve to provide me some enjoyment as I watch you all squirm.' She made a great performance of whisking herself over to the far corner of the room and flumping into the armchair there, although a mere second later, she realised that there was no wine bottle within reach and had to repeat the process to retrieve one.

Emeline and Maud did not react to their mother's childish actions, but rather seemed to take them as a victory. 'Uncle,' Emeline said. 'What say you? I think it important for us all to be in agreement.'

'What say I? What say I?' David seemed to have realised that he was the lone soldier prepared to die on the hill. 'Marjorie is correct – you have pulled the rug from under us. You appoint the chef as the detective, but who is behind the chef? Is his true objectivity certain?'

If it was not for the squirrelly nature of the man, it was possible that David would be a great mind. However, no one could get past his inherent sickly disposition – slimy to the point that a person could get mucus on their clothes simply from spending time with him.

'I wouldn't want Jon to treat me, or any of us, differently as per the results of this election,' Emeline attested. 'In championing him, I only want what is best for everyone.'

David snarled. 'Well, look who's the least likely suspect, and at this point in the proceedings isn't it so often true that the least likely suspect is in fact the most?' David's footing was starting to become unstable and over his next argument his voice reflected it. He was growing tired, showing his age. 'I see the wheels of change, and

I will not stand in the way for one simple reason. This does not matter. Once Speck and his cavalry arrive, it will matter naught what any of us have said – it will be dealt with properly, legally. So I will concede this little thing to the chef, if I can hear from you all on one matter. Tell me you do not think for one solitary moment that the chef is the one we are hunting for – the one who murdered my dear brother.'

The room fell silent.

Martin stood up. 'I don't think he did it.'

'That's good enough for me,' Thomas Crockley said.

'Not for one second,' Matthew said.

The princesses were in agreement. 'We have no doubt,' Emeline said. 'Though if I did, I surely wouldn't have presented the idea in the first place. Jon is practically part of this family, but that last bit of distance is what suits him to this. It appears we are all in agreement?'

David was truly lost for words – it seemed that this was the moment when he thought his nieces' proposal was going to unravel, but his plan had backfired. Jon could hardly believe the faith that the majority of the royals had shown. In another timeline, another situation, he would have felt touched. 'What have we become?' David was saying. 'The Royal Family putting their fate in the hands of an immigrant. You all deserve what is coming to you when this all turns.'

David stalked away, following in Marjorie's path – going to meet the prime princess in the far corner. He swiped his own bottle – this time, champagne – on the way to his end point.

'Right then.' Maud had barely even watched the old royals retire to their corner, but she definitely seemed to delight in carrying on without them. 'Shall we proceed?'

Jon felt so incredibly hot all of a sudden and it was nothing to do with the now-substantial fire crackling away behind him. 'Excuse me, Your Royal Highnesses, I must . . . I just need . . . I must get some air.' With that, he started away from the spotlight and was to the door before any of them could deny his dismissal.

The last thing he heard as he barrelled through the doorway was a familiar snort from Marjorie, followed by David laughing – 'Seems you all failed to ask the man himself.'

XX

Doubt and Duty

The hallway didn't quite provide the air that Jon craved. He would have liked to take a brisk walk outside, but that was impossible – and not only because of the raging blizzard. It would have taken Jon five minutes to get to a door that led outside, and he wouldn't have liked to open a window in this weather. This thick viscous air was the closest he was going to get to fresh.

How could events spin so quickly out of control? The king was dead, the royals were at each other's throats, and now Jon was being elected for a position that he did not even stand for. He could not be an investigator, a detective. He had forever been a chef and a chef alone – never desiring to step outside of his lane. Now the day was calling for him to take a leap.

He paced down the corridor and back, repeating the action over and over. Almost on impulse, he reached for the walkie-talkie on his belt. It was hopeless, but he was in a hopeless kind of corner. 'Come in, Speck. Come in.' That static again. 'Please, Speck. This is your damn job, not mine. You are security. I should be tucked up in the servants' quarters about now, not doing your work. The Bridlepath Causeway has Flooded, do you hear me? Do you hear me?' He depressed the button and the resulting hiss indicated that Speck did not hear him at all. 'Where the hell are you, Speck?'

He dropped the walkie-talkie to his side and clipped it back on his belt. There was no point even having it, really – a fundamentally redundant thing.

He paced a little more. He noticed that the grandfather clock at the end of the hall had stopped. Maybe it needed to be rewound. He stepped towards it, having seen how to do so once before, but then paused. Instinct had kicked in – he was not a simple worker now. A stopped clock could wait.

He didn't want to be the investigator. He couldn't be. But what else could he do? Everyone in that room was a suspect. The princesses who championed him, the spouse who would echo anything said, the old guard who both had showed varying degrees of contempt for everyone else, not to mention impaired, alcohol-soaked judgements, and (although it seemed the most unlikely) the two young royals, who stood to inherit the most.

All he could think of then was how not one of them could do such a terrible thing. Even David, who had jumped back and forth across the line of the law as though he were playing skipping rope in a playground, and Marjorie, who had grown vile and twisted in her elder years, had no place in his mind as possible murderers.

This was the Royal Family. The Windsors.

The pain in Jon's gut was becoming too much to bear. Suddenly, he had the undeniable sense that someone was watching him – that feeling of eyes boring into him,

147

privacy gone. He looked up and down the halls, but there was no one there – he found them as decadently empty as they had been since the previous night. The feeling of being watched was one that took some getting used to at the king's residences, because it was a common occurrence. It was something to do with the size of the spaces, the high ceilings, the dark corners – even the smaller, pokier corridors felt as though they held centuries of secrets. There were many places for someone to squirrel themselves away. It was always important to remember that it was just a feeling though – an overactive sensory reaction.

Jon found his eyes raising to the walls, following his new-found intuition. Eric Windsor smiled down at him, in watercolour, framed by a gold prison. Eric hadn't liked the painting – in fact, he had always joked of doing a 'Winston Churchill' and burning the blighter at the bottom of the garden – but Jon found it endearing. It was slightly more alive than any of the other paintings of the king, painted by a relatively young artist for some event or other. The thick brushstrokes in places and the deliberately light ones in others created a motion that showed how Eric never stayed still, the playful colours echoing Eric's vibrant personality, the youth that lingered in his face, although he was already of an advanced age when he'd posed for the portrait. There was a magic to it – just as there was a magic to Eric Windsor.

Jon's eyes threatened to water again, but instead he stood to attention. The king gazed down at him, with his frozen smile. Jon had lost sight of what this was all for.

'Of course, Your Majesty. I will do it for you.' Jon didn't add that everything always had been for him.

How could Jon abandon the king now – his legacy – in his time of greatest need? Jon was not one for vengeance – even thinking of it made him feel queasy – but he was one for justice, and maybe that meant he could actually do what needed to be done.

This new conviction, along with the new-found intuition, fuelled him. He paced some more, but this time it was for a more tangible purpose. With one final look back at the kinetic king, Jon went to the drawing room doors and stepped inside.

In the drawing room, it appeared as though nothing had changed, in a very literal sense. The royals were all waiting like they were part of a play, and when Jon had walked off stage, everyone was left confused as he had the next line. That was indeed the case.

Jon cleared his throat, although he had their attention already. 'I accept the role. For the king and for the Crown.'

XXI

For the King and for the Crown

Princess Emeline spoke first, as no one else moved an inch. She provided the best smile she could, given the circumstances. 'Thank you, Jon. I know Father trusted you with his entire being. It is time for us to do the same.'

'Everyone's complete co-operation will be necessary,' Jon said, trying to sound like an investigator might. 'Otherwise this will not work.'

Emeline nodded. 'You have mine. The truth and nothing but the truth.'

In turn, the other royals gave their consent just as Emeline did – all but the two usual suspects. Those two suspects sat in their corner on two chairs they had moved specially, and watched proceedings with interest – as though they were disconnected from what was happening in the rest of the room.

'Uncle? Mother?' Maud inquired. 'Is anybody present?' The two of them looked to their youngers with expressions that could only be described as utter barefaced contempt, and almost comically shrugged in unison. Maud sighed, 'They'll do it, Jon. They're just making a scene, because, all of a sudden, this is not completely about them.'

'Go and suck an egg, Daughter,' Marjorie said, before breaking down into a horrendous cackle. Her grief was taking her on a very twisted path.

'It's the Wild West, Margey. The walls are coming down,' David muttered. His comment prolonged the princess royal's hysterics – a scene that was completely neglected by everyone else. It seemed to be an unspoken agreement between the others to place those two in an echo chamber, and throw away the key.

Princesses Emeline and Maud, Thomas Crockley and Princes Matthew and Martin – the more amenable of the family – seemed united in support. That at least was a blessing. Jon did not know what it meant in terms of the task he had before him, but it was nice in the moment.

'Very well,' said Jon, hoping to conjure a heading. To attempt to look like he had succeeded, he quickly moved over to the coffee table between the two chaises longues. The serving decanter offered no grand epiphany. The whisky inside – still half a bottle's worth – seemed normal. He retrieved a glass and poured himself some. There was a slight murmur of panic from someone as he lifted it to his face, but it was unnecessary. He raised it to his nose, not his mouth. He couldn't smell anything intrusive that was not meant to be there – in the profile was the familiar wheat smell, almost overpowered by the phenolic smoky scent. There was nothing that screamed poison, although Jon would hardly know what that smelled like. The only scent he associated with poison was almonds for cyanide – common knowledge – and there were no nutty tones of any kind in the whisky

151

(at least none that should not have been there). Of course, Jon knew that cyanide was not the only kind of poison, but maybe it would have simply been the easiest solution. Without drinking the liquid he wouldn't know what it did internally, although he had some idea, given the state of the king.

He placed the glass and the bottle back onto the tray, defeated by his first act as investigator. Nothing was gleaned at all. He guessed the next action should be to go and look elsewhere – but on glancing around, he realised that his actions in his new role and his actions as the sole protector of the Royal Family would collide.

In a foolhardy attempt at retrieving a new bottle of wine, David had crossed the age divide and was about to stumble into a storm with Princess Maud. Jon could see it coming, as David, freshly tipsy and desiring to continue his odyssey, tripped into the princess. What followed was a barrage of insults from both sides, which would be barely repeatable in a 'common' household, let alone the king's. As the symphony escalated, and Crockley stepped in (as ever, a little too late), Jon understood that getting too far from this embarrassment of a scene would be unwise. Temperatures were running high, and if they rose any further, things would start to get ugly – the family's status be damned. Even if he was not present in the room, he had to be seen to be doing something more to actively impact not only the investigation but their current predicament.

He thought entirely as he spoke – an action that was very foreign to him while on duty at the castle. He usually composed and vetted a complete thought before voicing it. He had to shout for his voice to rise above David and Maud's battle. 'I think it would be best now to talk to you each individually, and get a clearer picture of what happened.' That sounded like something an investigator would do.

The current scene and everything that had happened since the king's grand exit had showed him that he must separate the royals if he was to have any hope of finding out what had happened. He was starting to understand how much he did not know about this family. He saw the king die, he saw that one of these people had killed him, but he was unsure who. Family bonds were strained, but he did not know how exactly. Loyalties were being tested, but how far? These people were being torn apart, but where did it start? He looked around and saw strangers – as if the king had been the only connective tissue between him and them. Jon had dedicated his life to a strange family who had kept him at arm's-length.

'I will talk to you first,' Emeline said, stepping in front of her quarrelling family members, who had still not stopped their war of words. 'I feel that me being the first interviewee is somewhat apt, given that this was my idea. Where shall we go? I do think that we should put some distance between ourselves and the very room in which the crime occurred.'

Jon, again, found that Emeline was trying to take control – a side to her that was not unwelcome given the circumstances, but was also slightly at odds with her usual easy-going temperament.

A great sigh seemed to fill the room. 'Little Miss Perfect goes first.' It appeared that Emeline's mother also noted her attempt at authority. 'Watch out for that one, Chef – she has a temper.'

'Mother, please,' Emeline snapped in such a way that Jon had never heard before. Jon had never heard Emeline so much as raise her voice, but she was surprising him of late. Was it possible that Marjorie was right? Emeline, who reinforced her question of where to go because of the interruption, mused for a second and then said, 'We could go to the hall.'

Having just been in the hallway, Jon knew the eerie nature of the corridors of Balmoral, the feeling of eyes resting on him even though there was no one else present, the fact that he felt overly exposed. It was hard to think any work could be done in the hallway. 'No. Let us go to the visitors' study down the hall.' The study was a perfect centre for his operation – it was vacant, having once upon a time been the princesses' private secretary's office. However, now that the princesses had moved away to their own similarly extravagant abodes, the study lay empty, forgotten. There were so many rooms in the 'Moral, it was startlingly easy for one to fall into obscurity. It was now repurposed for visitors to use – but visitors rarely came.

They started off towards the doors, an odd couple, but Marjorie staggered into view, and refused to move, seeming to undulate in her righteous indignation. 'I would not say anything you do not want in the papers, Daughter. The staff can never be trusted.'

'Mother, we are beyond that. What is it about this situation you do not understand?'

'Oh, I see plainly, Emeline. I see a great deal more than you give me credit for.' Marjorie said this triumphantly, before giving a great hiccup, jostling her wine. Despite this, Marjorie did not move from their path.

'Come on, Grandmother.' Matthew appeared from beyond them and took Marjorie by the arm, somewhat haphazardly. 'Let us get you sat down.'

'I do not need coddling!'

'I shall get you sat down and then get you another drink.'

She brightened at this. 'Oh. Well, all right then.'

Matthew guided Marjorie away, sat her down and nodded back to Jon with a somewhat satisfied smile at a job well done. Jon couldn't help but give a grateful one back.

'Excuse me, sir.' This was Thomas Crockley, who was attempting to appear fine with Marjorie being seated near him. He was still looking impossibly pale. 'Can we just maybe have a summation of what is going on?'

'I am going to talk to each of you one by one to get a general idea of the history that could have been involved with the king's death. We are going to the study just down the hall from this room,' Jon announced. 'I recommend that no one else steps foot outside this room until I am back. The fact that there may be a third party in the castle is a possibility that is still very much in play. You will be safe if you band together.'

'You are aware that you may be leaving us here with the killer.'

Jon was absolutely aware of that – he didn't like it, but there it was. 'There's one thing that we have over the killer. The killer is alone. If you don't let anyone out of your sight, then you will all be safe. I promise.' As soon as he said those last two words, he wished he hadn't, because a new possibility had just announced its arrival in his mind.

What if it was more than one of them?

Jon hastily had eyes on everyone in the room, realising that Emeline had already exited. When had she left? He had to get after her. However, there was one last thing he had to ask.

Matthew was crossing to Jon's abandoned drinks tray for Marjorie's sustenance, and Jon caught his eye, 'What were you going to say, sir?'

Matthew stopped in his tracks, emitting two very different countenances. He plainly appeared to know exactly what Jon meant, but on the surface, he appeared confused. 'Hmm?'

Jon knew to tread carefully. 'Just before we entered the drawing room, you said that you must say one thing before this goes any further, and then Marjorie dropped the glass and interrupted you. What was that one thing?'

'It barely matters any more.'

'Sir, please, if it may help.'

'It will not help,' Matthew said, 'it can only hinder.' Jon was confused, and with a sigh, Matthew explained. 'I was going to say that if we find out who killed my grandfather, I may not be able to wait for the authorities. Because when the killer is unmasked, whoever they may be, I'm going to kill them.'

XXII

A Private Audience with Little Miss Perfect

They were in the hallway, walking down to the vacant study. Jon hesitated before leaving Matthew alone with everyone after his promise, but he saw no other way.

'Oh, to be free of that room,' Emeline said. 'I half asked to be first just to be away from it.' They passed the painting of the king Jon had stared at, and the grandfather clock Jon had not fixed. The study was the next door they came across. Before going inside, Jon stopped a moment. Something about the hallway was . . .

'Jon? What is it?'

Jon shook his head. 'It's nothing.'

Inside, the study was small and dusty. The maids still cleaned here, but not quite as often. A small wooden desk sat in the centre of the room, with a desk chair behind it, and a rather less comfy chair in front of it. It was just as if someone had set it up for the very purpose of interrogation. There was nothing else in the room at all – the sideboard bare, the bookcase empty.

Jon instinctively went to sit in front of the desk, but Emeline shook her head and guided him to the desk chair behind it. He sat. It was easy to forget the mere joy of being off his feet. His legs were singing with gratitude. He immediately regretted it, already dreading the battle that would be getting up again.

'I have not had time to offer my condolences, Your Royal Highness.'

Emeline waved them away. 'Thank you, but it is not necessary. I am sorry for what you are going through, too – I know you and my father had an unlikely friendship. And I am particularly sorry for you having to see the rest of us at our worst. It is hard to believe the Royal Family can be so barbaric, but there it is.'

'How are you coping, if you don't mind me asking, ma'am?'

'I am broken, Jon. And I know my family is hurting too. But that does not make it any better for me. At least Maud has her husband and her sons – even Mother and Uncle seem to have each other. I am alone. I just wish Anton were here. He would know what to do.'

Jon did not want to make light of the situation, especially from his very unique vantage point, but he felt that they should press on. Anton was not here, and even Emeline would admit that that was probably best for him. 'Let us start with earlier this morning. We crossed paths in the drawing room when I was lighting the fire for your uncle. You came in with your sister.'

'Yes,' said Emeline, a little more content now Jon was asking questions. What an odd thing – content with interrogation? 'We had just made breakfast, although cereal does not take much making.'

159

'So you had breakfast, and then Maud's timetable says you went to find the king?'

'Yes, we were in such high spirits, just for pouring our own cereal. Christmas Day in more ways than one.'

'Did you see any of your family before going to find the king?'

'I did not. I walked with Maud and went to my room just to freshen up somewhat. Maud had been talking about *The Monarch* – by all accounts, she would not shut up about it. I haven't watched it myself, so I put on an episode while getting ready, but I could not concentrate, so I just watched the morning news. It took me maybe half an hour to get ready – I am not one to spend hours worrying about my appearance.'

That was hard to believe. Although Emeline was, in the public's eyes, the lesser princess, she still appeared positively radiant. Even her sorrow could not cloud her beauty.

'Why did you go to see the king? You already knew he would call upon you, as he would call upon the others?' He was, of course, referring to the private audiences that many of the family had mentioned.

'No, I had no idea that was his intention. I simply wanted to wish my father a Happy Christmas. It is very hard to get Father on his own, given his station, even in a castle of less than ten people, but I knew he would be alone in his study in the morning preparing his speech. He always does that, as I'm sure you know. He'll write it all weeks in advance, and then, on Christmas morning, he'll get a kind of anxiety about it, and go back

160

and tinker. I arrived when he had just finished, and, by coincidence, when he was just about to find some way to call for me.'

'How would he have done that?'

'I'm not sure. He would have employed Martin to run around for him, maybe. It hardly matters, does it?'

No, he supposed it didn't. 'So, your father had his private audience with you? I'm afraid I am going to have to ask what you discussed.'

Emeline smiled genuinely – a beautiful sight that reminded Jon of days gone by, and almost banished this day entirely. 'I know. And I will be forthcoming about it, although I'm afraid there are others in my family who definitely won't. First, we discussed the very private audiences themselves – he wished to talk with Maud, my uncle, my mother, my nephew, Matthew and, for some reason, Thomas. Though quite why anyone would want to do that is beyond me. I was to bring them all to his study when the time was right. So I suppose I was to be the "Martin" instead – doing Father's busy work as usual.'

'Does that annoy you?'

Emeline's eyes snapped to Jon, with an angry fire raging inside her irises. Jon realised that it was possibly the first thing he had ever said out of turn. Emeline seemed to realise this too, remembering Jon's new station, and softening. 'Yes, I suppose it does. I have always felt like the worker-bee daughter, to my more preened counterpart. I have never been enraged enough to commit murder though.'

161

'I am not insinuating anything, ma'am.'

'No, I know you're not. I just . . . Maybe I just had to say that for myself.' It was almost as if she had to convince herself that she hadn't performed the act – very odd, but he supposed that grief manifested itself in many different ways. It was possible that Princess Emeline thought herself responsible in any number of ways, and they were hitting her one by one. 'Anyhow, when the plan was drawn up for the audiences, Father just talked about the day ahead. He seemed in high spirits. I don't have to tell you, but Christmas is his favourite holiday after all. Was – Christmas *was* his favourite holiday.'

An uncomfortable silence threatened to derail the whole conversation. Jon stumbled to hold on to it. 'Matthew mentioned that he thought the after-dinner speech was to be about naming the king's successor. Did you happen to see the speech, or did the king mention the content?'

Emeline shook her head. 'I had no idea at all. Father never usually discussed those things with me.'

'Before the change to the succession rules, you would have been queen. Maybe you still are in line.'

Emeline shook her head again, but this time it was far more deliberate – one might have said the motion was violent, even. 'I was never in line, never in contention. He made that perfectly clear. However, I am fine with that – who would really want to be queen anyway?' She sounded sincere enough. 'No, there only one person that Daddy would have announced to be next in line.'

Emeline sat on the information, clearly taking some power from withholding it, if only for a second. For that second, she had the authority back. It was clear that she was missing it more than she was letting on.

'And that would be, ma'am?'

'Father would have named Matthew to succeed him. He has never hidden the fact, even when it might have hurt Maud and me. He never would have said it, but he thought we were too old. A new monarch would have to be full of youth, he'd say.'

'That must have stung a little.'

'Of course it did. Thirty-nine, and being called too old! But he was right – he *is* right, I suppose, and as I said, I never had any real desire for queendom.'

'Thank you for your co-operation, ma'am. I have only two more things to ask at this time – who do you think killed the king. And, maybe even more importantly, why?'

Emeline thought on these questions for a long time. He could not blame her. They were not easy to parse, and, in truth, they scared him to death. 'I do not think I can answer the former question, but with regards to the latter – it must be one who would benefit from the king not speaking Matthew's name. One who did not want Matthew to be the new king.'

Jon had been thinking a very similar scenario himself, although there were a few flies in that particular ointment. Killing a king to prevent a specific successor sounded like an adequate enough motive, but only if the king's intentions could not be proven. He had to admit that he was also in the dark about the finer protocol of the succession rules, and would have been even before they had changed – would the king's words have to be followed to the letter? Jon then stumbled upon something he rather wished he hadn't. 'If the king was killed before announcing a successor, one may assume that the title of monarch would fall to the first in line, that being you, ma'am.'

'Yes,' Emeline said, as plain as a sky with no clouds. There really was nothing else to be said. 'You see, I am the prime suspect. I saw that very quickly. This is why I wanted to get this all sorted – so I can clear my name.' Emeline rose. 'If it is agreeable, I would like to leave now.'

Jon rose too. 'Of course, ma'am. It seems you have been retrieving people all morning, so I do not want to ask, but . . .'

'Of course, I will send another to you, Jon. I am actually more productive when distracted, so being put to work staves away the tears. Do you have any preference as to who to see next?'

Anyone but David or Marjorie, he thought, although their time must come eventually. 'Maybe I should talk to your sister next.'

Emeline nodded in compliance – an odd shift in the balance of power that was not lost on either of them – and went to the door. Jon followed her as she turned. 'Thank you, Jon – truly. I know this is far beyond your duties. The Crown thanks you.'

Emeline stalked off down the hall back towards the

drawing room without another word. Jon gazed after her through the open door, and was about to close it, before his instinct made him pause again. A rather loud *tick tock, tick tock, tick tock* filled the corridor. It took a moment to realise why this was so odd, but once he had, Jon strode over to the grandfather clock.

It was running perfectly, the small hand denoting the seconds snapping to each minute segment with a fault-less rhythm. Jon would have sworn it wasn't working before and the fact that it was not showing the correct time proved it. There were more pressing matters, but it was highly irregular. With one final look, he returned to the study as the clock ticked away.

XXIII

A Private Audience with the Young at Heart

Three short and light knocks at the door.

Maud started as Jon opened the door to her, even though she must have known it was inevitable. She smiled warmly to Jon and came inside. Anyone who did not know the princess well might have thought her sunny disposition to be an odd demeanour to adopt in a time such as this, but Jon knew better. Maud often used her outer warmth to mask her heart, and right at this moment, her smile was a little too perfect, her eyes a little too warm. In actuality, she was barely holding the facade together.

'Your Royal Highness.'

'I told you – you should stop all that, Jon. Nothing is gained from treating us any differently to yourself at this moment. Your Majesty this and ma'am and sir that, it's nothing but wasted words. Maybe that's all it has ever been.'

He gestured for her to sit at the desk, and she did – obeying his order. A princess bowing to a chef. 'It is a hard habit to break, ma'am.' He sat too.

'We have to get him, Jon. The one who killed my

166

father. We really do not have time for chats, although I see the value, I suppose. I'm torn by all this. How do we know which course of action is the best, which avenue is the best to take? This will only happen once – what if we've already scuppered it?' The words fell out of her in a heap so fast that he almost had to search around her and piece a sentence together, not unlike fishing for meaning in a can of that awful alphabet spaghetti.

'We can only forge ahead with the path we've chosen, ma'am, and hope against hope that we've picked the right one.' He sounded far more composed than he had expected.

'Daddy – he must have been so scared. His eyes . . .'

In a dark corner of his mind, a voice whispered to Jon that Maud would be no good to anyone in this state. She must be taken back to the well-trodden path she had mentioned. 'I would like to begin with asking you about this morning. Emeline has said that you retrieved some cereal from the pantry.'

Maud returned with a vengeance. 'Well, yes, and I suppose the whisky was there too, but it was still sealed, so you can't think—'

'I do not think anything, ma'am. I just need to see the full picture.'

'Oh. Yes, we got cereal from the pantry. We ate in the sunroom, and then we crossed your path in the drawing room. After that, we walked upstairs together and I left Emeline to go back to my room, where myself and the family were watching *The Monarch* for a time. You can see our movements on the timetable I drew up. Thomas

167

went first for a smoke, and found his way to the drawing room, it seems.'

'Yes,' Jon said. 'He also found his way down to my kitchen.'

Maud was not listening though. A hand was raised to her mouth. 'Oh no. *The Monarch*. They'll do this bit. This will be part of it. Who do you think will play you, Jon?'

Her train of thought was so hard to follow that Jon almost missed exactly what she was saying. *The Monarch* would indeed be dramatising these moments. He personally did not like the sound of the series, but hadn't had the time to sit down and watch it at any rate.

As far as he knew, *The Monarch* was still in the earlier years of the princesses' lives, but, yes, they would inevitably arrive at this very moment. This was pure television gold, he imagined. He could see this as a series finale. Television producers would grasp this event with both hands, not letting any of the drama fall through their fingertips.

'What did the king think of *The Monarch*?' Jon asked, less for the investigation and more out of genuine curiosity. He had never heard the king talk about it, outside of the small snippets of opinion he gleaned from dinner earlier.

'Daddy? He didn't often talk about it – well, no, actually, I tell a lie, he had been recently. For some reason, he had started thinking that someone from the palace was leaking information. You know that *The Monarch* is an independent production, yes – so it is not supported or affiliated with the actual monarchy in any way. Therefore, all research, of which there must be mountains, is done entirely externally and unofficially. Father started watching it when I told him about a particular scene – my twenty-sixth birthday, in fact. Do you remember it?'

Jon did, of course. 'The birthday where the Russian celloist performed?' He had served a buffet lunch that day in the gardens of Windsor Castle. He remembered that he didn't get the pastry on the sausage rolls quite right and that would irk him to his dying day.

'Yes. Well, that day ended in a particularly nasty argument with Daddy, Mummy and myself. The programme portrayed it more or less perfectly, and it is rather odd, but no one could have known about that argument. It was never noted down anywhere, no one was in the vicinity – but the programme got it spot on. I put it down to coincidence – an extreme case of art imitating life, but Daddy thought something more sinister was afoot.'

'I have not seen the episode, ma'am, but if it is on national television, I'm sure you won't mind my next question. What was the argument about?'

'Oh, what almost every conversation with my parents has been about since the event, of course. They don't approve of my marriage. Or, no! That is not quite accurate, they don't like my choice of mate one bit.'

'They approve of union, but not of Mr Crockley?'

'Exactly so. They hate Thomas, to put it plainly. It is not often my parents are in agreement, but when the topic of my husband rears its head, it is hard to tell Mummy and Daddy apart in their viciousness.' Jon

169

found it difficult to believe that Eric could match the tyranny of Marjorie, but there it was. 'Daddy called him a "pig-headed businessman" on more than one occasion. I refuse to even see that – I think he's a proper English gentleman. Don't you?'

It was almost as if she were asking Jon's approval, looking at him with expectancy. 'He has always seemed very agreeable, ma'am,' he said, although inwardly he was far closer to the king's assessment. Putting his personal feelings aside, however, he wanted to get back on track, and see if this newfound wrinkle related to the day. 'You mentioned that every conversation you had with the king was about Mr Crockley. Does this mean that you talked about your husband in your private audience with the king this morning?'

Maud had something like admiration at the corner of her eyes. 'Yes. It does. Daddy was very odd this morning. He was decidedly unlike himself – very un-Christmassy, and very shouty. He said that enough was enough and that I should open my eyes to who Thomas Crockley really was. I must have called his bluff though, as he would not actually tell me who my husband really was. He kept saying, "I must give Thomas a chance to explain himself." That was my father for you, gracious even when he was angry.'

'So you have no idea what your father could be referring to?'

'Not one bit. And what was worse was I had to take Thomas to him afterwards. I felt much like an executioner taking my husband to the axe. When he came out,

Thomas was a shade of white I've never seen on anyone and wouldn't say a word. You are to talk to my husband, Jon. Could you get to the bottom of this?'

A mystery inside another mystery. Jon recalled a set of Russian dolls that his mother used to have on the shelf in her room in Barbados. Little Jon always used to wonder what was inside, until one day he climbed up on a chair to look. He marvelled as he took the lid off the doll to see a smaller one concealed inside, and it kept going – smaller and smaller. Until – well, it was his mother after all. The smallest doll had a baggie of heroin lodged in it. He wondered if this mystery was similar – comprised of smaller and smaller ones until finally he'd get to the smallest and reveal its dark heart.

'I am sure everything will have its time in the light. These things often do. Thank you, ma'am, for your co-operation. I have just one question to ask before we part. Who do you think killed your father?'

Maud didn't have to think for even a second. 'It's obvious, isn't it? My disgusting uncle.'

'Prince David?'

'Of course. He blames Daddy for his exile, he blames Daddy for his diminished title, he blames Daddy for everything. Uncle killed Daddy – I would stake my life on it. He's a slippery criminal – we all know this already, and it made me sick to my stomach that I had to share a dinner table with him.'

Maud was correct, of course – David was a notorious character. Something about David killing Eric didn't sit quite right though. There was something in it, and Jon

171

could absolutely understand Maud making the leap, but there were pieces of the puzzle that were missing – pieces that may yet reveal themselves.

For now, however, Jon had to resist the urge to jump ahead. 'Thank you, ma'am.'

Maud took this as a dismissal – yet another sign of this new dynamic – and rose. 'Should I tell someone else that you would like to speak to them?'

'Well, I suppose I should talk to your proper English gentleman next.'

Maud smiled – an act that didn't fail to still inspire some warmth in his heart – and went to retrieve her husband.

Jon thought on the wrongs being levelled at Crockley and what exactly they were. It was lucky, then, that he would not have to wonder for very long.

XXIV

A Private Audience with the Proper English Gentleman (or a Private Audience with the Pig-Headed Businessman)

'So then I said to myself, "OK, old chap, you're never going to get this chance ever again in your life. You have to start this business right this very second. Or someone else will." So I pulled up my bootstraps, and I got to work. That was how Ride+ was born, and the sky has been the limit ever since.'

Jon was quite unsure what to say. Had he asked about Crockley's business ventures? Had he even said a word? He really couldn't remember. Even in Crockley's current state – pale and sweating – he was still on top form (his very unique version of top form, anyway). Regardless of what one thought of him, Crockley had this uncanny ability to weave an enticing narrative that was hard to escape.

'Right,' Jon said, rather awkwardly. 'I'm sorry, what were we discussing?'

Crockley did not answer, but instead spluttered into his handkerchief. There was indeed something very wrong with him. As if the man were responding to this directly, he smiled and said, 'I'm fine. I'm fine.'

Jon continued then. 'I think I asked about your private audience with the king, yes?'

Thomas Crockley's smile faded somewhat. 'That may be what you call it. I rather prefer it as the Longest Ten Minutes of My Life. Really, a dreadful waste of time. I should have stayed down in the kitchens with you where I couldn't be found. The old boy was lucky that it's Christmas and I didn't have business calls to make, otherwise I'd be billing him for lost revenue. Well, I mean, figuratively. He was the king, after all.'

'May I inquire as to the content? Princess Maud mentioned that you would not tell her.'

'No.' Crockley's energy had entirely dissipated. 'Look, it's a rather touchy subject, so I would prefer not to talk about it, if it's all the same to you.'

'If your audience has any correlation to the king's death, then it could be of the utmost importance. I am not necessarily accusing you, either – there could be information about someone else that you are overlooking.'

'I find that hard to believe, old boy. My ritual sacrifice was very much about myself and my father-in-law. Can you imagine how embarrassing it is to know that your wife's parents have never liked you? Now, take that embarrassment and multiply it by a thousand because your father-in-law's only the sodding king?'

'Was there any reason why the king chose to voice his opinion today, of all days?'

Crockley hesitated a moment, as if trying to catch himself, but then thundered on anyway. He was away now, the spinning top of gossip. 'Oh, yes, absolutely. The king, with all due respect, you understand, had a bee in his bonnet for a long time about something, and he finally felt he had to nail me to the wall for it.'

'Would this be the fact that the king thought there was someone leaking palace secrets to the producers of *The Monarch*?' Jon thought back to what he had overheard at dinner.

Crockley did not appear surprised at all. 'Yes, sir, it would. Maud told you that, did she? The old king has been talking about it for what feels like years, and I've always had a sneaking suspicion he suspected me for it. He's never had the cojones to come out and say it though.'

'But today he did.'

'Yes. He made quite a performance out of it – I'm surprised he didn't sell tickets. Don't know if the conversation went the way he thought it would though. He had this evidence, this file – don't know where it is, never want to see it again – where he'd compiled every interview I'd ever done and photos of royal events and correspondence of God knows who and who knows what else. He was brandishing it at me like a sodding gun. Apparently, it all meant that I was the only one who had been present at every single instance that cropped up in the show. Going senile in his old age, clearly.'

Thomas Crockley was getting vile, but Jon had to let him get on with it to hear his tale. 'Mr Crockley, you haven't been leaking secrets to the producers of *The Monarch*, have you?'

Crockley's insipid demeanour instantly eroded back into an agreeable one, as he gave a chortle. 'Well, of course not. I've never heard anything so ludicrous in all my life. There is no reason for me to leak secrets – none whatsoever. Eric and Marjorie Windsor have clearly always had it in for me, and this was how they intended to separate me from my wife.'

Crockley took a spluttering break before continuing.

'I will tell you what I told him and the rest of the family. A man approached me in my local haunt, The Gentlemen. I was there one afternoon toasting my business success. This man came to me, I think his name was Tippin, and offered me a significant sum of money to be the production company's informant. He placed his business card on the bar, and he said to me, "You don't have to say a thing, you just have to take that card as confirmation." Well, you know what I did? I ripped that card into little pieces and I told him to eff off. In fact, I got him thrown out and barred for life. I know the manager, you see.

'The king won't listen to the truth though. It doesn't fit his little narrative. That I may be loyal to this family.'

Jon wouldn't say that that sounded like the king at all, but with Maud and Thomas both corroborating about some kind of a vendetta, he wondered if maybe he had simply not been privy to a slightly sharper side of Eric Windsor. What was this evidence Thomas mentioned? 'Maud said that the king would not tell her what he had found out . . . or, excuse me . . . theorised. Is that true?'

'It would seem that way, yes.'

'And you will not tell her? Why?'

'That is simple – to even entertain this is giving it time that it doesn't deserve. A man should not meddle in the affairs of his daughter, and that is exactly what the king was doing. He wanted to destroy our marriage, but I would like to think he brought us closer together. Bringing up all this rubbish could only hurt her. I have not only a wife, but two boys to think about.'

Jon nodded – he could understand that, at least. 'Can you see how this might look? The king seems to have something to hold over you, even if it is untrue, he confronts you about it and a few hours later he drops dead.' He didn't know how he felt about Thomas Crockley's possible involvement, but he was mightily curious about his response.

'I see exactly how it looks, old bean.'

'What do you think the criminal charge is for leaking royal secrets?'

'I wouldn't know.'

Jon didn't really know either, but he could guess. 'I would think it very much depends on the severity of the leak, but I could see prison time, excommunication, public humiliation. Treason?'

'That sounds about correct. But it does not concern me as I did not do it. I have no reason to jeopardise my small position here at the side of the princess. My business is booming, for Christ's sake. I did not do it!' He shouted this last declaration.

'I am not accusing you of anything.'

Crockley paused and sighed, 'I know, my good man. Sorry about that, it's just, emotions are running high, you know. And I do not feel my best.' Jon could confirm that. As previously noted, the man most definitely didn't look his best either. 'Look, I'm very sorry that the man is dead, and I'm even more sorry that he seemed to die with a misconception of me. I had nothing to do with his death, and I fear that if you concentrate on this farcical thing, you may miss something truly important. I mean, I tried to bring him back to life, for God's sake!'

'Who do you think killed the king?'

'I'm going to be honest – I haven't the foggiest, and I am glad about that. I have enough to deal with by myself. It would seem that the question of who killed the king falls to you. You have my support in catching the bastard.'

'Thank you, sir,' Jon said, out of a matter of principle more than anything else.

Crockley dabbed at his forehead with his soggy handkerchief. 'I have been wondering though, the CPR I performed. Now we're out of the moment, I think I may have done it wrong. I don't think you're meant to breathe into their mouths anymore. Maybe I did more harm than good?'

Jon's stomach turned. Why had he not seen it? With everything going on, Crockley's problems had been an afterthought. Crockley had touched the king's lips with his own. Please, God, there was not a chance that Crockley was poisoned, was there?

'You know,' Crockley said, 'I think the day is catching

up with me. Would you permit me to go and lie down in my room?'

Jon would almost certainly not have if he hadn't just realised what may be happening to the man. Hopefully, if it was the poison, Crockley had gotten a small enough dose to pull through.

'Yes,' Jon said, 'I suppose you can.' It was dangerous, but Jon remembered those red dots on Speck's security tablet. The royal family were in the drawing room, and no one else was here. 'Go directly to your room, and it may be advisable to lock your door.'

Crockley, with one final splutter, nodded and shuffled out of the room, leaving Jon with a sinking feeling. Although he didn't particularly like the man, he did not wish him ill. But now Jon had to search through the forest of Crockley's many, many words. It was such a thick forest that he barely had time to search – such was the problem of Thomas Crockley.

Jon first wondered if the king and Marjorie's vendetta against the man was not unfounded, then wondered if it was greatly exaggerated. From serving Eric for over thirty years, Jon knew he had been a man with a strong moral compass, and one who believed in the correct treatment of others. If Eric was accusing Crockley of this leak, he must have had ample evidence to prove that he had his culprit, and he would have made sure he secured this to back up his claim, despite any personal feelings.

Jon hoped Crockley would get to his room all right.

For now, Jon needed a break from all of this – his brain

was still running overtime with all he had just heard. The forest of truth and lies. But was there something in the forest of words that his suspects didn't want him to find?

XXV

The Ghost of John Brown

Jon was in such a horrible state of mind that his heart leapt when he again saw the corridor. He rested against the far wall and rubbed his eyes with his right thumb and forefinger while taking some well-earned deep breaths.

Jon retracted his hand from his face, and sighed.

Movement out of the corner of his eye, from the junction of the corridors, made him glance around. He was sure it was a figure moving along that corridor, left to right. He had clearly seen a shadow, although he had not been able to pick out any discernible features. He did not even know if it was a man or a woman. All he saw was flowing clothes trailing behind the figure, like a dress.

His first thought was to call out. Maybe Thomas Crockley was still around, or maybe it was even Tony Speck. But some inner instinct stopped him.

A dress? Or maybe a kilt?

It is important at this point to address the very real superstition that many of the staff had when working at Balmoral Castle. This superstition pertained to the ghost of a former servant of Queen Victoria named John Brown. John Brown was Queen Victoria's favourite servant – in fact, some even said that she was in love with him. Their exact relationship was a matter of speculation, but Brown received preferential treatment, a badge of honour and even a statue of himself at Balmoral. No one else approved of the relationship, even years after the fact, with Edward VII trying to expunge Brown from history, destroying every mention of him. Others managed to save the statue, however, by compromising with the king to move it to a secluded area on the grounds. Maybe it was saved to please Brown's spirit, as it is said that Brown still inhabits the castle, with every monarch since having tales of sightings. Even Eric had seen him a few times, saying that he was unmistakeable, with his bushy neckbeard and constant kilt.

John Brown was Jon's very next thought as he stood there in the corridor. He usually wouldn't abide such a notion. He had never seen Brown's apparition himself, and did not believe in it, but his nerves were fried and it was simply that kind of day.

A chill went through him as he ignored his instinct to go back to the visitor's study. He walked towards the junction where he saw the flowing figure. He must catch up to this unknown entity – if only to prove it wasn't Brown. He got to the junction as quickly as his legs and his gut would allow, and moved into the next hall without another thought. The hallway was empty, but it was a small one, that ended in the entrance hall and the staircase up to the bedrooms. If he listened closely, he could hear footfalls on the stairs, and yes, a creak. Whoever this figure was, they were going upstairs.

Jon broke into a bizarre kind of skip – both to mini-mise any sound he himself would make and to alleviate any pain he might cause on his poor legs. He met the staircase and started up it, just as the figure seemingly completed it. The stag mounted on the wall watched him with interest. He heard the footsteps quieten as the fig-ure progressed down the hall towards the bedrooms. Jon was up the staircase faster than he had thought possible of himself, and as he reached the summit, he looked the way of the figure and caught sight of a flick of some-thing turning a corner. He was too late again, as he still was not able to see who it was – but his conviction was firm. He was not merely chasing a ghost – someone was stalking the halls.

Jon followed and rounded the last corner to see . . .

Nothing. An empty hall with doors to the many bed-rooms. The hall was long, with no way that anyone, no matter how spritely, could have got to the end and turned the corner before Jon got there. But there were the doors.

The separate bedrooms were laid out as such – on one side there was the king's, Marjorie's and Emeline's, and on the other side there was Maud's, Matthew's, Mar-tin's, Crockley's and lastly David's.

Jon listened closely, to hear nothing.

He went to Crockley's door and knocked.

'Who is it?' Crockley shouted from within. 'I have a gun, you know. I'll shoot you.'

Jon highly doubted he had a gun.

'It's me – Jonathan,' Jon said through the door. 'I am just checking you got to your room all right.'

'Oh, Chef, yes, I'm fine, thank you.'

'No cause for alarm at all, but you weren't just out in this corridor, were you?'

'No,' Crockley said, 'I have just got into bed.'

'Of course, sir, sorry for disturbing you.'

Jon retreated, and then a tremendous rattling came from the doorknob of the next room to the left. It was the stuff of a horror film, but he would not be fazed. He went to the door and reached out for the handle, and to his surprise, it stopped rattling. Jon cursed John Brown before all of a sudden the door opened and Jon stepped back in terror as the ghost revealed itself.

The old man was startled too. 'Butler? Are you trying to give me a heart attack? Dear God, you aren't here to murder me, are you?' David stood there, defiant as ever.

Jon was so disoriented by David (was the old prince quick enough to traverse the corridors at the rate the figure had?) that he almost missed the man slip something into the lining of his kilt. His kilt – he must have been the figure.

'No, sir, I am not . . . Were you just out here?'

David's brow furrowed. 'Well, given that I am now in here, yes, being out there was a necessity.'

'You have not heard anyone else in this hall?'

'Yes, there is a rather annoying servant in the hall at the moment.'

'And everyone else is still in the drawing room?'

David laughed. 'Well, yes, I suppose so. Apart from that oaf Crockley, who said he was going for a siesta. So don't look at me like that when others are shirking your rules too.'

'I'm not . . . I . . . Thomas is not feeling well. He asked permission to go to . . . Will you please return to the drawing room, sir?'

'No, Butler. I was just coming to get you anyway.' Jon evidently was blank, as David delighted in explaining. 'I am tired of waiting like a criminal in the stocks. If I must be executed, I have the right to ask you to bloody well get on with it. So I am next on your list.'

Jon could not argue, and besides, he would have to get to David eventually, no matter how much he didn't want to. 'Yes, of course, sir.' He was still preoccupied with thinking on the figure he had seen and sizing it up to David's frame.

'Well then,' David said, stepping out into the hall proper, and making a show of closing his door behind him, 'shall we?' Without waiting for an answer, the aged prince started back down the hall – slowly but purposefully.

Jon followed, but not before one final look at the empty corridor. Damn that John Brown!

XXVI

A Private Audience with the Exiled then Returned

Prince David had sat behind the desk, and Jon had not plucked up the courage to tell him that actually in this office that was his seat, so the man lounged in the desk chair while his interrogator perched on the small chair in front of him. Jon felt as though he were inherently on defence in this position, as if he were a policeman who had accidentally locked himself in a cell.

'Now,' David said, 'who has killed my dear brother?' He slammed the desk at every word. Given that David had remained silent for the entire trip from the bedrooms to here, his outburst seemed rather theatrical.

Jon composed himself – it was clear that this would take all of his brainpower. 'Sir, I hardly think that is the place to begin.'

'Well, that's all that matters any more, isn't it? So why not start there. Who killed my brother, Butler?'

Jon had to admit it. 'I do not know, sir. Also, I am not, and have never been, the butler. I am the chef.'

'Well, after our Christmas dinner, I can tell you're not much of either a chef or a butler. And now you call yourself a detective.'

'Sir, I never did anything of the kind. As you continue to mention, I am just a servant doing the best I can with what I have to keep you all safe. Admittedly, I am very much out of my depth. I can assure you, however, I will do my utmost to find out who killed your brother.'

David snarled. 'But what if your "utmost" is not enough?'

Jon thought that he would have nothing to say to that, but found an almost perfect answer escape his lips before he could even think. 'Then I hope you have all helped me so much that we make it enough together. And when we have all done our duty, and we succeed, or even if we fail, we can know we have done right by the king, and by the Crown.'

'You talk a big game, don't you, the butler-y chef detective?' David said, relaxing backwards into the plush chair. He reached for a drink that wasn't there, and then turned the motion into trying to pick something out of his teeth, as if Jon's dinner was still bothering him. 'I never did understand why my brother liked you so much. Now you seem to have bewitched the rest of my family as well. At least Marjorie still sees sense.'

'This, sir, is a necessity – not something I am enjoying. Now, I have answered your questions – may I ask you a few of my own?'

David guffawed. 'Here we go. You want to know about the allegations then, do you?'

'Not unless it is relevant to this situation right now, no.' Jon could die happily if he never again heard about the allegations.

'The allegations are the only thing that seems to matter any more,' David said. 'You know that there is not a shred of evidence that I attacked that woman?'

'The reporter?' Jon said.

Disgustingly, David laughed. 'Oh no, I punched that insipid reporter woman. Maud was right earlier, that particular attack is well documented. I punched her because she was saying the most abhorrent things about me. Well, I can tell you, there isn't a lick of truth to it. It is all lies. Not that anyone cares. I have been shunned by my family, forced to spend ten years exiled in disgusting New Zealand to secure a role I already occupied, and been made a laughing stock in the popular press. I have been threatened with legal action for things that I can categorically prove did not happen, I have been told to take long walks off short piers, I have had threats on my life. And through it all, I have not even had the support of my dear older brother, who just so happens to be the man with the power to make this all go away with a snap of his fingers.' David clicked his own fingers to illustrate this. His face had gone medium rare throughout his rant.

Jon remained silent. He tried to stay out of the Royal Family's drama as much as humanly possible, and David's stories doubly so. He knew the bare bones of the situation and that was how he would have liked it to stay. David used to frequent a bar back in the '90s – The Gentlemen. (The very same Gentlemen that Thomas Crockley visited in fact.) David used to get very drunk and, well . . . there were stories. The situation was corroborated by many of the patrons of the bar, but given that they were all intoxicated in some way, nothing could be said with any amount of certainty. Jon often wondered, as did a wide section of the press, if the palace had suppressed any of the accusers. David's misadventures in that bar were always a question mark hanging over the head of every member of the Royal Family, although, given his previous actions, many thought that the rumours and allegations were probably true. The Gentlemen was still a popular haunt, as was noted by Thomas Crockley, but David never went there again.

Apart from his somewhat alarming colour, David was calm after his outburst. 'I am currently surrounded by a family who wishes I were dead. Maybe that whisky was meant for me.' That was very final, and Jon did not quite believe that David really thought that. 'Ask your damn questions, Chef, or whatever you are. I fear I'm going to go down for this anyway, even if we catch another of my family members dead to rights.'

There was silence. David had drawn a line under everything before Jon was even close to finished. So he pressed onwards, although it felt and sounded weird to. 'Some people have talked about your demeanour after your private audience with the king, saying you were distressed. Could you tell me what you discussed?'

Sure enough, David said, 'Well, Butler, I already have really. This is the albatross around my neck for all time – that place. Always that place. How could anyone think that of me? And today I hear that my dear brother had somehow come into some new evidence that supposedly proved the accusations were true beyond any doubt. I told him that that could not be – one cannot have evidence of something that didn't happen. I said, "Ask Stellan, Stellan will clear everything up." But I was pissing in the wind.'

'Stellan?'

'Yes,' David said. 'Stellan Tharigold. He was there. Not even an MP at that time, and look at him now.'

Stellan Tharigold was Miss Darcy's uncle, and a prominent politician. He had just handed off the Minister for Prisons post, and it was reported that he was now aiming for the top job. For him to be there at The Gentlemen was not an odd occurrence, but the fact that he could have been a voice (whether for or against David) was a quandary.

'We're old friends,' David continued, 'and I told him that he must not get dragged into this business, that Eric would keep his name out of it. The honourable Eric Windsor would not listen to me, however, brandishing this . . . well, folder, this dossier of imaginary evidence at me. Lord knows where he got it. He said that he invited me here today to enjoy one final Christmas with my family, and tomorrow he would put in a word to excommunicate me from the family for ever. I would have to go back to New Zealand, with all its mud, and spiders, and hobbits. That might have been why I was a little snippy upon my exit, don't you think? Because I will be snippy upon my EXIT!'

David mentioning a dossier was something of a strange coincidence. Could this be the same folder that Thomas Crockley had talked about? Had the king compiled a scrapbook of sins on certain Royal Family members? If so, where was this dossier, and were any other members included within it? 'This dossier you mentioned – did you ever see any of the evidence inside?'

'Of course not,' David said. 'Because there was no evidence. Eric has always wanted me gone, and this is a simple way to get rid of me. He has never liked me, and my mere existence is a threat to the Crown apparently.'

'It may be still. You understand that what you have just told me makes you a very likely suspect.' Jon was underplaying this. He almost felt that everything, from David's words, to his actions, to his reputation, dictated that he should declare the investigation over. He would not have been surprised if Eric, in his digging, had not found even more instances of David's debauchery.

'I am telling you all this to absolve me, Chef. Why would I voice this if I were the one who killed him? Also, I have no idea if Eric has already shared his information with the palace, so my exile may already be underway. The one-way plane tickets may already have been booked. When you take that out of the equation, there would be no point in me harming my brother. The damage is already done.'

'Maybe you killed your brother out of anger. Maybe you didn't like the mirror he was holding up to you.' Jon knew he had overstepped his bounds before he had finished the sentence. David instantly launched forwards and attempted to grab Jon by the scruff of the neck. Unfortunately for David, his seating choice did not work in his favour – he only found his way partly out of the plush seat before falling back on himself. After the feeble attempt was over, he merely sat there looking more than a little sorry for himself – the irony that his little folly proved his violent streak not lost on him.

Jon decided to note this, of course, but move on, tapping into that politeness that he often used to mask his true feelings. 'Thank you for your co-operation, sir. I have but one final question: who do you think killed your brother?'

David snorted quietly, still unable to meet Jon's eyes. What a self-pitying creature he'd become! 'I would not attempt to do your job for you. However, if I had to throw my proverbial dart at someone's head, then it would obviously find its mark on young Matthew. We all know that he was the favourite to be next in line, and despite what he says, he wants it oh-so badly.'

'Have you ever heard Matthew say anything to that effect?'

'It is only a feeling. My feelings are rarely wrong.' Jon would argue that there wasn't anything about the man that seemed right, let alone his 'feelings'. Jon was starting to understand why Maud was so staunchly against him – he had always felt that slippery, sickly awareness when being around David, but had never known quite how bad it was. David made him feel disoriented, uncomfortable and altogether out of sorts. 'Is that all, Chef? I need another drink to wet my whistle.'

Jon could have remarked that he believed David's 'whistle' was far too lubricated as it was, but he just took victory in seeing the difficulty the broken man had in getting out of his chosen throne. 'One more thing, what were you doing in your bedroom just now?'

David, halfway around the desk, stopped and scowled. 'That is none of your business. I can go where I like.'

'It must have been important, risking your life for it,' Jon said. 'Knowing that there is a killer among us, and going off alone anyhow.'

David said nothing, stewing.

'What is in your pocket?'

David did not tell him, as Jon knew the man would not, but his reaction told him everything he had desired to know. There was indeed something in David's pocket – something he had thought important to retrieve from his room.

David seethed, knowing he had given too much away, and merely bade goodbye to his inquisitor and left.

Jon stood up and sidled around the desk, sitting in the desk chair. It felt somewhat tainted by scandal, but then, he thought, what in Balmoral was left untouched by the events of the day?

XXVII

A Private Audience with the Next in Line

Prince Matthew came next, with such punctuality that he must have set off before David had returned. The young prince sank down into the chair facing his inquisitor, looking troubled. He opened his mouth, but no words escaped his lips, so he merely shut it again.

'Your Majesty?' Jon asked, after a minute of Matthew's odd silence.

The young royal just peered at him, clearly troubled by a quandary. 'I have been thinking about what I said to you before you began these audiences. About whether I could actually kill someone, even if that person did kill my grandfather. I don't suppose I could. That took me on to wondering about the rest of my family – and their capabilities. That's what state I am in now – Christmas Day and wondering which of my family filled my grandfather's cup full of poison.'

'It is sometimes hard to know the lengths someone will go to get what they want.'

Matthew sifted a hand through his sandy hair, and let out a long sigh. 'How are you doing, Jon? Are you any closer?'

'I do not know, sir. I don't have a full picture yet. It will help if I can ask you some questions.'

'Of course. I will help in any way I can.'

'Let us start with this morning.' Jon felt like a botched time-traveller, cursed to go back to the same point in his history. This cursed morning. 'You were with your family?'

'Yes. I went to my father's room at around seven o'clock to wish him a Happy Christmas. My father and I watched *The Monarch* while my mother went for breakfast with my aunt. She came back to his room, and we watched maybe two more episodes before my aunt came to inform us that the king was holding several private audiences. She took my mother to him then, but I knew my time would eventually come.'

'How did you feel about it?' Jon inquired.

'Not fantastic, as you can probably surmise. I knew what it was going to be about. My grandfather has always groomed me to be the next king. I thought that time had come.'

'When it finally came time for your audience, is that truly what it was about?'

'Yes, I'm afraid to say. He was going to announce his withdrawal from power at the after-dinner speech. Then, naturally, it would be time for me to step up. However, here is where everyone in that drawing room is wrong. I'm sure they are all thinking, maybe not even knowingly, that I could have killed my grandfather to inherit the role of monarch . . .' Jon knew that to be true, at least somewhat. Prince David had expressed that very

195

sentiment. 'What they don't know though, is that I have been fighting with my grandfather for years over this issue.'

'In what way?'

Matthew sat upright in his chair. He had tears in his eyes, but it seemed that even he did not know quite who they were for. 'I do not want it, Jon. I never wanted to be king. I looked at my grandfather and saw nothing but a vessel – a man celebrated as a god and shackled as a prisoner. The sick truth is that he was both. For what would we do if we found ourselves in the presence of a god? We would bind it, imprison it and make sure it would stay.

'You had a special relationship with him, Jon – you were friends for years. You must have seen it too. Eric Windsor could have been a great man, and in some ways, he was, but in others, he was nothing. Did he ever tell you what he would have liked for his life?'

'Yes,' Jon said, as Eric had told him once. It was after a state dinner, not too long ago. The king was slightly worse for wear and he had stumbled into the kitchens, waxing lyrical about the man that could have been. 'He would have liked to be a doctor. He said that there was no greater puzzle than the human body, the fixing of the physical being and the fixing of the soul. That was where his love of puzzle boxes came from. It was the closest he could get to his dream.'

'Why would anyone willingly lock themselves in a prison?' Matthew posed the question. 'The lions willingly walking into that pen and limiting themselves, just for the pleasure of getting gawked at by the family that went to the zoo. There are those in my family who would want this burden – my grandmother, my father, my grand-uncle, my aunt, maybe even my mother. I do not understand why my grandfather was so fixated on me taking up the mantle.'

'He never told you why?'

'No, never. The closest he ever got was when he talked about the need for a new perspective on the role. I think maybe he wanted someone young and contemporary to become the monarch in the hope of trying to shake up the establishment. He had already started laying the groundwork – changing the succession rules. It is no secret that he had become slightly more disgruntled than usual of late with the old way of doing things.'

Jon slowly nodded as he thought back to his conversation with the king just this morning.

It's a big day, old friend, the king had said. *Thank you for being here with me.*

On the surface, the king was talking about Christmas, but looking deeper, it could easily be inferred that he was referring to his stepping down. The end of an old chapter and the start of a new one.

'My grandfather was always five steps ahead of everyone else in the room, he has that brain built for these kinds of things. Mysteries. It is almost apt that he became one himself.' Matthew ran the underside of his right hand under his chin. It was a very common motion for the young prince when he was faced with a problem. 'I wonder if he didn't tell Tony Speck that he had an inkling something was wrong.'

'Speck?'

'Yes. It stands to reason that he would tell the head of security, who is also the only security personnel on the property. That might also explain Speck's absence throughout this whole ordeal. If Speck learned that the king thought himself in danger, the last thing he would think would be that that danger would come from within, so Speck, in his infinite duty, would double down on—'

'Protecting the perimeter,' Jon finished, cutting in with such aplomb that he instantly felt ashamed. Matthew merely nodded though, showing no disapproval whatsoever.

The prince had definitely seized upon something here – Speck being almost obsessive about walking the grounds of Balmoral must have had a genesis and this would explain it, but the question still remained why no one else had been alerted and why Speck wasn't answering his walkie.

'It is only a working theory,' said Matthew, sensing the apprehension in the air. 'That is all any of these theories are, however. We need concrete evidence to secure any kind of truth.'

'You speak confidently in these kinds of matters,' Jon said.

Matthew broke his seriousness for a moment, for a crack of gleeful youth to shine through in a smile. 'I would like to think that I inherited some of my grandfather's love of puzzles – well, that and I watch a lot of television. I have too much time on my hands.'

Jon wondered if maybe Matthew's insight, albeit it in a fictional stance, could help further – indeed, he was wondering why Matthew was not the detective himself. 'Seeing as you have more of a background for this type of thing – who would be your prime suspect?'

Matthew laughed – a joyless thing that betrayed his feelings. 'That is simple. My grandmother. I would stake my entire life on the fact that she would hold such hate in her heart. She has always resented my grandfather, for as long as I can remember. She wanted to be queen, she wanted the power, and she expected to get it. But then my grandfather, for reasons unknown, did not allow it. Oh, how I wish I was a fly on the wall for that conversation.'

'Do you know why the king denied the Princess Royal this?'

'No more than you, Jon. No more than any of us. That was between King Eric and Marjorie. *Princess* Marjorie. Or the bloody princess royal or whatever she calls herself. I almost understand how that could foster a special kind of loathing.'

'Thank you for your answers, Prince Matthew.'

'Of course. Are we done? Should I send another along?'

Jon braced himself. Maybe it was time to talk to the matriarch herself.

XXVIII

A Private Audience with the Sloshed Princess Royal

'So, you fancy yourself a detective, Alleyne? I must say, I would have never foreseen that you'd trade your big poufy white hat for one of those tweed ones that look like they'd go down to your ears but actually don't. You know what I mean, don't you?' Some rosé tipped into her mouth, some onto her chin – none actually went down her throat as she spluttered it all back up. 'What are they called?'

Jon regretted bringing the wine. It was the only way he could get her to come, however. He'd had to go and fetch her, after she had refused Matthew's request.

'You mean a toque for a deerstalker, ma'am.'

'Yes. Both of those words seem to fit the bill, Alleyne. Well done.' She gathered herself. 'I'm afraid if you are looking for answers, you won't find any here. I'm only here for the free drinks.' She snorted. 'David and I agreed to a vow of silence and it still stands.'

'Ma'am, Prince David has already talked to me. Indeed, everyone else has, apart from Prince Martin. You are almost the last person on my list.'

'Oh.' This was clearly not what Marjorie had expected

to hear – her front line of defenders had all conceded, and now she was all alone, which, by her face, was not somewhere she wanted to be. Had this been the Marjorie of five bottles ago, let alone five years, maybe she would have made a show of standing her ground, but that Marjorie had vacated the premises, and as it was, she threw in the towel, while eyeing her glass, of course. 'Well, maybe just some very short and to-the-point questions. I don't have all day.'

'If I may, I would like to start with this morning. We crossed paths in the drawing room when Prince David and Princess Maud were arguing. I was stoking the fire, and Princess Emeline was sorting the presents under the tree, if you recall.' He was including these seemingly innocuous details to try to seize something in Marjorie's mind, as he knew alcohol had a habit of erasing key events.

'Yes, yes,' Marjorie said.

'Was this your first port of call upon waking?' For his sanity, he was trying to find different ways to phrase the same questions.

'Yes, it was. I walked the halls in search of a glass of water, and heard the perfectly shrill voice of my youngest calling to me like a siren guiding a sailor to some jagged rocks. I thought it my duty to intervene. The situation with the children and David is becoming so banal that I simply cannot stand it. So, my headache be damned, I entered. And I found something better than a glass of water. I stayed in the drawing room with David until my loving husband called me to his study.'

'You are referring to the private audiences in which several of you partook?'

'Yes,' Marjorie seethed. She clearly was not happy with this particular line of questioning.

'Do you mind if I ask you what was discussed during your private audience with the king?'

Oddly, she conceded. 'No, I suppose not.'

'Good,' Jon said, and waited for any kind of revelation.

However, Marjorie stayed silent, seemingly revelling in some unspoken victory. Finally, she must have had enough, as she spat, 'Well?'

'Ma'am?'

'Are you going to ask me what we discussed during my private audience with the king?'

'I think I just did, ma'am.'

'No. You asked me if it was all right to ask me what was discussed during my private audience with the king. You did not actually ask me what was discussed during my private audience with the king.'

Marjorie was being difficult for the mere sake of being difficult. He'd expected nothing less. He wanted to shout at her. Instead, he voiced: 'I'm very sorry, ma'am. What did you discuss during your private audience with the king?' Those words had been said so many times in the past minute they had lost any and all meaning.

'It does not matter what we discussed, as it has no relation to what eventually befell him. It does not matter how snippy we were to each other, how he didn't even say goodbye, how he brandished that damn folder. It is all inconsequential.'

'I'm sorry, ma'am. You said a folder?'

'We all come to nothing in the end, Alleyne. Everything said to one another, the way we treat each other, our love and our hate, all becomes dust on the wind. We can only hope, for the ones left behind, the dust does not blow back into their faces.'

'Was the king showing you a folder? A dossier of sorts?' Jon pressed.

'I know what people think – yourself, the rest of my quaint little brethren, the establishment, the family outside the lion pen. They think we hated each other, and maybe we did – towards the end. But we had some damn good years – years of love.'

Jon tried to change tack, although all he wanted to do was talk about the folder. He knew that he was not going to get her to, though. 'I saw that you loved each other. And you shared your two wonderful daughters.'

Marjorie paused. 'Shared? Oh, yes, I see what you mean, Alleyne. It's your accent.' Jon had the faintest Bajan accent, and was perfectly understandable. There was something odd about what Marjorie had just said, and it wasn't even the casual racism. 'Yes. The twins were a blessing. And to come so late in life. They were panicking, you know. The government. They thought that once Eric turned forty it would all be over. No heirs. And then they came along, like gifts from above. So yes, we had years of love, and even if we did hate each other at the end, that does not diminish what we had.'

'Quite right, ma'am.'

'In some ways, I still loved him. Eric always liked to

203

think that he was the cleverest man in the room – but he rarely ever was. It wasn't entirely his fault – he's a Windsor.' Marjorie, incredibly, drained the last remnants of the wine from the glass and started to eye another. Jon, against his better judgement, poured her one.

'As are you, ma'am.'

'Yes, I am a Windsor. But I was a Nueberner first.' Marjorie's family hailed from Austria, a fact that was more than a touch controversial given the time when she and the king first started their relationship. 'It is a good job I never wish to forget where I am from, because I would be constantly hounded by it regardless.'

'On that subject, ma'am, do you think the Nueberner connection has any relevance to why you have never been named queen?' It was like walking on the crisp top of a crème brûlée, trying not to crack it, but sometimes secrets lie below and they need to be broken free. Maybe one of those secrets was the key to this case.

'I beg your pardon, Alleyne! I will not talk on such matters with you.'

'A king's wife is usually announced as the queen. Do you know why King Eric denied you that? And did it lead to you resenting him?' Now he was overstepping. But in some way, it did feel as though he was running out of time. He only had one audience left after Marjorie and such rash measures were justified.

'Alleyne, that has nothing to do with you.' She seemed to realise her mistake, giving any voice to this notion, making it a reality. 'But, no, Eric loved me. He knew of my family, and did not care.'

'Then why deny you queen?'

Marjorie knew why. Jon could see it on her face.

'Does it have anything to do with the king's death? Were you resentful, vindictive, angry?'

'All of the above. And I admit there were times when I wanted to kill him. But I didn't kill him.' Marjorie threw back her neck and another glass was gone. She poured her own this time. 'We are done here.'

Marjorie staggered to a stand, taking the bottle with her. In a second, she was gone.

Jon simply sat there. He did not know what to think. Marjorie had a secret and Eric had known it. But what was it?

The princess royal was like one of the king's puzzle boxes.

Unfortunately, he did not have time to solve her.

XXIX

A Private Audience with the Generous Whippersnapper

Martin sat there clutching his quarry. He was still holding the wooden Interregnum puzzle box – it didn't seem as though he'd put it down since the king had died. The thirteen-year-old was treating it like a comfort blanket.

Jon did not know why the boy had fixated on the box, at least until he said, 'I got him this.'

The mystery gifter, solved. It was unfortunate that it was no longer the biggest mystery of the day. 'What a fabulous present, sir.'

Martin nodded. 'I knew he'd like it. It has Christmas smells inside it, you know?'

Jon smiled. The king had loved the smell of roast potatoes and garlic. 'Why didn't you come forward to say that you got this for the king, Martin? Why stay silent?'

The boy was regretful, it was clear to see. After all, the king had died not knowing who had given him his favourite present. 'I knew he'd solve the puzzle box quickly – he always does. I wanted him to have a bigger puzzle to solve. I would have told him eventually. It was a dumb idea.'

'No, I don't think so,' Jon said. 'I think it was very thoughtful.'

'Hmmm,' Martin said, clearly not agreeing.

'The name of the puzzle – Interregnum – means "between reign", yes? It's a little coincidental, don't you think? We appear to be in a period of interregnum right now?'

Martin's eyes grew wide. 'I swear the puzzle came like this. I didn't do this. I couldn't kill him. I just thought he would find it funny – he's always joking about how old he is . . . So . . . I just—'

'No, no, no, I know,' Jon said. The boy was thirteen, but a royal version of thirteen. That made him younger than his age in some respects, and older in others. 'I'm not saying that. I'm just saying it is a bit odd, isn't it?' It was a bit odd, and Jon had to admit he'd thought of the mystery gifter and the murderer as a probable culprit. Now, though, looking down at the small boy, he saw that was not possible. 'Let us move on to something else, hmm? Did you see your grandfather this morning?'

'No,' Martin said, a little too quickly. He realised what he had done. 'I mean, not for one of these official private things that the rest of my family got. He grabbed me as I was going past his office after all the audiences, that's all.'

'And what did you say?'

'Happy Christmas.' Martin sniffed and ran a cuff under his nose. 'Do you know who did it?'

Jon shook his head. 'I'm afraid not.'

'But I'm the last one you're talking to. And you still don't know?'

The boy was giving voice to Jon's exact fear. He really didn't know. Even after all he'd heard, Jon could not extract an exact motive, an exact cause and effect, to the king's murder. He saw them all much as he had when he'd first inspected the timetable Maud had drawn up for him. He both saw them all as capable, and none of them.

Martin seemed to hear this, although Jon had said none of it aloud. 'Then what now?'

Jon was sure the young prince was not intending to unnerve him, but he had nonetheless. And all he had to do was tell the truth – *what now?* indeed.

'I think it was Aunt Emeline,' Martin said.

'What? Why would you think that?'

'I think she's angry that Matthew's going to be king. I get why she is. It should be her, right? I heard her last night, in the drawing room with Grandad. She was very angry about something, started threatening that she would expose something. Before I could listen for what, though, my dad went into the drawing room and ruined it all. He started talking about his stupid business. Ride+. Total Bust, more like. You know that he's going bankrupt?'

'What?' Martin had intended to shift the focus onto Emeline, but this revelation shifted it to Crockley. 'Your father just told me how great his business is doing.'

'Well he would, wouldn't he?'

Emeline was angry with the king, holding something

over him, and Thomas Crockley was going bankrupt, no doubt in desperate need of money. 'Maybe you should be the detective instead, Martin.'

'Just like Enola!' Martin said.

'Is there anything,' Jon asked, 'anything at all, that you saw today, that was suspicious in any way?'

Martin thought, but didn't say anything.

'I am thinking that maybe you were the most travelled royal this morning. Were you exploring the castle?'

'It's boring around here. Mum didn't let me bring my PS5. Me and Wilson were just playing around. You know, stupid kid stuff.'

Wilson the cat – Jon hadn't seen him in a while, same for Churchill. It was easy for them to get consumed by the castle, sometimes disappearing, being left to their own devices for days at a time. He hoped, wherever they were, they were safe.

'I saw you coming out of the pantry.'

Martin's eyes grew to saucers.

'Martin?'

'Uh . . . yes . . . I suppose . . .' The boy seemed to be grasping for some kind of innocent explanation, but it was too late. Jon was highly interested.

'Did you go to the pantry for a specific reason?'

'Excuse me.' They both jumped. Matthew was standing at the study door. Jon did not know how long he had been there. They hadn't heard the door opening. 'I'm very sorry for interrupting.'

Martin set his eyes back on Jon and clutched Interregnum hard. His last connection to his grandfather.

'It's all right, sir,' Jon said. 'We were just finished anyway.' They were anything but finished, but Jon provided a supportive nod to Martin. Martin smiled to him.

Matthew smiled sadly and quickly, and then it was gone. 'I just . . . Jon, there's a situation developing in the drawing room.'

'What is it?'

'You might need to come and see. Right now.'

XXX

The Winchester Among the Wolves

It is impossible to describe the impact the sight of a fire-arm has on any type of situation, but Jon felt it then as he entered the drawing room along with the youngest royals.

David was standing there, with an engorged smile upon his face, and a Winchester rifle on his shoulder.

The other occupants of the drawing room, which at this point was only Marjorie, Emeline and Maud, had retreated as far away as they possibly could. Marjorie was attempting to use the Christmas tree as cover.

'David, what are you doing with that thing?' she shrieked.

It was at this moment that the other three had entered, but David did not concern himself with them. He had a gun, after all. Everyone else had to concern themselves with him.

'Oh, this thing?' he said, shaking the rifle as though it were of no consequence at all. 'Well, I was just pottering around, and had the bright idea that we may need it. What with a killer on the loose, a man has a right to defend himself and his family. At least the innocent ones.

It is really that simple. I remembered that there were a couple in the store up by the tower stairs, so I decided to bring one back with me.'

'Put it down, you facile man,' Emeline said, 'unless you intend to use it, of course.'

'What? No, Niece. You have the wrong end of the stick. I am going to protect the innocent among us.'

'Maybe you should put it down, David?' Marjorie said, peering through the branches of the tree. 'Even if your intentions are pure.'

'Martin, Matthew,' Maud gasped as she saw her children close to David. 'Come here quickly.' They obeyed their mother and she grasped them just as tightly as she could. 'You're a madman, Uncle. Bringing a gun into this.'

David scanned the room, even acknowledging Jon by the door. He saw every scared face. 'What? I'm no threat to anyone here. In fact, the complete opposite. I am trying to protect you – why can't you see that?'

'Protecting us would have been leaving the Winchester where it was, you idiotic buffoon,' Emeline remarked. 'A gun is now in play and thus guns plural are now in play as well.'

'What?'

'You have just announced where to find more guns, have you not?'

'I . . . well . . .' David realised his mistake. 'Ah . . .' The Winchester wilted slightly on his shoulder. 'I see that was a misstep. But my acquisition was not one. Don't you see? Is everyone else going mad?' David betrayed

212

that he wasn't sure himself, making his hurried and slightly panicked tone not match his expression. It was decidedly strange. 'Yes, this is a deadly weapon, but it is a deadly weapon we can use. The good guy against the bad guys.'

'You do not look like a "good guy" right at this moment, Prince David,' Jon said, in as level a voice as he could muster. 'I'm sure everyone else in this room would agree.'

There was a murmur of assent from all corners – a level of synchronicity he was not used to.

'Give the gun to Jon, Grand-uncle, please.' Martin stepped out from his mother's clutches to the centre of the room, standing in front of the coffee table and the whisky. He was standing directly where the king had been when he died.

'Little field mouse, I am not going to hurt you.'

'We all elected for Jon to sort this out. To question us, to accuse us, sure. But also to protect us. He should have it,' Martin said, refusing to back away.

Rather than bearing any ill will for his grilling, Martin seemed to have grown a budding respect for the chef. It was almost heart-warming to see, had it not been for the situation surrounding it.

'I do not particularly want a gun either, sir,' Jon said to him.

'I vote for Jon too,' Emeline said.

'Me too,' said Maud.

Matthew simply nodded.

David gripped the Winchester. 'Margey?'

213

Marjorie did not meet his prickly eyes. 'I'd rather the chef had it than you.'

David gasped. 'You think I am more likely to have killed . . . than this . . . this . . . common . . .' Whatever insult he was cooking up died somewhere between his brain and his lips. 'We are all doomed.' He held the rifle out for anyone to take.

No one came to take the gun, and Jon had to force himself to step forward. He slowly took the Winchester from David, sliding his fingers around the base to hold it upright. He pulled it free from the other man and was almost toppled over by the incredible weight of the thing.

As if the gun were the focal point of the scene, Jon found the attention returned to him, and expectation at his feet. 'Right.' The rifle was cold, unwieldy. He hated it. 'I will return the Winchester to where it belongs, while trying to secure any further stock. In the meantime, please will everyone remain in this room? It is for your own safety.'

'Wait,' Maud said. 'You have seen all here now, as well as my husband. May we ask what you are thinking?'

I don't know.

That was the first thing that came to mind. The rifle weighed Jon down, but not enough. He wished it would pull him through the floor. 'I need some time to think on what I have uncovered. And to consider how to proceed.'

There were still so many unanswered questions. Where did one of the Royal Family procure a poison? What kind of poison was used? When exactly did they lace the whisky and how did they know they would not be discovered before the time was right – or kill the wrong family member?

The mystery was still as wild as the weather outside – with no hope of clear skies.

'He has no idea what he's doing,' David muttered, 'and I just gave him the gun.'

It seemed that the mood in the room was turning again, and this time Jon was in the firing – albeit he was the one now holding the gun. Marjorie, having entertained a brief sortie against David, was now back on his side. Emeline and Maud glanced unsurely at each other. It was only Matthew and Martin who seemed still in support.

Emeline was opening her mouth to say something, when—

'Who is that?' Prince Martin said, pointing.

This stopped everyone in their tracks. Martin was pointing out of the window, into the blizzard. Jon made his way around the Christmas tree to see the figure for himself. The window being so frosted up made the figure seem almost dreamlike. But it was unmistakeable – someone was standing out there in the torrential snow, staring in at them. What was more, the figure was wearing Jon's red coat.

Suddenly, the figure seemed to realise that it had been noticed and started moving backwards into obscurity.

And that was when the lights went out.

XXXI

Terror in the Dark

Now Jon was glad to have the gun. As the lights snapped off, and the world was only lit by a dying fire and the snow outside, the Royal Family panicked. It was not pitch black by any means, but it was enough to inspire terror. Marjorie screamed first, followed by Emeline, and then a male cry. The family bundled together, even David and Marjorie gravitating towards their youngers, and then suspicion tore them apart.

'What happened?' Emeline cried.

'The lights!' Maud shrieked.

'Who is that?' Marjorie was flailing her arms around.

'Me,' Martin said flatly. She had accidentally slapped him in the face.

'Assassin! Outside!' shouted David. 'He is making his move! Cutting the power!'

Jon couldn't blame the man – he thought much the same himself at first. But he remembered Tony Speck's security system. The red dots. They were the only people there on the entire grounds. Not even a skilled assassin could survive miles upon miles of blizzard to get to the castle in the time since Jon had seen the read-out.

'It could be Speck?' Matthew suggested.

'No. It's Thomas Crockley out there,' said Jon. 'He must be having a cigar. I let him borrow my coat earlier in the day. He is doing it again.' It didn't sound like the right explanation, but it was the only possible one. It had to be him.

'That idiot!' Surprisingly, this came from his wife. 'Why would he do something so reckless? He's risking his life out there. For a smoke.'

'What about the lights, Jon?' Matthew said.

Jon's eyes were finally adjusting properly. Everything was dark greys and blacks, apart from Maud, the closest to the fire, who was blessed with colour playing on her cheeks. 'It's the blizzard,' he said. 'The power system wasn't built for this kind of weather. The breaker must have tripped, that's all. I just need to go and turn it back on.'

Did he believe that it was just the blizzard? He had no idea. He was simply guessing about the power system. Or maybe he was hoping?

'Are you sure, Jon?' Emeline said. 'This really could be some kind of . . . sign.'

'Exactly,' David pounced. 'In the films, the lights go out and a second person dies! I'm going to need that gun back, Butler.'

'This isn't a film,' Jon said. 'I will go and turn the power back on. The box is down in the servants' quarters. It'll only take five minutes.' He had to leave them again – but it had to be him who took the gun.

'The gun!'

217

Jon shifted the gun on his shoulder. 'The gun is going back to the store.'

David seemed as if he were about to combust. Even in the black and white of the low light, he was crimson. 'How dare you defy me and take away my ability to protect my family.'

Matthew stepped between them, standing up to his grand-uncle, maybe for the first time. 'You don't want to protect us, you want to protect yourself.'

'I—'

'Go, Jon,' Matthew said.

There was a disgruntled moan from David as Jon stalked away. Jon looked back at the family before he left. They were all cowering, terrified, in their own way. They were broken.

The corridor was darker, not having the benefit of the light from the fire or the window. It had to be nighttime, but the white snow clouds were still acting as if it were day.

Jon fished around in his right-hand trouser pocket for his torch. He never used his right pocket much, being left-handed, so he mostly put things in there he didn't need as often. He happened upon something thin and metal, and had no idea what it was. All that mattered in that moment, however, was that it wasn't the torch. A few more grasps and he found it.

He set off with torch in his left hand and the rifle slung over his right shoulder. Balmoral was always the eeriest of the king's castles, even in the bright light of day. The dead animals mounted on the walls watching you; the disorienting tight corridors juxtaposed with the bigger ones, inspiring a discomfort; the constant draughts as if an ethereal force were guiding you somewhere. There was always some sound happening throughout the castle, even if it was completely empty. A creaking, a moaning, a groaning. As if Balmoral itself were alive.

Jon passed the pantry, where he had met with Martin earlier. Something about that location, and Martin's cageyness, piqued his interest, but the darkness was not the right moment to take a look. Besides, he soon forgot all about it.

Something clattered in front of him. Just beyond the torchlight. It sounded as though something had been thrown from a side table.

Jon stopped. The pain in his gut was throbbing with every step now. He could even convince himself he was stopping for that, and not because he was utterly terrified. 'Crockley?' he whispered into the dark. 'Speck?'

Churchill the cat came trotting into the light, looking up at him and miaowing.

Jon shook his head at himself for being so silly.

He got down to the servants' quarters with a renewed bravery, and was shadowed by Churchill every step of the way. At finding another living soul, the cat had started purring, and it felt as though Jon were being followed by a biplane.

The kitchen was just as he had left it – in a state of disarray that he couldn't quite accept. It seemed even worse in the light of the torch, like some kind of post-apocalyptic bomb-site. He would not have allowed any of his chefs to leave the majestic beast in such a disrespectful way, and he felt ashamed of himself for doing so, regardless of the feats he had achieved this morning. It was ungracious, making a beauty into an eyesore.

Jon had no time to mourn his loss of standards, however – there were things to be done before he lost his nerve. He propped the Winchester against the counter and went out into the hall, starting as Churchill jumped up onto one of the kitchen counters and mewed in his face. The breaker box was just beside the entrance to the kitchen, so Jon had seen it being maintained almost every time it was serviced. He opened the box.

The breaker box was much like a larger version of the kind of electrical box anyone would find in a standard British home. The only differences were that there were far more switches and the primary trip switch was less a switch and more a lever. It seemed exactly like the sort of lever one would use to activate some kind of evil plan, or to create a Frankenstein, and many of the chefs had remarked similar sentiments. Jon shone the torch on the box to see that none of the smaller switches had been tripped, but the large lever had been set to off.

Jon pushed the lever back up to the 'on' position, and power came back instantly. His vision was flooded with white, and he blinked away sunspots.

Could that lever have moved down on its own? And if so, why were none of the smaller switches off too?

'Meeew.' Churchill seemed to be offering his input. Jon went back into the kitchen to see the cat sitting in the sink licking at the bowl Jon had used to make the bread sauce.

'You're hungry?' Jon asked, picking Churchill up and putting him back on the counter. 'I think I have some food for you around here.'

Cats were not usually allowed in the kitchens, especially the lower kitchen, but Jon did have some sachets of food somewhere. He thought maybe he had put them in the top cupboards with the empty jam jars. An odd two things to group, he would have been the first to admit, but even in a kitchen so big, he was starting to run out of cupboard space.

Jon got the stepladder he used to access the top shelves and climbed it, reaching up. His gut groaned as a ripping pain pulsed through him. He doubled over and almost fell from the ladder. That was not psychosomatic, whatever the doctor might say.

Churchill regarded him impatiently.

Jon rolled his eyes and reached back up to the cupboard. Curious – inside he found the pack of cat food just as he thought. The rest of the cupboard was empty, however. All of the jam jars were gone.

As he fed Churchill, he cursed the maids. They must have mistaken all the jars for recycling. How was he going to make more jam now? But then, that was hardly important. Nobody loved his jam more than the king.

As Churchill tucked into his own Christmas dinner, Jon thought on the lever and the whole idea of the power going off. They had seen Crockley outside, so no one was here to turn the power off. And what would be the reason for turning it off when it could be so simply turned back on?

Jon's heart thrummed against his chest.

What if this were . . .

Jon grabbed the Winchester and charged out towards the stairs.

What if this were a distraction?

Jon ignored the pain in his gut and forged ahead, looking upwards to his destination.

He stopped in his tracks.

Crockley was standing on the stairs, looking down at him. Well, the figure in the red coat was. And Crockley had the hood pulled all the way up and down over his forehead, so it was pretty much impossible to see his face.

How was he here? When he was just outside?

'Crockley,' Jon said reasonably. 'What are you doing out of bed?'

Crockley said nothing. He started coming down the stairs.

'Were you behind this? Did you turn the lights off? To what end?'

Nothing, but getting closer.

Jon raised the Winchester. 'Did you kill the king?'

Crockley got to the bottom of the stairs, maybe thirty feet from Jon. Jon remained steadfast. All of a sudden, Crockley launched himself at Jon and the chef found he did not have the fortitude to pull the trigger. He braced himself for the collision, but, instead, Crockley ran straight past him.

Jon whirled around to see Crockley already at the end of the corridor, pulling open the door and letting the blizzard in. Crockley dove into the white. Jon was not far behind, acting on pure instinct and, thankfully, pure adrenaline.

The door stood open, already unable to shut, as a cavalcade of fresh snow was forcing its way in. The icy wind whipped through Jon. His coat was gone, of course. If he were to give chase, he would be exposed to the elements. But was there any doubt any more that this was the king's murderer?

This was it.

Jon raised the Winchester and braced himself, muttering the mantra, 'For the king and for the Crown,' before thrusting himself out into the wilds and wrenching the door closed behind him.

XXXII

Crawling Through Baked Alaska

Jon strode out into the courtyard, although no one would recognise it as such. The snow was up to his knees – soaking his dress trousers with the regret of the day. The ground had seemed hard, compact, but as soon as Jon had placed one foot onto it, the crust gave way to the softness below and he sank down and down into it. Jon wondered, momentarily, why he could not see any of the pathways that his prey had taken, but then the torrential wind and snow on the air responded by instantaneously removing these tracks like a pencil eraser. The only thing perceptible to Jon – not that his visibility extended much further than arm's-length – was the cavernous holes made by Crockley's steps, which were slowly being filled in as well.

Jon followed the holes and tried to use them to navigate the terrain more easily. He could not lose focus for even a second – the grounds of Balmoral were not exactly treacherous under normal circumstances, but now they were deadly. If he ended up wandering onto the River Dee, he could be in trouble. He did not want to get turned around and meet it, even in this weather, when it was most likely solid ice and covered. His legs were frozen, yet also on fire with pain as he battled against the snow to make any progress at all. Jon felt like he was crawling through baked Alaska – the crust bearing a striking resemblance to meringue, masking the softer consistency underneath. He knew it would not be easy, especially with the icy wind and his lack of any protection, but even so, when he stopped to see the progress he had made, and realised that he had only managed about a hundred yards, he despaired.

The only thing stopping him from resigning this fool's errand was the fact that Crockley must have been having a similarly difficult time on his trek. The holes left behind by Crockley's feet were getting deeper, and messier, indicating some trouble. Jon was also staggering, with the snow around him shredding and clinging to him, wanting him to stay. On occasion, he used the Winchester to push himself out of a particularly deep crevasse, even though he knew he should be keeping the rifle ready for action.

Jon kept along the path that had been laid for him, unsure where exactly he was going, or even if he would eventually reach his goal. He could no longer see Balmoral behind him – when he looked, all he saw was whipping snow, and the failing light of Christmas Day. He wondered what time it was, with natural light all but gone, but the white sky remaining almost luminescent. It gave a timeless quality to proceedings, as though the whole world had paused to mourn the king's passing.

There was barely any discernible difference between the sky and the ground. All around him – pure white.

Which way had he come from, which way was he going? The holes he was following were disappearing – the snow had picked up the pace at filling them, leaving Jon with nowhere to go. He staggered around, trying to find his breadcrumb trail, but to no avail. He turned around and around, knowing that with every revolution, he was becoming more discombobulated, but he was unable to stop himself. Everywhere was the same. Crockley must have been long gone by now – catching up to him had always been impossible. Maybe that was why he had come out here.

Could one survive out here? Could Crockley, could he, could Speck? In desperation, Jon thought to his only lifeline. The walkie-talkie on his belt was the only link he had with anyone, and although the person on the other end had not been particularly chatty of late, he knew that he had to try – and maybe if Speck was out here, a closer proximity would help, although Jon now realised he would probably not be able to hear it with the thundering of constant wind against his ears. Still trying to forge ahead, now in a direction he thought was most likely to be back to Balmoral, he reached to his belt and pulled the walkie-talkie up to him – the entire process made harder by the oppression of the gusts.

Jon finally achieved his goal and pressed the button, shouting as loud as he could – knowing it would not carry an inch. 'Speck, can you hear me?' He tried louder, his voice cracking. 'Speck, can you hear me? Speck, please. I need help.' Why did he have to sound quite so pathetic? He released the call button, and could barely hear the static over the wind. 'Speck, there's someone out here in the snow with me. With you, if you are still out here too. They're running, and I think there can only be one possible reason.' Static. 'Damn it, Speck. Where the hell are you? You were supposed to protect them. You were supposed to protect us. And look what's happened. This is all your fault.' Nothing, but then Jon didn't think he would have answered to that one either. He was getting too emotional – his eyes would freeze if he dared to cry. He said one last thing, as businesslike as possible. 'The Bridlepath Causeway has Flooded, Speck. I think Thomas Crockley is the murderer. I'm out here following him.'

He didn't wait for a response. He just clipped the walkie-talkie back to his belt, and received something in the way of a sound. There was a great rustling ahead of him – the movement of a formation of branches, or bushes. Someone was there.

Where was he, then? He could not still be in the courtyard. He must have ventured slightly further than he had given himself credit for, because there were no bushes or outcrops until the entrance to the castle. Had he somehow come to the front gate?

Another rustling in the branches responded – it was close, indeed had to be for him to be able to hear it. Jon pulled himself forward, pushing with the Winchester to get himself unstuck from a particularly nasty hole. The snow was coming down even faster now, the wind even more ferocious. As the tall bushes at the opening promenade of Balmoral came into view, Jon realised that maybe he should be walking, running, with all his might in the opposite direction.

The bush, a brilliant vibrant green, even in this white apocalypse, stood still and he wondered if there weren't all manner of logical explanations as to the rustling. The aforementioned wind could have been the culprit, or maybe even a small animal.

Suddenly though, the bush seemed to shake itself — the snow that lay on every branch was expelled into the air, only to be replaced moments later. Jon stared in horror, as the branches undulated and writhed, and then, once again, it was still. This was not the wind, and it was not any animal, not even a bear — there was someone walking around behind it, inside it.

'Speck?' Jon said, though more for himself than to inspire any affirmation. 'Crockley?' The wind took his words and carried them somewhere far away behind him.

The revelation of a human presence seemed to only make the sporadic jostles of the bush harder and faster. The branches started to bulge outwards, being rearranged by some force inside, and it was clear that someone was getting closer.

Jon was once again pinned to the spot — the snow in his current position winning its war to keep him just as he was. All he could do for himself was raise the Winchester to his face, his finger closing around the trigger, his sight now framed with a metal circle. He was begging with fate not to have to fire it. He was begging with fate for this not to be happening at all. He did not believe fate liked him very much.

The branches heaved and swelled with one final great crescendo, and then something – someone – began to be uncovered. The first thing Jon saw through the branches was the unmistakeable shadow of a figure, staggering out towards him on unsteady legs. Another step and Jon started to notice features. The figure was wearing a coat, but it was not red, it was grey with a fluffy hood pulled up – a parka.

Jon, still looking through the crosshairs of the rifle, faltered. 'Speck?' The figure did not seem to notice his question, although this time he would have liked some kind of answer. He didn't need it a second later, though, as his brain caught up with the image in front of him. The figure was nowhere near as tall as Speck, or as burly, so why were they wearing his parka? What had happened to Speck?

He readjusted the rifle, ready to press the trigger, still unsure if he could. 'Stay where you are. Don't come any closer.' His voice sounded like it wasn't even convincing itself, so he was not surprised when the figure did not adhere to the statement.

The figure took another step towards him – not seemingly threatening, but almost pleading. What was happening here? The wind showed him – as it whipped against the two of them, catching the parka's hood and pulling it away from the figure's head. As it settled on the figure's shoulders and the figure's hair whipped into a frenzy around her face, Jon lowered the rifle in confusion.

'Miss Darcy?'

Miss Darcy Tharigold, the king's private secretary, stood there, in Speck's parka, looking the very picture of exhaustion. She staggered towards Jon, saying nothing, before the snow claimed her and she started to fall. Jon caught her.

'Let's get you inside.'

XXXIII

The Heavens Open

Jon couldn't quite believe his luck when Balmoral – the great hulking castle that it was – appeared out of the snowy mist. Miss Darcy was leaning on him, so it almost felt like he was walking for two through the impossible storm surrounding them. The Winchester had now gone from a formidable weapon and sometime walking tool to an imperative part of this hybrid machine, clearing the holes that Jon used to navigate.

Miss Darcy was not offering help – he did not know if she even really understood what was happening. She was incredibly cold – even more so than himself – as she must have been out here in the elements for most of the day. Even the parka was not offering her enough respite, as it was caked in snow, and also soaking wet, perhaps indicating that she had fallen at some point or another. He had tried to ask her what had happened, but she did not respond. Her nose was blue in the stark white of the dying day, and her mouth could have been frozen shut for all the words she had spoken.

When the castle came into view, Jon had all but given up hope of ever seeing it again. His mind had half convinced him that it had never existed.

231

He rested Miss Darcy against the castle wall, as he collapsed against the servants' door, hammering an arm that felt far too heavy and far too strong. He felt no pain as it collided against the cold wood of the door, but knew he would in time – like the rest of him, it was numb. The snow had done to his body what the death of King Eric had done to his soul.

On the fourth thrust of his arm, the door finally gave way and he found himself sailing through the air, onto the comparatively warm white tile of the hallway. He could have whooped with joy then, entirely forgetting himself, and maybe he did – the only other soul who could have confirmed this was staring at him with cold, glassy eyes.

Back in the kitchens, Jon instantly set about making Miss Darcy a cup of cocoa, for the sugar intake, and a cup of tea, for refreshment. The young woman sat there shivering in her soaked work suit. She had shed the parka at the door, rightfully so, but now she was almost worse off for it. The right thing to do was to change into a whole new set of clothes, or at least remove the wet ones, but there were no new clothes down here in the guts of the castle, and Miss Darcy was not one to suffer the indignity of nakedness, no matter the cost. Luckily, for a reason that escaped Jon at this current moment, he did have a bath towel down in the kitchen, under the fresh tea towels, which he fished out of the linen drawer and draped around Miss Darcy's shoulders. He was unsure if she even noticed – her stare had not faltered since he'd found her.

The kettle boiled, and Jon put aside his differences with the microwave to warm the milk. Almost simultaneously, the tea and cocoa were ready. Jon, aware that he did not want to appear on an upper level to Miss Darcy, brought two more stools over to her, one to sit on and one to act as a table for her drinks. The moment he placed the mugs down, Miss Darcy's hands shot out for the tea. Her brittle fingers caressed the mug and slowly relaxed, warming into an embrace. She brought it up to her face and took a long drink, although the liquid still had to be scalding.

'Do you want anything to eat?' he asked, not that he could offer much more than stale toast and friendly service.

Thankfully, Miss Darcy shook her head – a swift movement of the head twice. 'There was a KitKat in my glovebox.'

'Oh, good.' He connected the dots, but wouldn't begrudge anyone who didn't. There were far more important issues than that, and Miss Darcy finally seemed in a state to answer them. 'Miss Darcy, what happened to you?'

Miss Darcy sniffed, running a hand under her nose. He had seen her reprimand a servant for performing a very similar gesture, calling it 'common' and 'not befitting of the place'. Now, the gesture only served to illustrate the depravity of the situation. 'The snow was already coming down something fierce when I left this morning. However, I thought I would be OK to get back to the village where I was to spend the day.' So there was definitely a unit down in the village waiting for any signal that something was wrong. Well, a great help they had been, and would continue to be, if the weather did not let up. 'I have snow tyres, but I had trouble getting out of Balmoral even.' Jon could attest to this – watching her out of the king's window. 'Once I reached the front gates, the snow had increased in speed. The road was almost impassable. The gates barely opened. Yet I still persevered. I do that too much – not accept defeat. I think giving up will make me a smaller person, and look where it got me. Right back where I started.'

Jon knew that he must steer Miss Darcy back on track, just as the snow seemed to be steering her past self off it. 'Did you crash, Miss Darcy?'

'No,' she said simply. 'I started driving and very quickly I could not see exactly where I was going. I knew I was on a road, and I thought it was the right one, but I did not know for sure. I went as slowly as I could, while going as fast as was sensible to get through the snow. At some point though, it was merely too much. The snow surrounding me and the car was piling up so quickly that I could not go fast enough to get unstuck from it. I did not crash – that would almost have been preferable. No, I merely stopped, and there was nothing to be done to get started again. You've never seen anything like it, Jon. The snow. It is as if the world is ending.

'I sat in the car for maybe an hour, watching the snow bury me. I was only safe inside as long as I could still escape. I had the heat on, yes, and could have happily stayed in there until the battery died. Eventually, it seemed like I would have to make a decision, a move. I didn't quite know what to do. It was terrifying, sitting in that tin box, knowing that safety was either closer forward or backwards, but I had no way of being sure.

'I decided that I must not have come that far, probably even less than I had thought. The snow diluted everything, stretched it, warped it. I decided to try to come back to Balmoral. My phone had already died, even before I got in the car. The plugs in the bed and breakfast, they don't work. I didn't have a coat, more than my suit jacket, but I knew I had to go, so I did.

'It seemed like hours before I reached the front gates. The wind, the snow, the white light coming from the sky – it all just sought to slow me down. I was wet, frozen, and stupid. I did not even think that I would not be able to get back into Balmoral. My set of keys were back in my hotel room, as I knew I would not need them this morning when I came to deliver the box to the king. Also, I could not chance being seen with them as I was supposed to surrender them for the day, as per the king's ridiculous request to be alone.

'God must have sent Tony Speck down to me then – I am not even religious. but that is the only thing I can think of. I must have been there for maybe fifteen minutes, screaming through those gates for help, before Speck came sauntering out of an outcrop as if he were taking a leisurely stroll. He had not heard me, of course, did not even see me at first, but when he did, he rushed over to open the gates. He understood what had happened almost instantly, and he took me to the watchtower.'

The watchtower, a name Speck had coined, was not a tower at all – it was a small untidy shack on ground level covered by uniform bushes, which was a base for the guards at the gates, with sleeping facilities and a wall of CCTV. 'He made me a tea, not unlike you have just done. Soon after that, the power died in the watchtower – it is on a different grid to the castle, a slightly less important and more temperamental one, so I was not particularly surprised.'

Jon could have cut in and told Miss Darcy of the power troubles the castle had experienced, but it was hardly relevant in the middle of her tale.

Miss Darcy finished her tea, in one final great slurp. She immediately began on the cocoa.

'I asked why Speck was even out there on the grounds in the first place and he said something about the king not stopping going on about how he thought someone would come to try to take his life. Speck had it in his head that he needed to be out there, and to his credit, the man has never been wrong. If he needed to be out there, then he needed to be out there. I said that I was going to try to make my way up to the castle, and he said he would not come, but he did offer me his parka. After some arguing, I accepted.

'That was hours upon hours ago. How much distance is between the watchtower and the servants' door? – maybe a quarter of a mile at a stretch? That is the power of the snow though. When I left that shack, I was back into that disorienting landscape, albeit with slightly more protection. I staggered around not knowing which way was right and which way was wrong, sometimes which way was up and which was down, left or right. Once I lost sight of the railings behind me, that was that. Nothing but white, and the occasional shrub to get lost in. I was on the grounds of one of the most secure castles in the world, and I had never been more scared for my life. How does that happen?

'Anyway, I believe that brings us up to speed. If you were not outside to meet me, I would have likely staggered around out there until New Year's Day, or died of exposure. You have my sincere gratitude, Jon.' She set down the cocoa. It was gone too. 'How are things here, anyway? Has the king made his speech yet?' She checked her watch and despaired. 'My God, is that the time! Yes, I suppose he has then – hours ago. I'm rather glad I missed that, truth be told. I do hope he won't mind me being here – I think he can shirk his rules in the circumstances. Jon, what is it?'

Jon could not move. He could not say anything. He could not even think. How could he even begin to explain the events that had occurred?

'Jon, you look as if you've seen a ghost and I assure you I am very much alive. Not only am I alive, I wish to be informed of today's events, which tells you I am still capable of doing my job.' Miss Darcy smiled, indicating that there was a joke in there somewhere. There might well have been, but Jon could not hear it. He hadn't really registered any of her words.

'I . . .'

'Jon, please, if this is some Christmas hijinks, I'm not

in the mood. I've been outside for so long, my wick has snapped off and . . .' Miss Darcy's face lit the colour of the sky. 'Wait, why were you outside anyway? And why were you outside with a rifle?'

Miss Darcy was starting to understand that something was wrong, and that helped to unlock Jon's lips, his voice a cold, hoarse thing. 'Something terrible has happened, Miss Darcy, and I've been the only one here to deal with it.'

'What has happened?' Miss Darcy got up – her life force restored by hot milk and powdered chocolate. The roles were reversed now, and Jon was glad. Finally, someone was here with a higher station than him.

'I've tried to keep it together for the sake of the Crown, but this day is a terrible mess.'

'Jon, stay calm, and tell me exactly what has happened.'

Jon opened his mouth then, the tears falling faster than the words, faster even than the snow. To the day he died, he could not recall exactly what he said to Miss Darcy then, but he would come to imagine it was something about a flooding on a bridlepath causeway.

XXXIV

Up to an Unfortunate Speed

Miss Darcy surveyed the body with a coldness that was unusual even for her. Jon would have found it odd, but she had betrayed herself with one single tear that was currently rolling down her cheek. They were in the king's room – the site where they both had unwittingly had their final private audience with the man. This seemed to be a fact that Miss Darcy was dealing with now.

She took a shaky breath. 'Who else in the family knows?'

Jon had given her a short version of exactly what had happened, and she still asked this? Darcy Tharigold was the type of character who believed a scene didn't begin until she had arrived in it. 'We were all right there in the drawing room when it happened. Everyone knows.'

'Yes, of course,' she said, small and slight. She wiped that one tear from her face and straightened up as if that had let out all the emotion she was allowed. 'I'm sorry. I just . . . I've never been close to a dead body before, let alone the dead body of the . . . the king.'

'Miss Darcy, I have reason to believe that someone murdered the king. How he died, what happened to

239

him, falls in line with some kind of immediate reaction to something ingested. It was maybe an hour since Christmas dinner and the king had been drinking, along with everyone else. Drinking the same drinks and eating the same food. But the king died when he drank a glass of whisky just before his speech. Nobody else drank that whisky and he was dead in less than a minute.'

Miss Darcy was still staring at the king's face, which now had the look of some department-store mannequin, frozen in an expression it couldn't comprehend. Indeed, the king's body was almost just that – an inanimate object, all used up. 'How sure can you be that this didn't just . . . happen?'

Jon wished he wasn't sure at all – it would be so much simpler. 'I was there, Miss Darcy. This was not natural causes. From my experience, although it is largely culinary, there is no way that this was not as I described. The king was poisoned. And what is more, I believe the murderer to be one of the remaining family members.'

'Be careful what you say, Jonathan. This sounds dangerously close to treason.'

'I understand that, but I have uncovered things, Miss Darcy. The king called Emeline, Maud, David, Matthew, Marjorie and Crockley for private audiences this morning, and he saw Martin afterwards. Things were discussed. The king seemed to be tying up loose ends – he had a folder, apparently, that may have had some incriminating evidence inside.'

'A folder?' Miss Darcy said. 'Have you found this folder that proves your musings?'

'No. I haven't.'

'You have no evidence of anything, Jon. You said you were appointed to this new role?' She was suspicious of this, but then who would not be? He was still unsure how he had obtained the job himself.

'Yes, ma'am. I was the last employee, and the remaining Windsors came to understand that they were compromised in some way and could not lead themselves. I became investigator by a process of elimination.'

'Do you have any "detective" credentials?' She was being deliberately flippant, not even trying to hide it from view. Before this moment, Jon had not known Miss Darcy's view of him, but now that her shock of the day thus far had worn off, she seemed very keen to show him.

'I am a chef, Miss Darcy. I have never been a detective. In practice, there are very few skills that transfer between the two professions. Investigating a murder isn't like investigating why a soufflé didn't rise.'

'So you are not a detective, and it would appear you are not a security guard either,' she snapped, gesturing to the king.

Anger surged, momentarily, inside Jon's heart. 'No, I am not, ma'am.' He enunciated a little too much, a stronger tone for every hour he'd endured alone. 'However, Tony Speck is a security guard. Unfortunately, he was outside, chasing phantoms in the snow, and not protecting his king.' He regretted every word as soon as he was done. Thirty years of holding his tongue gone in an instant.

Strangely, Miss Darcy did not fire him on the spot.

Rather, she seemed a little less perturbed by him. 'You're right, of course. Tony has shown an extreme lapse in judgement today. He will be dealt with when this whole sorry business is concluded. Now, you said you were following someone outside? When the power went out?'

Yes, that was also almost forgotten. There were too many things – too many puzzles in this box. When Jon focused too much on one of these mysteries, he lost sight of the others, as though they moved while out of view.

'Yes. I was in the drawing room with David, Marjorie, Emeline, Maud, Matthew and Martin. We saw Thomas Crockley out of the window, standing in the snow.'

'And Crockley wasn't in the drawing room because he had retired? Due to feeling unwell?'

'Yes,' said Jon. 'I went to turn the power on and came across Crockley, who gave chase outside.'

Miss Darcy put her head in her hands for a few seconds, almost like when one played a peekaboo game with a child. When she reappeared from her cocoon, she was a different person. She still eyed Jon suspiciously though, as if she questioned the reality he was talking of. 'Let's go and see the family – see what they have to say about all of this.'

Miss Darcy turned away and started towards the door, leaving Jon with the sense that she did not believe he had done his best, because if he had, the king would still be alive. It did not affect him as it should have, because he had been living with that feeling ever since the king had dropped from his role. He looked down at the monarch, and apologised silently once again – *I should have done more. I should have known that you were in danger.* Unspoken and in between Miss Darcy's words was a slight perturbed tone, that betrayed that she thought that in some way she was having to unravel his mess. She was right, of course. Even if Tony Speck should have been there, the responsibility always fell on those present.

Out in the corridor, the atmosphere was even worse. As they started towards the drawing room, Jon stopped. 'Wait.'

'What is it, Jon?' Miss Darcy said, disgruntled.

'Crockley's room will be empty.' Jon went over to Crockley's room and knocked. There was no answer. He knocked again, giving Miss Darcy time to catch up. 'You'll see.'

She sighed as he tried the door. It was unlocked.

Thomas Crockley was there, wrapped in his sheets, stirring from sleep at the sound of the door. It appeared as though he'd been there all afternoon. He didn't look as though he'd been outside at all – no oddly rosy cheeks, or stiff frozen hair. An eye winked open. 'Alleyne?' A red coat was nowhere to be seen.

Miss Darcy shut the door without any regard for Crockley's question. 'Are you feeling all right, Jon?'

Jon had always found it cliched when someone's mouth dropped open at a surprise. Now he knew it to be true. 'I . . . I . . . don't understand. If it wasn't Crockley, then—'

'Let's just go and see the family. Maybe now I'm here, you can get some sleep, yes? Didn't the doctor tell you that you had to stop running around like this?'

243

Jon was confused. 'I never told you about the doctor.'

'No,' Miss Darcy said. 'But I make it a point to know the business of all the castle employees. Especially if that business could affect their work.'

Something was being said here, something beyond the words.

Miss Darcy smiled, but her mouth didn't match her eyes. 'Come.' She turned, but after a few steps came back. 'Oh.' She pulled something out of her pocket. 'Tony Speck asked me to give you this. He said you were so transfixed with it earlier and it's not doing him much good down at the watchtower.' She thrust the thing into Jon's hand and stalked away down the corridor.

Jon inspected what she had given him. A small tablet. He touched it, and a familiar image filled the screen. It was the security tablet with the read-out of the castle. The same wireframe map was on the screen. Balmoral and the grounds. Red dots denoted the heat signatures of the people present. One was almost off the map – Speck at the watchtower. There were six dots towards the front of the castle – Emeline, Maud, David, Marjorie, Matthew and Martin in the drawing room. There were three dots towards the back – Jon, Crockley and Miss Darcy. Miss Darcy's red dot was even moving as she walked down the corridor.

No one else was in the castle. Crockley seemed to have been in his room all this time. Everyone else had been with him when the lights went out and the figure appeared at the window.

Did Jon really just chase a ghost?

XXXV

An Adjustment to the Status Quo

The excitement on every royal's face as they saw Miss Darcy Tharigold gliding into the room was palpable. They gathered around her, as children would gather around a favourite teacher, asking questions, telling her how happy they were that she had arrived, offering her tears of relief. Jon would have been offended, if he did not pity Miss Darcy for now having to be the object of their attention. It was nice to be adored, but that came with a certain expectation. Everyone in this room understood that now.

'What happened to you, Miss Darcy?'

'Where have you been?'

'Thank the Lord you are here!'

'Did you turn the power back on, Miss Darcy?'

Not embroiled in the gaggle was Princess Maud, who was looking tentatively to Jon. He gave a slight shake of his head – *not Crockley*. She seemed to understand and run the gamut of emotions. Relief gave way to confusion, gave way to fear. She stood back from the rest of them, and remained deep in thought for a long while.

Jon stood back as well and watched the huddle of

royals embrace their new leader. He was forgotten, left behind, merely the chef again. This is what he had wanted, wasn't it?

He was at a loss for something to do.

Jon went to the dresser next to the fireplace. The right cupboard in the dresser was for anything the Royal Family might need in the room. There was a stack of the king's favourite board games – Monopoly, Scrabble, Cluedo – and a selection of stationery and paper. There was also a bundle of Marjorie's failed pursuits, such as a half-completed cross-stitch, a barely grazed puzzle book and several untouched paperbacks. In the left cupboard, however, were items that a servant might need for the room. He searched among the bottles of antibacterial spray and the extra linens to find a bin bag. He ripped one off and went about collecting up all the rubbish in the room. This was not usually to be done in front of the royals, but he doubted they would even notice.

As Miss Darcy explained how she came to be in the drawing room to her adoring audience, Jon collected up all the wrapping paper, organised the empty glasses and tided the presents, with the swiftness and uniformity of a seasoned veteran. It was nice to be good at something again.

'That was when I met Jon outside. Jon has brought me up to date with what has transpired here.' Miss Darcy commanded the room, more so than he ever had. The Royal Family were a collective organism then. 'I am truly and deeply sorry to every one of you for what has happened. In some ways, I hold myself responsible.'

246

'No, Miss Darcy!'

'You must not think that!'

'You were not here, how could you be responsible?'

'That is exactly why I hold some responsibility. I should have been here. I know the king requested for this to be nothing but a family affair, and I wanted to honour that request, but myself and the establishment had the power to overrule him and we did not.'

'Do not blame yourself, child,' David said. 'This could not have been foreseen.' It seemed as though the rest of the family echoed his sentiments, even the ones usually pitted against him.

Miss Darcy was leading them as a conductor did an orchestra. It was really a sight to behold. Jon did not see any malice in it particularly. Rather, she knew exactly what she needed to get out of this exchange, and she would stop at nothing to get it. If it was some kind of absolution from the situation, she had just obtained it, but Jon thought that there was more she desired.

'Wherever blame is placed,' Miss Darcy began, 'it will not change where we are. The king is dead, and now that I am here . . .'

'Thank goodness,' Marjorie said, with a flourish towards Jon.

'. . . there will be a change in tack to what came before my arrival,' Miss Darcy continued. 'I will act accordingly.'

'You mean summon us all and declare who the

murderer is?' Martin asked almost excitedly, and then in response to glares from his father and brother, 'That's what Enola did.'

'I will not declare anything, young Martin, because that is ridiculous. And we all seem to be under some kind of shared delusion here. A delusion perpetuated by your leader, Jon.'

'And what is that?' Emeline said.

'Why, simply, this delusion that the king was murdered.'

The room stopped.

'What?'

'Wait . . .'

Jon was staring at Miss Darcy – he didn't know who spoke. It didn't really matter. What was she doing? Miss Darcy's smile never faltered. She seemed almost like an emotionless automaton. If it wasn't impossible that Miss Darcy had killed the king herself, Jon would have thought this was something of a plot.

'Miss Darcy—' Jon started, but the woman held up a hand.

'We have heard enough from you, Jon,' Miss Darcy said. 'Now, Jon has recounted events and, to me, it is clear. The king died of some natural cause. Jon himself said that it is not beyond possibility. The king was hiding certain things from all of you. He was not well. His death was not caused by any whisky or poison. It was caused by illness and old age. I agree that it must have looked very dramatic, but death does. I am sorry for what you all have experienced. I should have prepared you all for what may happen, and if I was here, I could have offered support.

'I think you have all been led astray by a man who fancied himself more important than he actually was. Through misguided actions, no matter how well-intentioned, this man has used a family tragedy for his own ends. It is perverse, and it stops right now.'

Jon couldn't believe what he was hearing. Unfortunately, the family could.

'Finally some sense!' David laughed coldly.

'We told you all not to appoint this idiot as an investigator,' Marjorie shouted in victory.

There were two hesitant parties among the royals – Maud and Matthew. Emeline had taken a step towards her uncle and mother – a move that would have seemed unbelievable a few hours ago. Even Martin was peering at Jon with suspicious eyes. Miss Darcy's word meant a lot in these rooms. Jon was in trouble.

'Maybe I made a mistake,' Emeline said. 'It just . . . It looked like he was poisoned so . . . I thought Jon was the best option.'

'Your Royal Highnesses, the Royal Family is the most important commodity in this country. You all are the most important people in this country. Do you really think we would have left you all if there was any possibility of an assassination?'

Miss Darcy was building to a crescendo, and Jon did not like where the music was taking them.

'I am aware that your one protector seemed to like swanning around thinking himself some kind of detective, when he was simply the chef. He was acting out some kind of bizarre power fantasy. This will not stand any longer.'

David cackled, as did Marjorie. Now even Matthew was faltering. Only Maud stood with Jon.

'You all were following the lead of a man who needed to feel some kind of control. He has always desired to be more than he is. And now, just for one final time, he wanted to be important. You were following a dying man into battle.'

Jon's eyes were threatening to fill with tears. He must not show weakness against her.

'Is this true, Jon?' No, not Maud too. They were all turned against him now.

'Jonathan Alleyne is ill himself, you see. He's dying. Maybe seeing the king perish finally broke his mind.' Miss Darcy almost seemed as though she were enjoying this.

Jon couldn't find the words. There were none. No one reacted to his secret at all, like they didn't even hear it.

Miss Darcy's sunny disposition came back, snapping on just as the lights had snapped off. 'So we are going to spend the end of our Christmas as usual. Jon is going to serve you all some supper and you can all relax by the fire.'

They were really going to act like nothing had happened. Of course they were – they were going to do everything Miss Darcy said.

'We will salvage what festive spirit we can. We will try to remember that it is Christmas Day – we will eat, drink and be merry. We will celebrate the life of Eric Windsor. And when the blizzard is over and this day is behind us, Jonathan Alleyne will face the consequences for this foolishness. And he can leave this castle for good. Once and for all.'

XXXVI

Tables Turn

'I bloody well knew it,' David said. 'Leading us on a wild goose chase. Perverting the name of my good brother, and besmirching us all in the process. And spilling my whisky too.'

'I knew he was trouble,' agreed Marjorie. 'He's always had that shifty look in his eyes. They all do.'

Jon wished to simply disappear.

'I do not believe it,' Emeline said. 'But there it is.'

'I can't . . . I'm going to be sick,' Matthew announced. 'Excuse me.' He stalked out of the room and did not return for five or ten minutes.

The other royals seemed to want to voice their opinions too, not to mention that Jon himself would have rather liked to state his case, but as ever the maestro, Miss Darcy had the floor and held a hand up to silence the room. 'Now, I think we should all just put the television on and forget about this for the time being, yes? You may still be able to catch the end of *Strictly Come Dancing* if you do. Alternatively, we can stay here and play parlour games.'

Parlour games. At a time like this.

But Miss Darcy was saying things with such conviction

that it was hard for even him to remain firm. Had he really acted rashly? It was true that poison had not been confirmed as the method of death, and the whisky even less so. Was there some kind of truth locked inside Miss Darcy's harsh words?

'We are just meant to go back to how we were before?' said Maud.

'No, you misunderstand,' Miss Darcy asserted. 'I'm afraid you can never go back to how it was before. You have all witnessed the death of a beloved family member. You are all traumatised, exhausted and suffering a grief I could barely dream of. But isn't it to be British to endure? Isn't it to be the Royal Family? Wouldn't King Eric have wanted you to see this day out with joy and compassion for one another?'

Against it all, Emeline chuckled. 'If he could see us now . . .'

'He'd laugh at all of us,' Marjorie said.

'How many times do you think he'd have told his ruddy fable by now?' Emeline laughed.

'"One day, a common family went to the zoo to see the lions . . ."' David mimicked, in a surprisingly accurate impression. 'Yes, brother, we know. They go an awful lot.'

The family started to reminisce about Eric, and one by one they softened. Maud was the last to get consumed by nostalgia, but she did eventually, cracking up as Martin remembered Eric's sour face while talking about *The Monarch*.

Jon simply watched them. Once again, he was on the

outside looking in. He hated how that made him feel. And then he hated that he thought Miss Darcy might be right. He'd felt 'among' them for a moment, even if it were in dire circumstances. And now he was not, and never would be again.

Miss Darcy stood next to him, her smile never changing physically but meaning something completely different.

'You did not have to do that,' Jon said, regretting the fact that his tone sounded more dejected than hostile. At some point in his life, he had become this – the one that gets happened upon by other people. 'You did not have to say that.'

'No, I did not, but it is done now, and I think we are all the better for it.'

'I would respectfully disagree.'

Miss Darcy smiled that awful smile and chuckled. 'I don't care about your opinion, Jonathan. I never have. Nobody in this castle ever has, unless it has to do with food. Speaking of which . . .' Miss Darcy raised her voice. 'Who is hungry? It has been a long day for all of us.'

There were cries of happiness from all of the family.

'Treat them like schoolchildren,' Miss Darcy muttered to Jon. 'That's the secret.' She clapped him on the back. 'I expect your resignation on my desk by the time I've cleaned up your mess. Unless you'd like to be fired.'

Miss Darcy walked among them. 'Jonathan will do his job for a change, and go and fix us all up some supper. I'm assuming there are a fair amount of leftovers from dinner, yes?'

Jon silently nodded. He was in disbelief.

'Then off you pop.'

And Jon found himself doing exactly as Miss Darcy ordered. His legs seemed to carry him on autopilot, with a mind of their own, as he bowed to the Royal Family and took his leave.

At the door, he looked back to them. They had already forgotten all about him. All except Miss Darcy who raised a hand. 'Oh, and Jon, extra sprouts for me.'

XXXVII

Leftovers for Supper

Over the next hour, the family ate around the coffee table where the king had taken his last breath. Jon had concocted a platter full of leftovers and put them on the sideboard. The family filled their plates. He made Miss Darcy her own Christmas dinner and she sat down and ate with the family. She was one of them, just as he had always wanted to be. When he was done, there wasn't anything left but meat and gravy.

Jon was starving. He didn't know if the pain in his gut was the tumour or his stomach screaming. But he didn't have time to eat – and wasn't interested in the scraps. He probably wouldn't have been able to keep anything down anyway.

When the doctor told him it was cancer, he didn't cry. When he was told it was inoperable, he didn't even flinch. He only cried when he thought of leaving the Royal Family behind. Now, he saw they were more than fine without him. They were flourishing.

The younger ones were playing Monopoly. The king couldn't be further from the topic of conversation. It was almost as if it had never happened. All was the same, except his favourite armchair, which remained empty.

Martin was already out of the game – he was pestering his elders. David and Marjorie sat furthest from the table, their plates perched on their laps, deep in muttered conversation. 'Did you know that gorillas don't beat their chests with their fists, they beat them with their open palms?' The two of them barely heard the boy, and definitely didn't acknowledge him.

Miss Darcy had just finished her meal and was currently buying a swath of houses to put on her purple set. She was winning the game.

In more ways than one.

'More wine, please, Jon.'

This from Emeline. At one time, she was his chief defence. It was her idea that he become the investigator.

He came over and poured her a glass, making sure everyone else was topped up as well. Maybe David had been right all day – he *was* the butler.

Not one of them had questioned the food they had been brought. Jon had gotten back to the kitchens to see the leftovers all exposed, and he had thought long and hard about whether to serve them. Any of the family could have poisoned the leftovers – they all had ample opportunity. But no one else seemed concerned with that any more. And he would have been lying if he said that he didn't simply serve it because he was expected to.

A life of doing as he was told. That was the life he'd left Barbados to find – apparently. Ever since he'd left, he'd sought out someone to lord over him. Well, he had hit the mother lode here.

'That's not fair,' Matthew wailed as he landed on one of Miss Darcy's populated spaces. 'I'm bankrupt. No – I'm not mortgaging anything. I'm gracefully going down with the ship.' He thrust himself back on the chaise longue, laughing.

Could Jon blame them? The family were mourning. They were suggestible. It was highly likely that at least some of them were putting up some kind of shield. Jon had seen it plenty of times – that shield. They were all acting like they were in public. He'd also seen the shield come down.

Matthew shuffled back so far on the chaise longue that he ended up losing balance and falling off the end. He fell to the floor in a tipsy bundle of limbs. Something that had been placed under the chaise longue skittered off to the side and collided against the right wall. Matthew burst out laughing, and everyone else did too.

But the laughter soon stopped when the tinkle of a music box tune started. 'God Save the King'. It was the puzzle box, Interregnum, that had skittered to the wall and its impact had triggered the tune to commence.

The shield came down.

The family let the day back in.

'I may turn in for the night,' David said, finishing his drink and swallowing a sob along with it.

'Good idea,' Marjorie said – her liver, no doubt, rejoicing.

'Bloody hell, it is late, isn't it?' Matthew said, getting up, dusting himself down and looking at the clock on the mantel. It was almost 11 p.m. Almost Boxing Day.

'Maybe we should all go to bed, yes?' Miss Darcy said. 'Everything will seem a trifle better in the morning. Maybe the blizzard will have even stopped.'

They all started collecting themselves and filing out of the room. Emeline went first, eyeing the music box and drying her eyes with her handkerchief. Maud collected her family group and ushered them out. David strode out the room. Not one of them acknowledged Jon, standing at attention by the door.

The only ones left were Jon, Miss Darcy and Marjorie. The princess royal was trying and failing to get up from the chaise longue. 'You know, maybe I should just sleep here tonight.'

'Nonsense,' Miss Darcy said. 'Hardly a bed fit for a queen, is it?'

This was the right thing to say.

'I'll help you to your bedroom, ma'am.'

Miss Darcy had bent down to help her, but stopped and turned. She stared directly at Jon, that damned smile still haunting her face. 'Jon, what are you still doing here? You are dismissed. If I were you, I'd have half a mind to stay out of everyone's way from here on out, yes? Why don't you go back to your little kitchens and say goodbye?'

Jon didn't glorify that with a response. He merely nodded to her, 'Miss Darcy,' and Marjorie, 'Your Royal Highness. Happy Christmas to you both.' He liked to think that that stuck in them somehow – him taking the high road – but the reality was that they probably didn't even care.

Out in the corridor, Jon dropped the decorum. He sank to his knees and let out a sob of pain. His gut was on fire. Standing so still for hours had physically exhausted him, the scene had destroyed him. It was over. It was all over.

Wilson the cat trotted up to him out of nowhere and started rubbing himself on Jon's shin. At least someone was still on his side. Jon went to stroke him, but Wilson seemed to have other ideas — he went to the drawing room door and started pawing it, trying to get it open.

Jon went to the door, and was just about to open it, when he heard the conversation from within. He picked up Wilson to stop him scratching the door. At first the cat resisted, and then settled into his arms purring softly. Even so, Jon had to strain to hear.

'Oh, leave me alone, silly little girl. You do not know what you're talking about.' One did not have to point out that this was Marjorie.

'I do not want to speak out of turn, Your Royal Highness, but would now be a good time to let go of that secret you have been holding on to so firmly? The barriers are down now, it could almost be some kind of redemption story.'

'What would be the good of that?' Marjorie snapped.

Miss Darcy applied the sweetness, of which she had an infinite supply. 'This family is cracking — we need a new glue to hold it together. For you. For the country. For the British public. This could be that glue. A new chapter.'

'And I suppose you know everything of this secret, do you?'

'I know everything about you, Your Royal Highness. It is my job. And everything about every other member of your family. I could let you know things.'

'Do you know where my daughter was that day in Plymouth?'

'What?' It seemed Miss Darcy was caught off guard by this.

'Did I stutter? Do you know where my daughter was that day in Plymouth? She was thirty minutes late for the opening of that stupid cat place. How does that happen? Do you know where she was?'

'No . . . No, I don't.'

'Then what use are you to me? You know what – how dare you? I see your game, Tharigold. You are trying to threaten me. Well, curse you, and curse Fairfax before you. I can give as good as I get. My secret is just that – mine. I'd like to spill some of your secrets too. Your family has plenty – the mighty Stellan Tharigold's niece, hmm? How many skeletons are in his closet? Be gone. I will stay here for the night. I rather think a nightcap is in order anyhow. Be gone. Unless you have a wine bottle opener. A corker. A skewer. One of those things.'

'Ma'am, I did not mean—'

'Be gone.'

Miss Darcy's footsteps could be heard coming closer, and Jon shrank into the nearest alcove as she appeared out of the door. She stalked past him, before stopping. She couldn't have seen him, but she had. 'Jon, you're still here.'

Jon stepped out of the alcove, making a show of

drying his eyes. She seemed to believe that he wasn't eavesdropping. 'I'm always here. Or I used to be. For the king and for the Crown.'

Miss Darcy rolled her eyes. 'Give me your walkie-talkie. I am going to try to hail Tony. I'll get a signal if it kills me. I'll climb to the top of the tower if I have to. This all needs to end, I'm sure you'll agree.'

Jon let Wilson jump from his hands and unclipped the walkie from his belt.

'It's better this way, Jon,' Miss Darcy said as she took it. 'You may even see that one day. Now, off to your kitchens.'

Jon obeyed, never looking back – thinking on Marjorie Windsor-Nueberner's secret every step of the way.

XXXVIII
Defiance

The washing-up was done. The counters were cleaned. Jon had nothing left to do but sleep. He had never hated the sight of a sparkling-clean kitchen so much. Sleep would not come, and if it had, he would have sent it away anyway. He wanted to spend as long as he could in these old walls, and he wanted to do so conscious. This had been his life, and it wasn't hyperbole to think that, in a way, he was dying with his job.

He was so hungry. Maybe now he could try to eat something. Maybe one last time, he should make the king's breakfast. He grabbed two slices of bread out of the bread bin and slotted them into the toaster. Where had he put the jam this morning? He had the strangest feeling he could have put it anywhere other than where it was supposed to be. Sure enough, it wasn't in the side of the fridge where he usually kept it. The morning had been in such disarray, he didn't know where it had ended up.

Maybe he could solve the mystery of the missing jam at least.

As he got to work on that, his mind drifted back. There were still so many things that didn't make sense.

263

The chief thing was the figure in his red coat at the window. If it was not Crockley, then who could it have been – bearing in mind that no one else was here? It was proven.

Jon reached into his pocket and brought out the security tablet. The red dots of the Royal Family, Miss Darcy, himself and Tony Speck off in the watchtower. No one else.

How was that possible? The figure had not been some kind of group delusion. It had happened. Something had run past him, something had gone off into the snow – he had not been following nothing. He was not going mad.

He also just couldn't believe that the king had died naturally. He had foamed at the mouth. He had clutched his throat. Directly after drinking the whisky. That could not just happen. Also, Crockley got sick after touching his lips, although it seemed that he had pulled through. Jon stood by it – the king was murdered. And people in this castle were holding back secrets – secrets that could easily transform into motives.

He found the jam but he slammed it down on the counter so hard it almost shattered the jar. Luckily, it didn't break – he didn't have many jars left after all. Correction – whoever was to replace him didn't have many left. Maybe his replacement could solve the case of the missing jam jars.

His toast popped up, but he didn't notice. He re-examined the tablet. Red dots. No more, no less than there were before. He was starting to show signs of paranoia.

He put it in his off-hand pocket, to try to quell the urge to keep looking at it, and the tablet collided with the small, metal thing he'd felt earlier but entirely forgotten about.

He pulled it out.

A Windsor family crest.

Where had this come from? It was identical to the ones that the family had on them throughout the day. He'd never had one, of course, and had absolutely no idea where this one had manifested from. And then it all became clear – the king must have slipped this into his pocket as a Christmas gift. A Windsor family crest, maybe a symbol that he was closer to the family than he thought.

For the king and for the Crown – maybe now was when that was tested.

Jon put the crest back into his pocket. He was not done as investigator quite yet. Miss Darcy was already going to crucify him – already going to try to pin him for treason, no doubt. He would not go down without a fight. He would not go down without finding King Eric's murderer and bringing them to justice.

He didn't care what happened after. All he needed was that.

He stalked out into the hall, toast abandoned and gut trying to get him to turn around. But he would not. This was it. The final act. His final act. It was time to find what was at the centre of the Russian doll.

Jon felt something akin to happiness. No, it was not happiness, it was merely a tremendous contentedness that he was doing what he must. He glanced up to the stairs that he would take two at a time. And jumped out of his skin.

Someone was standing there. Shivering and sniffling.

It was Maud. He had never seen her in such a state of undress. She was just in her nightie, looking like she'd run here all the way from her bedroom. She was still wearing her crest as a necklace.

'Princess Maud?' Jon said in surprise.

Maud grabbed him by the shoulders. 'Jon.' She burst out crying and pulled him into a hug. 'It's Thomas. He's disappeared.'

XXXIX
The Redacted One

Thomas Crockley's room was empty. His bed was unmade, as if he had just rolled out of it. His drawers were open, as though someone had rummaged through them. Maybe it was the man himself. Nothing else was amiss, and Jon found himself comforting Maud. The woman had been beside herself, all the way to the bedrooms.

'He will have just gone outside for a smoke, you know him.'

Did he really believe that? Well, yes, he did. He took out the security tablet and showed Maud. Quite how Thomas Crockley had gotten outside, Jon did not know, but there was indeed one red dot just outside the castle walls.

'What is this?'

'It's the read-out for Speck's new security system that I told you about. The red dots are heat signatures. Human heat signatures. And there is your husband.' The dot darted around somewhat. Jon could just imagine Crockley falling over in the snow at that point. The red light was smaller, probably because he was freezing.

Maud put her head in her hands. 'I'm going mad.

Jumping at shadows. I'm sorry, Jon. I'm so sorry for everything. You must have felt so betrayed by all that in the drawing room. Damn Monopoly, for God's sake. I cannot speak for everyone, but I just wanted to escape for a while and Miss Darcy offered us that, but that puzzle box brought it all back. I will do everything I can to help you keep your job.'

Jon shook his head. 'I'm afraid I think that ship has sailed, ma'am. Miss Darcy has me in her sights. And we both know that she won't stop until she gets what she wants.'

Maud knew. 'Was it true what she said – that you are dying?'

'That's a very blunt way of putting it,' Jon replied.

'That's not a no.'

Jon said nothing.

'You've always been so good to us, Jon. And how do we repay you? With snide remarks and lies. Even I do it.'

'Lies, ma'am?'

'Yes. I knew that Daddy was going to announce his abdication today. I'm betting that most of my family did too. I would also assume that they all kept their stance of knowing nothing about it – just as we all did in the drawing room. I didn't even necessarily lie to you because it would make me more of a suspect. I just lied to you because it was easy. Almost second nature.'

Jon considered this. If they were all lying to him, there was no chance he could find the king's killer. However, it seemed like Maud was not lying to him now.

'Can I please ask you a question?' Jon said.

'Of course, anything.'

'I overheard your mother and Miss Darcy talking privately just before I was sent to the kitchen. Your mother appears to be holding something back from the rest of the family.'

Maud relaxed slightly at this – a very odd reaction. She sat down on her husband's bed. Everyone at Balmoral had to sleep in separate rooms, regardless of marital status, and even sitting on the bed of someone else was forbidden. Maud did not care though, or even notice. 'Well, of course she is holding something back. She is the great Marjorie Windsor-Nueberner.' She sang the name in mock awe. 'The woman collects secrets as though they were commemorative coins. She once told me that the trick was to have so many secrets that your adversary didn't know which ones were important. I imagine a psychologist would say that's why she drinks so much. To lighten the load on her soul.'

Jon's legs would rather have liked to sit down too, but there was only the bed, and as Maud was in her nightie, there was no way he was going to do that, even if he was further than arm's-length away. He made do propping himself against a wall. 'She also is rather interested in something else. Something to do with you.'

Maud froze. 'What?'

'She wants to know why you were late for the opening of the RSPCA cattery in Plymouth. She asked Miss Darcy if she knew anything about it.'

Maud glanced about her in disgust. 'I knew she

269

remembered. She has been toying with me for months, for my entire life. They both have.'

'Princess Maud?'

'I will tell you, Jon,' she said, crying. 'I will tell you. Here is my motive.' And she started. 'When I saw that I was to go to Plymouth, I knew that I must seize a chance to follow a hunch. There was something in my past, now in Plymouth, that everyone here wished to bury. I was not supposed to know about this, but I happened upon it one day. One day far too late.'

'Plymouth, ma'am. But what could possibly be in Plymouth?'

'Poppy.'

'Poppy?' He searched back. She had said that name already today. But when? At the dinner . . . 'Wasn't Poppy a dog? Your mother said she was a golden retriever, or a lab, or something?'

Maud snorted. 'That's my mother for you. Poppy wasn't a lab, or a golden retriever. She was a girl. She is a woman.'

'I'm sorry. Please continue,' Jon said.

'Poppy was my age. We went to the same school when we were thirteen or fourteen – you had started a few years earlier and were training a lot of the time, that's why you don't know her. Poppy even came to Windsor Castle a few times, stayed over for sleepovers. We got close. Too close. Daddy walked in on us once. Nothing sordid, you understand. Just a kiss.

'The next day, Poppy was gone. Not just from the castle, but from the school, and from her home. From the face

270

of the earth. Daddy told me that her father worked for a very important law firm and they had to move away. I never saw her again. A year later, it got back to me that they'd been in a car accident. The whole family had died.'

'I'm sorry to hear that, ma'am,' Jon said. He was surprised he had not heard of Poppy before. Maud seemed very distressed by the situation. It very much sounded like the king had sent this girl away — that, or it was extremely bad timing.

'Poppy faded from my memory. How could she? I don't mind telling you, Jon, but I loved her. And what hurts even more is I think she loved me. But being royal is to live a mile a minute, especially when one is young. I almost forgot her.

'That was until a note was slipped under my door when I was staying with Mummy and Daddy in Windsor Castle. I found it very odd and almost thought it some kind of mistake, to be tossed away without looking at it. Luckily, I didn't. It was an address in Plymouth. With one name at the top. Poppy.'

Maud stood up and strode over to the window, looking out into the white. She couldn't possibly see anything through the darkness and the whipping snow, but it seemed enough for her to be doing something. She was silent for a minute.

'The stars aligned. The order came that I was to travel to Plymouth the next week. I knew I must go to this address and see what this note wanted me to see.

'So I did, and I'm almost ashamed to say there was something thrilling about it at first. The security detail

271

checked me into the hotel across from the cattery to get ready for my public appearance, as it had been a long journey. We were also early. I told them I wanted to catch forty winks before the appearance. They left me alone in my room.

'I quickly dressed in plain clothes and snuck out. Almost forty and feeling like a naughty little schoolgirl. Thrilling. Rather the same feeling as getting to make my own breakfast this morning. What an odd emotion.' Maud smiled at memories of trivial things.

'It took me longer than it would an average person to find the address. Maps on your phone are very strange, aren't they? Eventually, after walking through the whole town and thinking I'd be recognised at every step, I came across a side street that was lined with quaint little brick terraced houses all in a row. They were probably hundreds of years old. I remember thinking – who was on the throne when all these were built?

'I came to the address. One of those identical houses. There was a small concrete front yard with a dead hanging basket next to a purple door. I had never experienced such surety before. I thought maybe I'd arrive to an address that was a cemetery. But she was alive. This was her house.

'This was her exile.'

Jon listened quietly to the tale, with shock. This did not sound like the king he knew – sending an innocent girl away, making his own daughter think someone she loved was dead. Maybe there was some other explanation.

'I half wanted to run away as fast as I could. But after

all I had done, I knew I had to see. So I knocked. Do you know who answered the door? A little girl. Maybe six or seven. Wearing a tiara. I said I was in the wrong place, but she saw who I was and screamed out my name, "It's the princess." So excited.

'And then her mother came to the door. It was her. Poppy Stilwell. Older, but still no less beautiful. Perhaps even more so. Funny how age can do that to some people, isn't it?

'She wasn't as shocked as me. She said she knew this day would come. There was a coldness in her voice I didn't expect, had never heard before. She asked me what I wanted. I just burst into tears – I didn't know what I wanted. Once upon a time, I'd wanted her. I'd wanted to spend my life with her. But we were young and maybe it wouldn't have happened, but isn't it human to mourn all the lives we do not live?

'I told her what happened. That they said she was dead. She laughed, and she said, "They? They said that?" And then she said, "Talk to your father about what *they* said." I brushed that off at the time. I was just so confused, so happy to see her, so sad at the life I lost.

'And then it all just came flooding out. I said I would renounce everything. I said I would divorce Thomas. I said I would change my name and move to Plymouth. I said I'd do anything to be back in her life. I said I still loved her.

'And do you know what she said?'

Jon shook his head.

'She told me to piss off.'

XL

John Brown Strikes Again

Jon had never heard an expletive escape Maud's lips before, even a relatively light one. She had always been mild-mannered and polite. This word broke her. But not for reasons anyone but her could understand. She sniffed and raked her hands through her hair and the perfect princess persona slipped back onto her face.

'I would have been on time for the opening had Google Maps not decided to direct me to the wrong one at first. Two RSPCA catteries in one town? Plymouth has a feline issue, Jon. I really should try to do something about it, if I could summon it in my heart to like the little creatures.'

'Princess Maud, I am so sorry. I had no idea.'

'No, of course you didn't, Jon,' Princess Maud said, with the saddest smile that he had ever seen. 'That was quite the point.'

Jon had always assumed himself King Eric's confidante, being told of issues and concerns that he didn't think graced the ears of even the highest members of the establishment. This day was showing, however, that that thought was entirely false – the king hadn't told him anything of the issues he had with his family. Of course he hadn't. Not a confidante at all. Jon was just the chef. Just the chef.

'Poppy was like a ray of sunshine, if you will excuse the tired simile. There are a million things I regret in my life, but I don't regret the kiss.' Maud smiled a sad smile. 'But why did they have to say that she had died? Why could they not leave it at the fact she moved away? You do not have to answer, Jon – I know it. The establishment has the stick and they love to draw lines in the sand. Their files must be full of the phrase "The End". To tell me she had just moved away would be leaving things far too open, leaving the sentence without a full stop, as if inviting more words to come and join.'

'Ma'am, why did you not tell me this before? I am under the assumption that this is what you talked about in your private audience with the king?'

'Yes. Of course.'

'Then why hide it? Why lock it away in your heart?'

'Jon, is it not obvious? It is simply too painful for me to talk about. It is not shame, never shame. It is having to accept that my father had a hand in this. Even if what Poppy told me last week is untrue, and Father did not give the order to send her away, he was the only one who witnessed our true relationship. He would have had to go and run and tell the puppet masters. They had such a hold on him. Then I enter that room today, and my father has the audacity to complain about my choice of husband.' She was seething with anger now. 'A husband that I only had so I would appear proper and prim. And to sire my children. I had a husband for the British

275

public, for the king and for the Crown. I've lied to myself for so long that I even believed it myself. Poppy is right, Jon.'

Something was inside Princess Maud, something he had never seen before. A pulsing, radiating fury. Jon did not know what it inspired more inside himself – fear at what she could have done, or sadness at what she had become. Could Jon believe that Maud – the young at heart, the free and joyous – had hurt her father?

No. She was not confessing to murder here. She was confessing to being broken.

'Do you see, Jon – the grand image?' Maud wiped her nose, this time with the back of her hand instead of the handkerchief, abandoned in her pocket. 'This place is Hell. I will not stand for it any more. I am done with this establishment, but I am part of the problem. For example, I disagree vehemently with Miss Darcy's strategy, but I did not say a word because I was scared to go against her.' Maud tried to stand, tripped and fell to the floor, her anger used up and her exhaustion overwhelming her.

Jon rushed to her, forgetting his own fatigue, and pulled her up. 'Maybe you should get some rest, ma'am. I will wait here for Thomas to get back. Maybe Miss Darcy is somehow right. Maybe everything will be better in the morning.'

Maud hugged him. 'Thank you, Jon. You have been so good to us today. Please don't let anyone make you think otherwise.'

They left Crockley's room as they made their way over

to Maud's. With one final smile, she entered her room, and shut the door behind her. Jon hoped that she could find sleep somewhere inside. Maybe he would find rest someday soon too.

He went back into his pocket and checked the security tablet again. All the red dots were in order. Thomas Crockley was still outside and had even moved slightly away from the castle. Jon had no idea how a smoke could be worth braving that tundra. No quantity of cigars in the world could make him take a single step outside before the blizzard let up.

Still, the screen gave him an uneasy feeling. He was still haunted by the image of the—

Footsteps. Ahead of him in the corridor. His eyes shot up. A kilt again? Flitting around the corner of the corridor. John Brown was back, he thought. But no – it had to be Prince David again.

Jon made his way over to Prince David's door and knocked – three times.

'Who is it?' came the familiarly cowardly voice. Jon cursed to himself – the figure was not the old prince. 'Go away, won't you? I have had enough of this blasted Christmas. I just want to sleep.'

Movement again. A figure – the figure – had just moved down the corridor, darting around the corner of the hallway. How sure was he that it was the same person? How sure was he that he had even seen it? He couldn't be sure of it at all, but he knew something had drawn his gaze and sent his inner alarm into turmoil. He listened and heard carpeted footsteps hurrying away from him, with flashbacks to the footsteps he had heard last time he was up here. John Brown was lurking around the bedrooms today, it seemed.

'Hello?' he asked, as loudly as his frayed nerves would allow. His voice did not carry anywhere near far enough. The footsteps remained, and it might have been his imagination, but they quickened. Jon started down the hall, ignoring the fact that David was wittering something beyond the door in response to his question. 'Stop!'

He rounded the corner in the hallway onto another vast expanse that stretched the entire length of Balmoral. If any figure was here, it should have come into his sight, but there was none. Nothing. The footsteps had ceased. Was his mind playing tricks, or had the figure simply ducked into one of the many doorways littering the hall?

On this hallway, having passed the bedrooms, were illustrious studies, a dusty library and decadent meeting rooms where the family took their callers. The only room of any consequence, however, was where Jon set about travelling to.

The king's private study was at the far end of the hall, much farther than the figure could have moved in the short time that they were out of sight. This made it odd then that the closer Jon got to the room, the more he became sure that someone was inside it. Jon heard a shuffling sound at first, as if someone was searching through a stack of papers at a hurried pace, and then he heard the unmistakeable creak of the study floorboard.

This floorboard was famous among the family, especially the princesses. When they were younger, around ten or so, and lamented the amount of time that their father had to spend working, Eric would have a habit of pacing around as he underwent his royal duties. Whenever they heard the floorboard, they knew that their fun would have to wait.

Now, the floorboard inspired something else – fear. An entity was indeed in the king's study, and as Jon get ever closer, his legs carrying him as if on some fateful conveyor, he knew that somehow it was this mystery figure. There was something in that study that the figure wanted, and as per the shuffling sounds, they were ransacking the room to look for it.

Closer still and able to peer around the frame, Jon saw that the door lay open. Even closer, and with the sounds getting louder, met with scurrying, and the occasional thumping of drawers being flung open, Jon began to wonder if he could manage to confront this phantom alone. He was an older man after all, physically exhausted after being on his feet all day without food or rest, and mentally exhausted from an unwanted career swerve and the loss of a friend and employer. He was barely a formidable threat to anyone, let alone a figure who, most likely now, had killed the king. A loud bang from the study seemed to inform his decision, as his instinct was to run the last few steps to the study and round the door before he could even think about what he was doing.

He stood there, in the doorway, feeling like the very intruder he was attempting to stop. The study was in complete disarray – it had been thoroughly ransacked.

The cupboards stood open, the chairs overturned, the desk a mess of loose papers. Stood over the desk was the culprit, with their hands on the desk curled up into fists. The bang Jon had heard was this culprit, thundering his fist into the mahogany in utter despair.

'What are you doing?'

Jon forgot his suffix.

The young man started with a desperation Jon had never seen woven into any man. His aura had gone cold and tainted, like stagnant water in a forgotten plant-pot. His eyes betrayed a truth that Jon was only beginning to understand.

Prince Matthew had the nerve to smile.

XLI

The King's Private Study

All at once, Prince Matthew was five years old again, being caught doing something naughty – an assailant seized red-handed, and a young man who had all the suspicion in the world thrust upon him. These somewhat intangible concepts all coalesced and swirled, like cream in a soup, until they were represented in a simple smile.

He was still dressed in his formal Christmas attire, but he had removed his jacket with his family crest pin (as if he didn't want it to see what he was up to). He had rolled up the sleeves of his dress shirt.

'Jon,' Matthew said, clearly trying not to look at the mess of the king's private study around him. 'I wasn't expecting to see you up here. I thought Miss Darcy would have you under lock and key in the kitchens by now. Look, Jon, I don't believe a word of this nonsense about you, so don't worry about that.' Matthew was mumbling, rambling. The young man was still leant over the desk with his fists down in an oddly simian pose, as though all but his face was frozen. It gave the effect of him looking like a cheap animatronic with too few mechanisms.

'Your Highness,' Jon said. The entire contents of the king's desk seemed to be on the floor surrounding it – files, papers, puzzle books and plans strewn everywhere, unwanted and forgotten. The cupboards and dresser drawers stood open, and their innards were similarly hanging out. Matthew had well and truly cased the entire place. 'What are you doing in the king's study?' It was fairly obvious – the young man was looking for something – but Jon needed to hear it from the culprit's mouth.

'Well.' This one word seemed to encompass Matthew's assessment of what he presumed he could get away with. 'I'm here for much the same reason as you are, Jon, I assume. I do not really rate Miss Darcy's decision-making.' It was just as Maud had said. The spell of normality had been broken, everyone was back to being suspicious of each other. Everyone was back to thinking the king was murdered. If only they had spoken up for him in front of Miss Darcy. 'I'm looking for clues as to what really happened to my grandfather. Would you like to join me?'

Jon started to pick his way across the carpet, dodging stray papers and upturned drawers. 'I understand that, sir,' Jon said, understanding it more than anyone, 'but did you have to be so . . . violent with your investigation?'

Matthew finally moved then, his fists dissolving back into open hands, his stance straightening to fight the desperation. He wheeled around, seeming a bit shocked at the scene he so actively had a part in, as though he were not conscious of it. 'Oh, well, I must have let my ambitions get the better of me. I thought I really might find the key to everything in this room, and, well . . . I'm sure you can feel it too, Jon. We are approaching some kind of apex. I just wanted to be prepared.'

Jon did indeed feel it too. Emotions were running incredibly high, relationships were fractured and, if Miss Darcy's spell were truly broken, they would be worse than ever. Jon did not feel ashamed to admit that he was afraid – afraid of a denouement that was coming faster than they could cope with. Would the mystery be able to hold steady until the blizzard broke and the police came? Somehow, he didn't think so.

'You were looking for the folder?'

'Of course. This folder seems to be the key to everything. It's all anybody can seem to talk about.'

'Did the king show you this folder in your private audience with him?' Jon asked. Was there anything in there that Matthew didn't want other people to see?

Matthew started clearing up his mess, picking papers up from the floor and forming a pile on the desk. 'He didn't wave it at me, if that's what you're saying. But it was right here, on the desk, the whole time he was talking to me. And now it has just disappeared. I've searched high and low. It isn't here.'

Jon started helping to clean. It was instinctual. 'Did you find anything of any interest?'

'No,' Matthew said. 'Most of these papers are . . . nothing. You know how he liked to scribble, or else they're just standard things that a king would have. Oh, where is it? There's only one thing I found which is even slightly odd.'

Matthew undid all the tidying he'd done by rummaging through his organised pile. He finally located the piece of paper he desired. He handed it to Jon without a second thought. 'I think it's a doctor's report. Dated a week ago.'

It was not actually one piece of paper, but a number of them stapled together. Jon flicked through them. It was indeed a doctor's report – a comprehensive breakdown of King Eric's physical and mental health. There were many paragraphs, spanning everything one could ever want to know about the king. Jon didn't have time to dive into it all, so luckily the doctor had summed everything up rather concisely in the final paragraph on the last page – 'For your age, you are a remarkably healthy man.'

Jon read it over and over and peered up at Matthew. The young prince was similarly perplexed. 'He was healthy?'

'Apparently so.' Matthew choked on something as he said this. He went back to his pose, with fists on the desk. 'If he hadn't . . . If he hadn't . . . He could have lived ten more years. Hell, he could have lived fifteen more, maybe even twenty. He could have sent himself a damn letter on his hundredth birthday. I don't understand . . . He told me that he was . . .' Matthew glanced around the room sadly. 'I have to be honest, Jon, maybe this was all more of a cathartic exercise. I'm sorry for the mess.'

Jon shook his head. It was all right, and the doctor's

notes were actually a good find, if a little invasive and offering up more questions than answers. 'Not at all, sir. Might I suggest a good rest? Leave this mess to me.'

Matthew thought for a moment and then nodded. 'Yes. Yes, I think that is best. I am exhausted.'

Jon knew the feeling.

Matthew left in silence, comically picking his way across the room as though he were playing a game of hopscotch designed by Picasso. Jon didn't watch him go. He was too busy thinking, and by the time he heard Matthew's muffled footfalls up the corridor, he knew what he must do.

There was something that Matthew had been entirely right about. The folder. The king was murdered and the folder had gone missing – the folder that seemed to have most of the motives inside. If this mystery were to end, they had to find the folder.

Where was it?

The king had spent all morning up here in his study – when Jon met Matthew just before dinner, he was coming from his private audience. So the king couldn't have had time to go anywhere other than the drawing room and then straight to dinner. If Matthew was looking for the folder so ferociously, and believably so, it stood to reason that he didn't have it.

Then where was it?

The king could have slipped it somewhere hidden, inside this room – somewhere Matthew couldn't find. But Jon knew most of the king's hiding places – they were crafty, but the king was usually so proud of them that he told Jon all about them. Also, the king would be clever enough to know that if anything happened to him, the study would be the first place the others looked.

So the king had put it somewhere else on the way to dinner? That was the only explanation, seeing as Matthew was the last one he saw.

No. Matthew was not the last.

Jon's eyes lit up. He knew where the folder might be, and with that, a potential end to this sorry day.

286

XLII

The Missing Motives

The sorry day did indeed end, but only in the inevitable sense. As Jon hurried through the castle, all the clocks struck twelve. All except the grandfather clock between the drawing room and Jon's makeshift study. It had stopped again. It was a new day – 26 December. Boxing Day.

Jon got to his destination, out of breath. He didn't even feel the pain in his gut any more. His body was nothing but pain, exhaustion and sweat. It was better not to think about it. He was too busy thinking about whether he would run into Miss Darcy on his journey.

Jon stopped for a second, allowing himself a few blissful breaths, and then pushed the door open to the pantry.

He remembered the panic in Martin's eyes when he had seen him earlier in the day. It was almost as if Martin had been caught doing something he shouldn't. Or maybe hiding something.

Inside, Jon turned on the lights. The pantry was much as it always was – a small cupboard room lined with shelves and packed with dry foods and non-perishables. Through a narrow conjoining passageway, a bizarre piece of connective tissue in the room, was a small wine cellar, where the fateful whisky had once sat ready to play its part. The light in the wine cellar portion of the room flickered and refused to come on. It was always temperamental.

Jon searched the food store more meticulously than he usually would in such an unremarkable room. Once again, he found the room entirely in line with how he had always known it to be. There was no evidence that anyone had been in here who shouldn't have been, or that anyone had engaged in any kind of suspicious activity. His eyes scanned the shelves – the tins, the boxes of cereals, the miscellaneous foodstuffs, the . . .

Jon inspected the cereal shelf. Something was poking out between two boxes of Shredded Wheat. He reached up and slid the boxes apart, slipping out the intrusive object. It was not the folder. It was a small book – *101 Fun Facts for Dinner Parties*. Martin had definitely been here.

Jon quickly emptied the shelf, starting to prop up the cereal boxes on the floor and then simply pushing them off the shelf. He did not stop until it was empty. Nothing. No folder.

'It's gone, isn't it?' Jon jumped and whirled around. Prince Martin stood in the doorway, still fully dressed, his hands in his pockets dejectedly. He started to cry. 'I can't even keep my promise.'

'The folder?'

'Yes,' Prince Martin said, coming into the pantry and

kicking one of the cereal boxes in desperation. 'Grand-father caught me just as I was walking past his office this morning. Really, I was hanging around. I thought maybe I'd get a private audience too. No, though. He just wanted me to take the folder and hide it somewhere. I didn't ask what it was, I just did it. I wanted to impress him – I know I'm not the favourite. Not for any of them. Not even my mum.'

'Why didn't you tell me you knew where the folder was?'

'My grandfather said it was top secret. He made me promise. He told me not to tell anyone as long as I lived. When he died, that almost seemed even more important.'

Jon smiled. 'You did a good job. I didn't even notice you had a secret.'

Martin snorted back tears and smiled too. 'I know. I'm good.'

'Are you sure you didn't look in the folder?'

Martin shook his head. 'It wasn't part of my job. I just put it there. Behind the cereals. It's gone, isn't it? Someone took it?'

Jon looked at the bare shelf, standing back and crunching some Shredded Wheat beneath his shoes as he did. 'Yes. It's gone.' Which of them took it? And where could it currently be? The answer was almost disgusting to him – any of them could have taken it, and it could be anywhere in the castle.

'I'm sorry, Jon. For lying to you. For being a dick.' Martin absent-mindedly picked his *101 Facts* book off the shelf and tried to put it in his pocket, as if for something to do. When it wouldn't fit, he simply shoved it into his waistband.

'It's alright,' Jon said. The wine cellar light flickered again out of the corner of his eye, attempting and failing to turn on. If he were to search the whole castle, he thought he might as well start there. He fished his torch out of his pocket and angled it into the surprisingly dark wine cellar. 'Can you do me a favour, Martin? Could you go and turn the lights off and on a few times? The wine cellar light is temperamental.'

Martin went over to the lights, while Jon moved through the small connecting alcove into the wine cellar. There was something in the air – an odd metallic smell. Maybe a bottle had been spilled?

The torch was dying too. He wouldn't be able to see much until Martin got the lights on. He was turning the lights on and off with abandon, but the wine cellar bulb was refusing to co-operate. Jon shone the torch around, and the beam caught on something on the floor in front of him.

In the pocket of light, the thing was beyond his comprehension. A beige colour in the circle of brightness – whatever it was, it was textured. Jon would think it was merely the floor, if not for a crease that ran the length of the circle and beyond.

An item of clothing, then?

He inched closer and closer, and as he did, the picture became clearer. His shoe slipped on something, a viscous liquid, but he hardly noticed. He was too busy peering at the light. The beige fabric was part of a mass that was on the floor, it seemed. What was it? He moved the torchlight along the mass.

And almost dropped the torch as it fell upon a face.

The light snapped on, but now he wished, more than anything, it would turn back off.

Jon started backwards from the horror in front of him and collided with Martin, who had followed him into the alcove in triumph. Jon turned to him, blocking the scene that would stay with him for ever. 'Your Highness, don't look. Do not look.'

But it was too late. Martin sidestepped him, and saw. He went white. 'Dad?'

On the floor of the wine cellar, propped against the back wall of wine racks, clutching an empty vial, lay the body of Thomas Crockley.

XLIII

A Tragedy in the Wine Cellar

Thomas Crockley's face, white and frozen in a choking expression, was propped up by one of his arms. Around his mouth was a pool of blood, which Jon had stepped in. His left hand was outstretched, palm closed around a long thin glass vial – like a test tube. It was empty.

A theory was already forming in Jon's mind. He wished the theories would stop.

He checked on the young prince. Martin was frozen, standing in the small connective corridor between the pantry and the wine cellar. He was silently panting words. Jon didn't know what he was saying.

'Prince Martin, you should leave.'

Martin shook his head forcefully. 'Is he . . . Is he . . . Is he . . . ?' *Is he dead?*

Jon would have given anything at that point to shake his head with the conviction that the prince had just displayed, but instead he nodded. 'Yes. He's dead, Martin. I'm so sorry.'

Martin held back tears.

'If you won't leave, can you stay here while I search the bod— while I look at what happened here?'

Martin said nothing, but an unspoken confirmation passed between them.

Jon turned back and let the tragedy in. Another dead body. Another soul to put on his conscience. Thomas Crockley – the man no one seemed to like, but everybody put up with anyway. Jon had to confess that he did not particularly like him either, but he would not have wished this upon him.

He examined the room now there was light in it and the shock of the main attraction had settled in. The floor of the room was a mess – some wine bottles had been dislodged from the rack that Crockley's back was rested against and they had rolled across the stone floor and were teetering there. Jon counted five wine bottles in all, and among them was something else. Smaller things – still glass. More vials – about twenty of them strewn all over. It was a miracle he hadn't stepped on one in the dark. He stooped down and picked one up. It was three-quarters full of some kind of colourless liquid and had a small cork in the top. All of the vials on the floor were the same.

He took a step back and inspected the floor again. The wine bottles had come from the rack, that was certain, but where had the vials come from? He glanced around to see the answer almost immediately. To the left of Crockley's body, in an antique drinks cabinet, a bottom cupboard sat open. A vial was wedged there so the door couldn't shut.

Jon went to the cupboard and opened it, having to shine his torch inside as he was blocking the light from the bulb hanging in the centre of the room. The cupboard was empty. Jon was about to look elsewhere, when he saw that the back of the cupboard seemed odd. It almost looked slightly misplaced. There was a seam at the back and Jon didn't exactly know how to comprehend it at first. But then it came to him – it was a false back! In their haste, someone had not returned it to its original position.

Jon reached in and pushed the false back aside to reveal a secret compartment. He shone the torch inside, and the light was reflected back to him from dozens upon dozens of jam jars full of the same colourless liquid as the vials. The missing jam jars from the kitchen, Jon barely had to time think as he noticed that, rather garishly, whoever was responsible for these jars had stuck labels on each and every one with a skull and crossbones emblazoned on them.

He took out one of the jam jars and held it up to the air. The liquid sloshed around inside. These were the jam jars that had held the king's favourite jam. Now it was clear what they held – the person responsible had made sure of that. He regarded the small and almost comical skull and crossbones watching him with hollow eyes.

Poison.

The vials were full of poison. A single serving of death.

And Thomas Crockley had an empty one in his hand.

Crockley. Jon put the jam jar down on the cabinet that had housed it and stopped over the body of Thomas Crockley. Although all signs pointed to him dying in the same way as the king, there was something infinitely more violent to how Thomas Crockley had died. Bleeding from the mouth. Face almost more pained. Crockley had gotten a more concentrated dose, it seemed.

Jon knew that he should search the body, and with one tentative look towards Martin (who was doing everything not to look), he inched closer. He searched Crockley's pockets, sad that he still had to quell his suspicions. But then suspicions were rife here. If this was what it appeared, Thomas Crockley had killed himself with the same poison used to kill the king.

There was nothing in any of his pockets except his wallet. Why he thought he needed his wallet for Christmas Day in Balmoral was anyone's guess, but it fit Crockley so well to have it close by. Jon opened it and saw that he was carrying his cards, no cash and not much else. Except . . .

One card drew Jon's interest. A white matte card that shone something gold in the dull light. Jon took it out. It was a business card embossed with gold lettering. *George Tippin, Sunwing Production House, Researcher*. It had this Tippin's phone number on the reverse. Jon thought back to what Crockley had said – this Tippin had put the business card on the bar and said Crockley didn't even have to say anything, he just had to take it.

Crockley said he'd ripped it up. Yet here it was.

He'd taken it. He was the leak to the production company.

The king had known. Motive.

Jon stood back, thankful to be away from him.

Crockley was the killer, and as he had seen the noose tightening, he had killed himself. After one last long smoke.

It was perfect, clean.

Jon slipped George Tippin's business card into his pocket.

It was almost too clean.

Crockley's eyes were open, eternally staring ahead of him, with that horrifying look on his face. If he had ingested the poison willingly, would he look like that? He'd already seen what a weaker dose of the stuff had done to the king, he had to know that it was going to be so much worse for him. But then maybe it was just so painful that he couldn't help but look like that. But not even to shut his eyes?

One final thing interested Jon. The blood was surrounding Crockley's head, just as though he had thrown it all up after swallowing the vial. So then, why was there no blood on his lips?

Jon could not investigate further – there was no time and he couldn't disturb the body, especially with Martin present. A new fork in the timeline presented itself in his mind. He knew he was right.

He hurried over to the young prince, careful to block the view of Crockley. As he spoke, he guided him out of the pantry by almost forcing him to backstep as he advanced. 'Prince Martin, I need you to do something for me.'

The boy's eyes showed no recognition, but Jon knew he was listening.

'This may be difficult, but I need you to gather your family and bring them all to the drawing room. If it is easier, don't mention my name. Tell them that Miss Darcy wants to see them.' They were outside in the corridor now.

Martin said nothing.

'Prince Martin, can you do that for me?'

Again nothing.

'Prince Martin?'

Martin snapped out of it. 'I'm sorry . . . um . . . Yes, I can do that. But why do you need everyone back there?'

Jon laid a supportive hand on Martin's shoulder. The boy was shaking. 'Because no one else is getting hurt. It is time to end this.'

'We don't have the folder. How can we end this?'

'Because we don't need the folder any more. I think your father just led us to the real murderer.'

XLIV

Jonathan Alleyne Sits Back and Thinks

Jon was back in the vacant study which had been temporarily bequeathed to him. Martin and he had parted company not five minutes ago. Jon had repeated his instructions to the prince and sent him to his task. Martin had faltered slightly, but then ran off, each step becoming more confident. The boy was stronger than he gave himself credit for. Jon didn't know how he hadn't broken at the sight in the wine cellar.

There was no real need for Jon to be in the study, but he wished there was. He could have convinced himself the stop was necessary and not just because he needed a sit-down. His body was starting to fail him – exhaustion consuming him. His legs felt like the jelly that he had made for the trifle, all those years ago, this morning.

He collapsed into the desk chair, and instantly his body thanked him. He didn't think he could ever get up again, but he knew he would. There was still work to be done. When he'd woken up this morning – or yesterday morning, he supposed, now – he had had such high hopes for the day. He knew it was to be difficult, and stressful, and tiring, but just as he had every day serving under the king, he was looking forward to it. He was looking forward to being a small part of something bigger. Once upon a time, this was a day as stuffed with joy and optimism as the turkey was with stuffing. He was a chef – imagine that? He cooked a fabulous Christmas dinner and was happy to serve the family he had loved so much. He not only had a king that he would have gone to the ends of the earth for, but he also had a friend.

In actuality he had been part of something bigger. Just not something he wanted.

Still, there was no use mourning the day – not when there were two very real bodies in Balmoral Castle to mourn instead.

Jon's thoughts went to Crockley. He was sorry that he had to leave him there on the floor of the wine cellar. Had Crockley really taken that poison himself? And, if the answer was yes, that meant that Crockley had killed the king, didn't it? Why would it not?

Crockley had taken the business card. He was the leaker of palace secrets and he was no doubt being paid handsomely for it. If the king had found out, then that was reasonable motive, but he just couldn't see Crockley having the backbone to kill anyone, let alone the king. Also, Crockley had tried to save the king, even if he'd had to be persuaded to do so. Why would he touch the king's lips if he knew they had poison on them? He could have killed himself then. Was it possible that Crockley had stumbled upon the killer and their supply of poison, and their only course of action was to kill him? So Crockley went into the pantry – why?

There was a reason, but it didn't fit with the timeline.

The red-coated figure came to his mind next. Jon had thought it to be Crockley, but it couldn't have been, could it? But it also couldn't have been anyone else. There was no one else in the castle. Unless it was one of his fellow family members. And how did this figure fit into the puzzle of the day?

First, Jon thought of Princess Emeline. At a swift glance, she was the least likely of the suspects. She had put up a discerning shield, that she didn't want to be queen, but Jon saw through it. Would she kill for the chance of the Crown, especially if she knew that another would be announced to be the recipient? He thought she was far angrier than she had wanted to appear.

Her twin sister, Maud, had given up her motive freely. A young Maud had fallen in love with a girl, and the king had sent this girl away. It was clear that Maud held a certain amount of sorrow for the event, particularly recently. Could that sorrow have turned to anger – could she kill her father, and what was more, could she kill her husband after he found out?

Moving on to Prince David, Jon thought back to the litany of allegations he had heard against the man in the past. The wax effigy of a man, melting around the edges: he was a deviant. He was a slippery character, the bitty fug at the bottom of a teacup when the bag had burst, but could he be a murderer? David was no stranger to seething jealousy, usually directed at his brother, but jealousy was not always enough to breed murderous intentions – killing the king would not move his chess piece up the board, so to speak. But then, maybe he would just do it for the chaos it would cause.

Matthew and Martin. The young royals. The next generation. The elders of the family didn't understand them, but they were doing their best. Jon had seen them grow up, from adorable babies, to troublesome toddlers, to the young men that strode the halls today. Their bodies coursed with royal blood. They had lost a grandfather and a father. It was hard to think that they had anything to do with any of this, but they were as intertwined as everyone else. Could it have been them, really? Jon thought he could discount Martin, and he so dearly wanted to discount Matthew – but was that naïve?

Princess Marjorie was akin to a ladyfinger biscuit – soaked in alcohol and hiding at the bottom of this sorrow-filled trifle. Ever since Jon had first met her, she had been a fickle and prickly soul. There was love in Marjorie and Eric's relationship – he had seen it himself – but it had waned over the years, as love so often does, and in its place came a special kind of resentment. However, Marjorie's motives were as elusive as the flames in the drawing room fireplace – changing and moving with such energy that one could be equally enchanted and mortally terrified. That, and she seemed to put up a very convincing performance when she thought the king was playing dead.

What was Marjorie's secret though? There was no way to know now, was there? A twinge of a thought. Jon went into his pocket and pulled out his collection of trinkets from the day – his torch, the security tablet, the family crest that someone had slipped into his pocket, his notebook and a folded pile of papers. That was what he wanted.

He rifled through the king's medical notes, not really knowing what he was looking for. Until he found it.

Jon found the strength in his legs to jump up in surprise. He couldn't believe it. This was it – and this explained a lot.

Jon stuffed everything back into his pockets. He couldn't stay still any longer, not after what he'd just read. It had been there all along – the key to Marjorie's secret. The key to her malice, and to her station. This was what the king had held against her.

He started to the door, and then turned back. He pulled the family crest back out of his trousers. He did not deserve it. He was about to accuse a Windsor of murder. He wasn't part of this family. And he was starting to realise that maybe that was a good thing. He left the crest on the desk.

Out in the corridor, the grandfather clock had stopped again. He hoped the servants would notice that in the days to come. He didn't think that he would be there to tell them. Miss Darcy would not like to hear what he had to say and would make sure that he was sent away as soon as the blizzard broke and the world descended upon Balmoral.

Where was Miss Darcy now? Was she still off somewhere chasing the white rabbit that was Tony Speck? The cold hard truth was that it hardly mattered. Jon had noted a surge of optimism when Miss Darcy entered the picture, but now she seemed to be an almost inconsequential addition. What was her place in all of this? Maybe there was none.

The drawing room felt soulless without the family inside, the only life in it being the flames licking in the fireplace. Jon found the room cold and uninviting, despite the imposing Christmas tree and the cheery decorations, so he gravitated towards the fireplace. Princess Marjorie was nowhere to be seen.

Wilson had found his way into the room at last and was stretched out on his back in front of the fire. Jon wondered where Churchill had gotten to. As if on cue, there was a tapping noise. A tapping against glass. Jon searched for the sound, finally finding the source at the window.

Outside, the blizzard was still raging. The sky had darkened somewhat – the night finally breaking through the clouds, but it was still abnormally light for past midnight. The source of the tapping caused Jon to run over to the window. Churchill was there, sat outside, looking cold and incredibly annoyed. Snow stuck to his fur. Jon opened the window and he ran inside, quickly finding his brother and joining him by the fire.

How did he get out? He must have slipped out when Crockley went for a smoke. It was a good job Jon found him or he would have frozen to death out there.

Jon slammed the window shut as the wind threatened to throw it back open. He locked it.

The two cats watched him – Churchill seemingly

already having forgotten his plight of a few moments ago. It was almost as if they'd assembled as part of the family, waiting for the great reveal.

Six royals – Matthew, Emeline, David, Marjorie, Maud and Martin. Two murders – the king and Thomas Crockley. More secrets than one castle could hold.

No sooner had Jon sat down in front of the fire than the door opened and Jon instinctively stood up. One always stood for a member of the Royal Family. What he did not expect was for all of them to start flooding in. David and Marjorie marched in, followed by a threesome of Matthew and Emeline, who had their arms wrapped around a freshly distraught Maud, who couldn't even walk for grief. Martin had told them about Thomas Crockley's demise – that was probably just as well. Everyone but Maud was still in their formal attire, even though Maud was still wearing her family crest around her neck. In fact, Jon could see all six family crests assembled – Matthew having put his suit jacket back on since the last time he had seen him. Six crests. Six Windsors. Murder among them, like one thorn growing in a field of daisies.

'Your Royal Highnesses,' Jon muttered, although not one of them gave a signal that they had heard the greeting. It was a second before Jon realised he had merely mouthed the affectation and it was more for himself than any of the souls joining him. His life was his duty, and he felt better for it, even if it were not noted.

Duty was so hard to forget. But one of these people had forgotten theirs, and soon they would reveal themselves. Soon? Yes. Jon saw the same realisation etched on every face, and echoed by his own. Of course everyone knew – the whole of Balmoral was singing it out, from the depths of the servants' quarters, to the highest parapet.

The end had begun.

XLV

Assembly of the Damned

Half past midnight is nary time for a denouement. By that time, one should be cosily wrapped up bed, in the throes of a pleasant dream. Most of Great Britain was, but the souls of Balmoral Castle were not permitted sleep, and only nightmares stalked the halls.

The influx of confused faces in the drawing room told Jon that no one living had guidance for him – all he saw painted on there was pain, loss and anger. It was seemingly an eternal truth that some of that anger was pointed towards him.

'I am starting to feel an odd kinship towards the humble sheep,' David spat, and upon seeing Jon gleefully added, 'I am assuming that makes you our sheepdog, doesn't it, Butler?' He guided Marjorie over to the seating area in front of the fire – from where Jon had just risen – and sat her down with an almost paternal force. Jon had to step back at David's scowl as he completed his task and rounded on him again. The weight of the occasion dragged them both down. 'You know, I am starting to wonder if Miss Darcy doesn't have a point and you are just playing around with all of us for your sick enjoyment.'

'Hear, hear,' said Marjorie, forcing the words through her ever-present alcoholic mist. It seemed the matriarch had used her time since they had all parted to do nothing but accelerate her drinking. She must have found some more alcohol beyond the drawing room in the interim.

'Uncle,' Emeline snapped, stepping away from her sister and her nephew. 'This is not the time for vendettas. Another tragedy has befallen us, and those of us' – she mouthed the next word, 'remaining' before returning to her usual diction – 'must remain steadfast. Thomas has . . .' She glanced at her twin sister and fell silent.

Everyone knew. There wasn't much of an outpouring of grief. It wasn't exactly the same as the king's passing. If Jon didn't already have a good idea who was the culprit of both killings, he would have had a hard time discerning anything usable.

Rather than remaining steadfast, David rounded on Emeline in complete disobedience as Maud provided a backing of sobs and wails. 'I am very sorry to hear about what happened to Crockley, but it is almost irrelevant. That common crabstick of a man was not fit to be in the same room as the king, let alone sully one of the halls with his own blood.' Maud's sobs and wails became ever-so-slightly more prominent in the face of this.

Emeline retaliated. 'Uncle, I have been holding back from speaking my mind because it is not the proper way to do things, but let me hold back no further. You are absolutely the most disgusting creature I've ever met in all of my thirty-nine years. You are abhorrent, cruel, cowardly, a shell of what my father was. The fact that

Windsor blood runs through my veins fills me with pride, but the fact that I share that with you almost makes me want to throw it all away. How Miss Darcy and the establishment at large have not forced Father to throw you out on to the street is beyond my comprehension.'

'Please,' Maud shrieked, 'stop it now. My Thomas is dead, Daddy is dead, we must get to the bottom of this before anything else happens!'

Marjorie exuded a little titter on the settee, and attention was once again on her. She seemed to grow at every pair of eyes that fell on her. 'Your Thomas. He was a cardboard man – a light breeze could blow his morals down. He does not deserve to share a thing with my husband, even if that thing is death.'

'You can say what you want about Thomas, Mummy,' Maud seethed, her tears steaming, 'but I did grow to love him. If you wished for something else for me, maybe you should have spoken up in the past, instead of lounging back and critiquing it.'

'It's so easy to be young,' Marjorie scoffed. 'All that fire and no worry of getting burned. I am here to tell you, Daughter, that that fire will come back to claim you in time.'

'Wait, where is Martin?' Maud said. 'Where is my son?'

'He went to get a glass of water, Mum,' Matthew said, his arm around her. 'You remember – he told us?'

'Going senile in your old age, Daughter?' Marjorie snorted.

'Shut up!' This was Matthew. It was so sharp and

unexpected that Marjorie launched an instinctual tirade of abuse back at him.

'Stop this, Mother. Matthew. Maud. Everyone!' Emeline shouted. 'This does not help us. This has gone on long enough. Jon, please, you have summoned us here – do you have a final verdict?'

Jon would have happily never said a word for the rest of his life, if he had been allowed to not say the next one. 'Yes. I believe I know who killed the king.'

The room dropped a few degrees. The only sound was the synchronised cats purring by the fire. Emeline guided her sister over to the left chaise longue and sat her down. Matthew did too. As if it were mandated, David and Marjorie came to sit on the right.

'OK then, Butler,' David said, all his sarcasm merely implied. 'Let us hear it.'

Jon did not even hesitate. He began. 'We all know what brings us here tonight. The king is dead. He died right here, on the coffee table we are all gathered around now. I think you will all agree that the manner of his death was very odd. In fact, he was murdered – murdered by ingesting poison, poison that was in that very whisky.'

He pointed to the decanter half-full of the tainted whisky.

'But,' David said, 'Miss Darcy said that my brother died naturally.'

'Are you really that naïve, David?' Marjorie snapped. The old man went white at his partner in snippiness betraying him. 'Tharigold is talking out of her arse. Even I can see that.'

'Continue, Jon,' Emeline said.

'We quickly ascertained that I was to investigate this matter, because the whisky was only unsealed in this room, and the only person who had cause to poison it was one of you. I couldn't accept it at first, but I have come to see throughout the day that one indeed was able to bring themselves to do it.

'You all have motive for the king's murder and that muddied the waters somewhat. I still could not see who had the most reason to dispatch the king, particularly just before his speech, which was going to announce who was to be the next monarch. We know that, from the updated succession rules, it could have been one of four of you. Princess Emeline. Princess Maud. Prince Matthew. Prince Martin. But I could not discount you two – Princess Royal Marjorie and Prince David – from the investigation either.

'I admit I did not know what to do after the private audiences. In fact, I did not know what to do until not long ago. Prince Martin and I were searching separately, and then together. Prince Martin had been tasked with hiding this elusive folder you have all mentioned. The king gave it to him and he hid it in the pantry. That is where we met and where we happened upon a tragedy in the adjoining wine cellar. Thomas Crockley – dead.

'By all accounts, it appeared as though Thomas Crockley had died by suicide. He had drunk a vial of poison, taken from a stash of jam jars of poison in a secret compartment in the drinks cabinet nearby. Thomas was collapsed against a wine rack, with a look of anguish

310

on his face, with blood pooled around his head, very much looking as though he had vomited it up. I believed Thomas Crockley had killed the king and then, when he realised I was close to figuring it out, he took his own life.'

'Well,' Marjorie said. 'There we are then.'

'No. It was perfect. A little too perfect. I started thinking about other options, different possibilities. Something just didn't make sense. If Crockley had known the extent of the poison, why would he have performed CPR on the king? He put his lips to the king's, he could have killed himself. Even more so, because in updated CPR, you are not even supposed to blow through the mouth. Crockley was so desperate to save the king that he did it anyway.

'So what if Thomas Crockley were murdered by the same assailant who killed the king. Crockley had been outside for a smoke. He had then come back to the pantry, because he wanted another. I had told him earlier in the day that there was a box of firelighters in the pantry if he needed a light. There, I think he must have happened upon the murderer making sure their stash had not been disturbed. I think Crockley threatened to unmask them, and the only course of action for this unknown was to kill Crockley.

'It seemed like Crockley was bleeding from the mouth, but only because of the angle of how he lay. I think the murderer lay him like that on purpose. I think, had I moved the body, I would have found that Crockley had been stabbed in the back with a fire poker. The murderer left the weapon in him so as to minimise blood flowing out, but then had to conceal the weapon. So they backed him into a place where they could slot the poker. Like a wine rack. The blood trickled only where it could. To the floor around Crockley's face – making it look as though he had vomited blood.'

'That's rather ingenious, Jon,' Emeline said, impressed.

Jon ignored her. 'So next I had to ask myself, who? Which I got to through the question – why? Why would the murderer be in the pantry and the adjoining wine cellar? And then I realised maybe it was to search for the folder of all of the family's sins. Where had the folder gone? Martin had hidden it in the pantry, as I said.

'Then I wondered – could anybody have known that? Well, there was really only one person. One person who'd had ample opportunity throughout the day to learn that. There is only one person who could have known that Prince Martin had done that, and one person who knew him well enough to know that he most likely had. This one person had not only seen his short conversation with the king, he had seen Martin come out of the pantry this morning, and he had walked in on my private audience with Martin when he was being cagey about the pantry.

'Isn't that right, Prince Matthew?'

'What?' Matthew scoffed as all eyes fell on him. The young man sprang up in something like disgust. 'I don't believe this. I've stood up for you all day, Jon, and this is how you repay me?'

'Tell me I'm wrong then, Matthew.'

Matthew's angry gaze broke like the break of day. He glanced to his family, and back to Jon. He had realised that it was futile.

'Tell me I'm wrong,' Jon urged. 'Please.'

XLVI

Spitting Venom

'There is something you all need to understand,' Matthew said, regarding them all in turn. Even David and Marjorie were lost for words as they listened to the young man speak. 'Firstly, it is not poison. It is venom. There is a very distinct difference, even if the outcome is rather the same.

'I will tell you what I saw, even if I now know it to be wrong. My grandfather was slowing, he was in pain — day by day, he was getting worse. We all saw it, we just wanted to deny it. One day, Grandfather called me to Balmoral. It was last spring, do you remember, Mother? You tried to come too, but he forbade it. "Just Matthew," he said.

'I didn't think anything of it. I was just happy to spend time with my grandfather. We had a lovely day, in fact. We went hunting. That day, we actually killed the stag that now hangs in the entrance. But when it was all done, the king took me to the wine cellar and he opened a secret compartment in the drinks cabinet and he showed me what was in there.

'I didn't understand. I picked up these jam jars with those comical skulls on them, full of poison, and I just

314

simply didn't understand. So all I could do was listen to my grandfather.

'He told me what was wrong with him. A rare heart condition called Ultimum Cor Subsisto. One day, it would claim him for its own, but until then it would creep up on him, slowing him down and impairing him.

'I asked what that had to do with the poison.

'"This is not poison, Matthew," he said, "so you may pick up your jaw. Not to you, anyway. To me, however – well . . . There is very little about me that is shrouded in mystery. You will come to know of that in time, when you take up my mantle and see that to be king is some-times very much a state of mind. The few secrets that I do possess I clutch hard and fast to my chest, never to let them go. A very select few know what I am about to tell you, as you should never advertise your weaknesses. I am allergic to a very specific type of wasp sting. The *Polybia plancalais* is not a particularly interesting wasp, but is the one that could end my life if it so put its mind to it. This is the sting ground up, the venom extracted, all mixed into this liquid you see here. This is my end, Grandson." The king regarded the jar, rolling the liquid from side to side. "How horrifying to hold such a thing in one's hand, but how freeing all the same."

'"What is it you ask of me, Grandfather?"

'The king looked regretful. "When the time comes, Grandson, when the pain is too great, when I am spent, I wish to bow out of this great performance on my own terms. I do fear that I am not strong enough, mentally, to do it myself though. Will you help me?"

315

'He was the king. He was my grandfather. What was there to do but assent? So I said yes.

'The king never asked me to poison him. I came to that conclusion myself. But not because of what he wanted. All signs pointed to him announcing the next ruler here now. I found a specific opportunity. I heard that he wanted a Christmas alone with minimal staff. The blizzard was what really sealed it for me. I would not get another chance like this. I knew I had to do this before I was announced as the next king.

'I never wanted to be king. I saw what it did to my grandfather. Shackled him. I had never wanted the throne – why would anyone? I want the complete oppo-site – I want to be free of the shackles of my family name and to live my life in peace. I wished to settle somewhere in the city, maybe meet a girl, get a real job and just live. The Crown is a life sentence to misery. Why would I ever want that? I tried to tell him this. But he would not listen. I loved my grandfather, and if he was dying anyway, why not accelerate the process slightly to my own gain?'

'Matthew . . .' Princess Maud said. 'Are you saying—'

'But, and here is the bit you will not believe, I couldn't do it. I did not poison the king. I had the vial in my hand, I brought it to this room, I held it over the whisky. But I just couldn't do it. I loved him so much. I would serve a life in chains to keep him in my life a little longer.

'But then he died anyway. Somebody else used the poison. And I knew that I was going to be framed. I went back to the pantry a few times throughout the day to check that the secret compartment had not been used. At least one other person knew of its existence.

'On one of my trips to the pantry, I found my father. I don't know how, but he'd discovered the compartment. He was gathering up vials to bring to everyone, to show them. I confronted him, I tried to make him see, but he would not. I did kill someone this day, but not the person I had first set out to. I killed my father – in much the way that Jon discerned. I did not set it up in this grand way to make it look like he drank poison. I . . . I did the deed and I ran. He must have somehow fallen into the wine rack. A convenient accident.'

That didn't seem right. The Crockley murder scene seemed engineered . . . calculated.

'So there it is. I killed my father, yes. But I did not kill the king.'

David sprang up. 'And after all that, we're supposed to believe you? You disgusting thing. You are the reason my brother is dead. You knew of this venom, you knew of his plot and you told no one. Why should we believe you when you say you didn't do it?'

'Killer!' Marjorie shrieked. 'Murderer!'

Matthew let the insults absorb into him and burst into tears. 'Of course, today I found a record of the king's illness in his study. Or, rather, I found a record of his perfect health. He wasn't ill. It was a test. And I'm not entirely sure if I passed or failed. You know what Ultimum Cor Subsisto translates as? Ultimate Heart Stop – he played me for a fool.'

Matthew might as well have been talking to himself for all the good it did.

'You failed, boy,' David said. 'I will see you burn for this.'

Maud jumped up to her son and, against everything, wrapped herself around him. 'Matthew, I believe you. I believe you. And I forgive you.'

'What are you doing?' Emeline said. 'Get away from him, Maud.'

'Cold-blooded murderer!' screamed Marjorie.

'No,' Maud screamed. 'You don't call him that.'

'He poisoned my husband!' Marjorie yelled back.

'No, he didn't.'

'How do you know?'

'Because I did,' Maud shrieked.

XLVII

The Devil's Daughter

Maud stepped in front of her son, shielding him from Emeline, David and Marjorie's ire. She didn't have to – none of it was focused on him any more. Jon forced himself to take a breath – this was something he had not foreseen. The kind and sweet Princess Maud – a murderer. What had happened to these people?

'Sister?' Emeline said, blinking through tears. 'What are you . . . Why are you saying this? Are you protecting him?'

Maud matched her twin's tear with her own. She shook her head. 'I did it. I put the venom in the whisky. I was so angry.' Maud ran through a quick version of what she had told Jon. Her trip to Plymouth. Poppy. The revelation that the king had been responsible for sending Poppy away. 'I was poisoned myself. Poisoned by this uncontrollable rage at the life torn away from me. Matthew is right – we are in prison. Father played the guards' game. And right then, I blamed him.

'I knew something was wrong that day Matthew came back from Balmoral. He was different, distracted. Next time we came here, he was even more so. I resolved to keep a close eye on him. I followed him one day to the

319

pantry, then to the wine cellar. I saw the secret compartment, I saw the venom. It took me a while to piece it together.

'I saw the opportunity of this Christmas Day in just the way Matthew had described. But I didn't have time to develop misgivings. Plymouth happened last week. My anger was fresh. I poured the venom into the whisky, and when I did, I felt something like peace. It wasn't until later that I realised quite what I'd done.

'I remember watching my father die and thinking, *I did that. I poisoned him. Now all I have to do is get away with it, and then that's it.* Such was the set-up of the day, by his own design. I didn't know that we would fixate on the whisky so easily. I didn't know that Emeline would suggest Jon investigate matters. But it was all right for the first few hours — my guilt had not claimed me yet. I'm sorry, Jon, but you weren't exactly much of an opponent, at least at the outset. I started to think that maybe I could get away with it, but then the guilt consumed, followed by the remorse. What had I done? What had I really just done? The anger was so fresh, the desire for revenge. My wanting to cover my tracks became less of a thrill and more a desperate attempt at keeping some kind of family. I had resolved to tell you, Jon — when I told you about Poppy. But then Thomas. And now my boys. It's all too much.'

'Your boys. The most important thing to you,' Jon said.

'I may not have loved Thomas as hard as I loved

Poppy. But Thomas gave me my two sons. And I would do anything for them.'

'You would even confess your sins when one of them is called into question.'

Maud nodded. 'I did it. I killed my father. I killed the King of England. What came over me? I do not know. But I do know this: whoever I was when I poisoned the whisky, that person melted away, she got to leave this place and Maud remained.

'A scared little girl without a father.'

'I do not desire pity. I desire the exact opposite. This is my confession, and I will tell the police this to the letter when they arrive. I desire them to lock me up and throw away the key.'

Emeline fell to her knees, retching. 'Oh, dear God in heaven, Maud . . . what did you do?'

Matthew stepped out from behind his mother, regarding her with distrustful eyes.

Marjorie gave a husky chuckle. 'Oh, Daughter. My poor sweet thing.'

This was not the reaction anyone expected.

'Is it not the way when you have twins? One gets the brains, and one gets the looks. I always thought you were the lucky one, but you may have appreciated a brain cell this once.'

'Mummy?' Maud said, with an alarm that stretched as far as her confusion.

'Do you honestly think your father would see you upset, or hurt or heartbroken? He wanted for you whatever you wanted for yourself. He would never hurt you.

The irony was that by his inaction he would have. You would have been tossed to the wolves, child, if your little affair had come to light. So I was the one who took the action that the king did not. I commanded the establishment to send your little plaything away, Eric didn't even know I'd done it until she was gone and I ended the discussion by declaring her dead. Poor poor little Maud, your poison found the wrong cup.'

'What?' Maud said. 'Then Father was—'

Marjorie chuckled again to interrupt but offered nothing further.

David, always the first to get his opinion registered, was evidently still trying to catch up. Once he had, he surged forward, towards Maud. 'You bitch. My brother!' He grabbed Maud by the neck and thrust her against the wall.

Maud cried out in pain as David dug his long fingernails into her neck. 'Ahh . . .'

David gripped even harder. 'This is for my brother, you disgusting creature!'

'Uncle!' Emeline was on him then, pulling at him, trying everything to make him loosen his grip. David did not relent, with a surprising amount of strength. Matthew could only watch, much as Jon did, frozen there in absolute shock. Emeline finally got one of David's arms to move, but the old man quickly batted her away. Emeline went colliding into the wall – her head giving a heavy thunk – and came to fall on the carpet, groaning.

Marjorie gasped as Maud's face turned purple. David was killing her, whether he meant to or not. Jon glanced towards Marjorie – she was letting this happen, she had the means to stop this. Jon knew it because he knew her secret. He had read it plain as day in the king's medical notes.

'Princess Marjorie, stop this,' Jon said. 'Please.'

Marjorie was suddenly completely sober. But she was wrestling with her secret, not wanting to let it go after so long.

'I am going to watch your life drain from your eyes, just like you watched my brother's,' David yelled into Maud's face, as she struggled for a breath that could not come.

Emeline was groaning on the carpet. Her forehead had a large cut on it and blood was running down her face.

'Your Royal Highness! Princess Marjorie!' Jon yelled, as Maud's eyes started to flicker like the light of a dying star.

For the first time that day, Marjorie saw him, and saw what was happening with complete clarity. Jon knew he didn't have to step forward and do it for her then.

Jon had stumbled upon the secret without knowing what he was looking for. The king's medical files.

'David, stop it,' Marjorie said.

'No, Margey, you will thank me in the end.' He sounded evil, like a devil had taken him over.

'Stop it!'

Jon had found her secret in a place he'd never have expected. King Eric's medical notes, in a part labelled 'Sexual Health'.

Maud spluttered. Everyone in the room seemed to know that this would be the last splutter.

Who knew King Eric's sexual health would be such a mystery. But it was.

David did nothing but tighten his grip.

Jon saw Marjorie realise that this was her last chance. And that was good. Her secret would come out finally.

Because the king was barren. He could not have children.

'They're your daughters,' Marjorie shrieked.

XLVIII

The Common Family

David faltered and that was enough. His grip softened on Maud's neck and she was afforded one small, life-saving gasp. 'What?' He let go of Maud's neck, and she slumped to the floor, spluttering and heaving, David's white handprints on her scarlet neck. A cut was gently seeping blood where one of his sharp fingernails had dug in to her flesh. It wasn't clear if she had heard her mother's admission.

Her twin had, however. Clutching her bleeding fore-head, Emeline had jumped up. 'Mother, what are you saying?'

'Yes, I would rather like to know the same,' said David, who had such a scowl on him, Jon wondered if he would not have preferred a bullet through the heart.

Marjorie looked upon her daughter with emotionless eyes. She had retreated behind her shield once again. 'I mean precisely what I said. He is your father.'

'No,' Emeline said definitively. 'No. That's ... That simply can't be. That is not true. That ... Oh God.' She doubled over.

Maud was propped against the wall she had fallen

against, and was panting, but she had wide eyes. She understood too.

'What the hell are you talking about, Margey?' David said, going to her. 'This can't be real. They're not my daughters. Look at them. I would have known . . . I would have—'

Marjorie snorted. 'I think you did know, you bloody idiot. I think everyone knew. Really. Deep down. No one wanted to see it though. Come on, David, you know what we used to get up to. Back in the time when Eric was only ever invested in his station. You know what we used to do. Have you never put two and two together? Eric could not have children. We tried and tried for so long, to no avail, and then the years ticked by. Everyone was panicking – a king must have heirs. The clock was running out for me – our union came just in time. David, how have you not seen it before? Did you not want to see what was in front of your eyes?'

'This cannot be true.' Princess Emeline rushed to the waste bin in the far corner of the room and proceeded to bend over and throw up the entire contents of her stomach. There was no way to fake her utter disdain for the man that was now purportedly her father. 'Mummy, this is perverse. Even for you.'

'Oh shut up, Emeline. Eric was not giving me love, not giving me affection, not giving me a child. What was I to do but stray, and I thank God that I did because it gave me what I so desired, what we all so desired. And if I hadn't strayed, you wouldn't have had a chance to exist at all.'

326

'What are you spewing now?' Emeline spat.

'Your father was dry, Emeline. As dry as the Sahara Desert. Useless to me. And, more importantly, useless to this country.'

'Shut up.'

'You see, there really was no option available to me. Now, either David is your father, or you choose to believe you were immaculately conceived. An altogether idiotic notion.'

Emeline faltered, seeing the options her mother was giving her. 'I need to see official documentation of this lie before I will even hear of it again.'

Marjorie looked to Jon. 'Well, investigator, I assume you have it.'

Jon shuffled uncomfortably on his feet. Emeline was staring at him menacingly as though he were the guilty party. Wordlessly, he took the king's medical notes out of his pocket and handed them to the princess.

Emeline quickly rifled through the pages as David paced up and down. Maud was still on the floor, but her breathing was finally getting softer. Soon, Emeline had found the pertinent paragraph and let out an eternal yowl. She fell to her knees and threw the notes into the air. 'No, no, no, no, no.'

'It's true?' asked David. 'It's really true?'

Emeline did not respond but to pummel her fists into the carpet. 'How could this happen? Who else knew of this travesty? Did Father know?'

David was about to combust.

Marjorie tutted. 'Of course he knew. Just like

everyone else, he stuffed it deep down. At first, anyway. Like his core was shielding him from the heartbreak of it. And then his core began to crack, and the truths leaked out. He started to openly confront me about it, and then he decided to get himself looked at, checked out – a full medical analysis. He could not hide from the truth then. And he saw the only option was his brother.'

'How could you, Mother? How could you do such a thing to Father? He loved you with all his heart! And now, he is gone. And we are left with a stinking wretch who is no father of mine. I want a full DNA test. I want to make sure this isn't some horrible trick.'

Marjorie shrugged.

So that was it. Marjorie's secret was out in the open. Eric's killer revealed. Crockley's killer revealed. There was nothing left. Done.

Wait. No. No, it wasn't. In some ways, it was too neat, but in others, it was too messy. There were still things that didn't make sense. The figure in Jon's red coat. Who was that? Was it really Thomas Crockley? And if so, why? Why turn the power off?

Jon thought back to the Russian doll on his mother's shelf. The Russian doll that in the end revealed itself to be her heroin stash. Jon had thought, throughout this investigation, that he were constantly getting deeper in a theoretical Russian doll. He was gradually getting a layer deeper, a layer deeper.

But now he saw that that wasn't the case at all. It was

the exact opposite. He had been in the smallest Russian doll and he was trying to get out. Maybe there was one layer left above him. Maybe there was . . .

It was odd that through all the chaos of the room, through Emeline and David and Marjorie still shouting at each other, Jon was distracted by a small tinny ringing sound to his right. He looked down towards the sound to see that Churchill the cat was up and scratching at his collar with his back leg. The tinny sound was what was irritating the cat. Jon bent down and slid his collar around.

Someone had clipped one of the metal family crests to Churchill's collar. Why would someone do that? Jon unclipped it and Churchill gazed up at him in thanks before collapsing belly up in front of the fire again and purring. Jon stood and turned the family crest over and over in his hands. Curious.

Jon thought back to the figure in the red coat, and then he thought of Miss Darcy and Tony Speck. Where were they? Things were unravelling even more than usual. He could really use them. He then remembered that he could see exactly where they were.

He dropped the crest on the table and pulled out the security tablet. Red dots filled the screen – the usual ones. And . . .

'Oh my God,' Jon said. It was so quiet he was surprised that everyone managed to hear and they all fell silent. The red dots. Miss Darcy still in the tower. Tony Speck still in the watchtower. The family and himself in the drawing room. But one more dot.

'How is that possible?' Jon said, realising where the red dot was.

'What is it, Jon?' Who said that? He didn't care.

'There's someone in the empty study.'

XLIX
Badge of Honour

Jon was out of the drawing room as fast as his failing legs could carry him. He ignored all the questions coming from the remaining family members and slammed out into the corridor. He chanced a look at the tablet – there was still a dot in the study.

How was this possible? How could someone else be here? He had been checking the tablet periodically and there was no one. Speck had shown him the tablet at dinner, and one fact was empirical. No one else was here.

But there it was, on the screen. The thermal dot of a person. The king was dead. Crockley was dead. Miss Darcy and Tony Speck were worlds away. Who could this possibly be?

He passed the stopped grandfather clock and was on the corridor with the study. Now there was no escape for whoever was in there – he could see the door, and he was upon it in mere seconds.

Jon steeled himself, with one final look at the tablet. The dot was in there.

He barrelled through the door, almost throwing it off its hinges. And stopped. The room was empty. He stared at the tablet. Still a red dot in the study. He wheeled around – behind the door, under the desk, anywhere a person could hide. No one.

He went back to the tablet. Still a red dot. But only one. Surely now there should be two. Now he thought of it, though, he had not made a dot in his journey between the drawing room and here. How was that possible? The map was thermal, wasn't it, and he was quite sure he still produced enough heat to show up.

Jon threw his hands up in frustration, and his eyes fell on the desk and what he had abandoned there. Suddenly he understood, and the rules of the day came crashing down around him. He had been so naïve, so stupid. He'd believed everything he was told.

What Jon saw on the desk was the family crest he had found in his pocket. He had thought the king had secretly given it to him as a gift, but no, nothing so quaint. If he had to guess, he'd say the actual person who had slipped it in his pocket was Tony Speck, most likely while they were standing outside the dining room, just before he had shown Jon the security tablet.

Jon picked up the family crest in one hand and held the security tablet in the other. He propped the tablet on the windowsill and opened the window. The wind ripped it open, but he didn't care. With one swift motion, he threw the crest outside. The red dot in the study travelled about ten metres away from the castle walls.

The read-out wasn't thermal. And the crests weren't decorative. They were trackers.

Crockley and the cat – Crockley had never been

outside, Crockley's crest had been put on Churchill's collar and Churchill had been outside. So then why didn't Matthew mention it? Because Matthew didn't know about the trackers.

Something Matthew said came back to him. Matthew had killed his father, but not made it look like suicide. Someone else had. Someone else had also transferred the tracker to Churchill.

The figure in the red coat.

The biggest revelation came crashing into Jon as a gust of wind whipped through the open window. He dutifully closed the window, grabbed the tablet again and started hurrying back to the drawing room. Anyone who didn't have a crest would not show on the read-out. Any number of people could be in the castle.

He started flying up the corridor, before skidding to a horrified halt. The grandfather clock ahead of him was opening. As the person inside unfolded themselves out of it, the pendulum started swinging again and the clock resumed. The person was at first all limbs, and then a familiar face roared at him. Speck.

Jon was frozen as Speck launched at him. 'You stupid meddling moron,' Speck snarled. 'You couldn't just leave well enough alone, could you?' Speck gripped him and managed to lift Jon off the ground with ease, his hands around his neck, just as David's had been around Maud's. Jon felt as though Speck were going to crush his windpipe. He braced himself for it. 'You have ruined everything.'

Death did not come. In fact, Speck's grip loosened.

Jon opened his eyes in time to see a blur of a boy come out of nowhere, jumping on Speck's back.

'Get off him!' Martin clawed at Speck's face, careful to keep hold of something in his hand. A folder. *The* folder. Martin had found it.

Speck got Martin by the back of his shirt and easily swung him over his shoulder. Martin slammed into the wall and yowled with pain. Speck started to go back to Jon, but there was a loud, distinctly feminine clearing of the throat.

All three males looked around. Miss Darcy stood there, in front of the grandfather clock. Unlike Speck, who had been cramped and squashed, it seemed as though Miss Darcy had just strolled in from a leisurely soiree. 'Boys, really. We don't want to get blood on the carpets, now do we? Shall we all return to the drawing room? I'm sure the others are getting worried.'

Jon coughed and heaved. 'I'm not going anywhere with you. We are not going anywhere with either of you.'

'Might want to rethink that, Alleyne,' said Speck, laughing. He pulled out a small silver handgun. 'The cavalry's here now. Best get back to following orders, yeah?'

L

Truth and Consequences

The drawing room was almost exactly the same as when Jon had left it. After all, he had only been gone for maybe three minutes. Emeline and David were still frozen in a paused argument. Marjorie was still watching them, with a glazed expression. Maud had clawed her way up the back of the nearest chaise longue and was still recovering from her assault. Matthew was standing there, not knowing what to do. The cats were still living their greatest life by the fire.

At Jon's entrance, they barely moved. At Martin's entrance, only Maud made a sound as the young prince rushed over to her. And then, suddenly, the room came alive as Tony Speck and Miss Darcy stepped in. At first the family seemed almost happy to see them, and then they realised that Speck was carrying a gun.

'Speck? Miss Darcy? Where have you been?' Marjorie asked.

They remained standing by the door, blocking the exit. This was an incredibly bad situation – Jon knew it, Martin knew it and it was just starting to dawn on the wider room. Before Martin had run over, Speck had grabbed the folder and now held it like a grand prize.

335

Miss Darcy ignored Marjorie. She just stood there, with her arms behind her back and that godawful smile on her face. For someone so young, she inhabited the malice of millennia. 'Why is everyone still up? It's very much past everyone's bedtime.' She sounded like a nightmare warden of a children's home.

'What is the meaning of all this?' David said, finally drawing his eyes away from Emeline – his daughter. 'You're blocking the door – it's a little menacing.'

'Jon,' Emeline said, 'did you find the person in the study?'

Jon glanced from her to Speck's gun.

Miss Darcy nodded to him. 'Go on, investigator.'

'We have been tricked,' Jon said slowly, thinking that every word could be his last. They were toying with them – the lions were now the mice being played with. 'Your family crests have all had trackers placed on them. What I thought were heat signatures were really just the crests.'

Realisation dawned on Emeline's face, 'That means—'

'Yes,' Jon said, 'I think these two have been here the entire time.'

'Would anybody mind catching us up?' Tony Speck said. 'This is the grand reveal of our great investigator, I assume?'

Jon refused to speak, so Emeline ended up giving a quick summation of what had been talked about. She still seemed to hold out some hope that Miss Darcy and Speck were here for friendly reasons. When she said that Matthew had killed Thomas Crockley, Miss Darcy nodded as if she'd already known, but when Emeline said that Maud had killed the king, Tony Speck snorted with derision.

'Is that so?' he mumbled. 'Well, I'll be.' What a reaction to finding out that your king, the one you had sworn to protect, was dead.

'Well done, Jon,' Miss Darcy said. 'I didn't think you had it in you. Well, Maud, you will be handed over to the police immediately when the blizzard breaks. Matthew, you as well. There is no room in the monarchy for naughtiness.'

'Naughtiness?' David said. 'Naughtiness? Are you playing with us? What are you saying that for? They are murderers. We should be restraining them, locking them up, keeping them under surveillance until the police get here.'

'You are under surveillance,' Tony Speck said simply. 'You have been under surveillance every moment since arriving at the castle.'

This took a moment to sink in. 'What?' said Marjorie.

'Well, I didn't keep it from anyone,' said Speck matter-of-factly. 'The new security system. I simply didn't correct you when you made a mistake. You thought it was outside the castle. Rather, it was inside. We have cameras in every single room and trackers to easily track everyone's movements. That's how we already know everything that happened. We know that Maud poured venom into the whisky, we know that Matthew killed his father, we know that David took this folder here from the pantry. So I took it back. I must have dropped it when I had to hurry to hide from you, Alleyne.'

'I found it in the hall. I couldn't believe my luck,' Martin said, as if to confirm this.

Jon shot a look at David. The old man shrugged. 'You almost caught me with it, Butler. You thought you saw me slip something into my pocket, and I was cagey about it. That's what I wanted you to see. It was easier for me to slip the folder back into my room. Simple misdirection. I didn't have time to look in it then. And when I went back to my room, it had disappeared. Seeing as I had stolen it originally, I could hardly raise any alarm about it.'

Jon didn't care. 'If you saw all of this, why didn't you stop it?' He said this towards Speck, but really it was more to Miss Darcy.

Something Speck had said out in the corridor stuck out to him – *You have ruined everything*. There was something else – something final, that he was missing. Why did he think it was back in the king's medical notes . . .

'Let us see what was in the folder then. All of your secrets, yes? Sounds juicy. Let us see your ruination.' Speck opened the folder and tipped the contents all over the floor. Sheets upon sheets of paper fell out and scattered. Eyes followed every single one, but there was no need. They were all exactly the same. They were all entirely blank. 'Seems like the king played you all. Just to see how turgid you all are. He never had any evidence.'

Eyes darted across the pile of blank papers. A realisation set into each and every one of them. The folder was empty. Nothing. Their secrets had been revealed by none other than themselves.

They must have all looked a picture, as Tony Speck started to laugh, but after the final piece of paper fluttered out, he was confused. He grunted like a caveman, and turned the folder in his hands. 'There was meant to be one thing of note in here.'

Martin laughed and held a swath of papers up. 'Do you mean this?'

'You little bastard.' Speck started advancing towards Martin.

'This is the king's speech, right? The speech he was going to give to us?' Martin said, dodging out the way of Speck's grasp. 'The one that's going to tell us who is the next king?'

There was a soft murmur that ran through the remaining royals. Even after everything, they were still so bloody interested in who was to get the Crown next.

Speck cornered Martin so he couldn't run away and reached for him.

'Tony, stand down,' commanded Miss Darcy. 'The damage has been done. I have been thinking that maybe everyone here deserves to hear the speech anyhow.'

The confusion was palpable as the muscleman wheeled around to her. 'Are you sure? That is a change of—'

'Just let them read it, Tony. It is time they all understood. This has gone on long enough.'

'Fair enough, boss. Little Marty, why don't you read your little speech out for the whole class?'

Prince Martin held up the papers and started to read,

before Speck interrupted, 'Wait. How about you let Alleyne read it actually? The poor chef must be feeling rather useless about now. After all, he has been prancing around all day playing detective and it seems all his working out was wrong.'

Wrong. Wrong. Was he still getting it wrong? There was one final doll to break through so he could see the sky.

Prince Martin did not quarrel with Speck, he merely plodded over to Jon and handed him the sheets of paper, before returning to his original position.

Jon thumbed through the sheets — typed up on the king's typewriter. He thought it gave a speech an air of occasion if it was typed on a typewriter. Jon automatically started to scan passages that jumped out at him, and before he knew it, he was enraptured in the voice of the king, speaking to him from beyond the grave.

'Well?'

Jon shook himself somewhat. The room was looking back at him, expectation weighing everyone down. From what Jon had just read, he thought they would not like what they heard, and he would not like the painful truth that this speech would unearth. Something was still horribly wrong here, and for some reason, he knew the identity of 'what' was locked within these pages.

He looked to Miss Darcy and Tony Speck, still projecting a powerful unity, and they nodded almost in sync.

Jon cleared his throat and began to read.

LI

The King's Private Speech (Not Safe for Television)

'The Royal Family. Such an enigma, yes? We spend so much time thinking of what the public thinks of us that we forget what we think of ourselves. So, for now, let us not be royal. Let us be just a family. Can we allow ourselves that? If we can, then it is an honour to spend a Christmas alone with this family of mine. Christmas is a time for happiness and joy, but it is also a time for forgiveness and looking towards the future.

'So firstly, let me wish you all a Happy Christmas. Let us take a moment to remember that we all love each other – no matter our place in this familial unit, and no matter how the sands of time have eroded us, our values, our devotion to one another. We are the Windsor family. We always have been, and we always will be – no matter history or future. And on this most white Christmas, let us be united and happy. So cheers to all. I love you – remember that throughout the next few minutes. And Happy Christmas.

'Now, to business, as some may call it. I'm sure the majority of you have some idea what the rest of the content will be about, and if you don't, I would wish you to just take a look at me, and that may give you some idea. I talked with some of you earlier this morning, in private audience, about various matters. In some ways, those were my parting words as king. In other ways, they most definitely were not. You see, I did indeed say what I needed to say to you as individuals, but not what I needed to say as a collective. When I get onto all that, remember the start of this speech. Remember, all, the love – but I am about to say some things that will be hard to hear.

'When I look at us, we have become something I would not wish on anyone. We have become engorged, dependent, out of touch with our subjects. Look at us – family. What have we become? The world has grown up outside of these walls and we remain the suckling piggies we always were. We allow others to wipe our mouths when we drool, we allow the government to dictate whom we park our rears next to at dinner, we allow the law to pervert itself for our own ends. Family, I want you to see that today could be the start of a new chapter.

'Daughters, I have done you a grave disservice. I feel like I have not been your father enough – maybe I have been here, but I have not protected you from the wolves at the door. Sometimes a bird must thrust his little ones out of the nest, but we didn't. We couldn't. And now I see that my nest may not have been my nest at all, but I want you to know that whatever happens, whatever happened, I am your father.

'Thomas and Anton (although he is not here), we have cultivated an atmosphere where your actions are constantly questioned. Whether you are genuine or just hungry for money and fame is a topic debated constantly in these halls by many, even regarding Thomas, who has been married to Maud for years and has children with her. I do not partake in this line of inquiry, but I do question one thing – your desire to be a part of this grand show, and that, I feel, is deeply odd. (And to Emeline, on this note, I am sorry that Anton is not here for you today. I did have a hand in it. I promise next year, he can come to Balmoral and have his Test and become part of the family.)

'Grandchildren, what have we done to you? Facing you is a life of red tape. You will be adored by millions, but hated by millions too. That is no one's fault but our own. And the worst thing is that I believe in some way you want this. Whether to fulfil yourselves or please us – you want this. I guess it is just as well, as it would seem you do not have a choice.

'Marjorie, my dear Marjorie, what has become of you? I think I know – the burdening of the soul. That has ended now, after what we discussed earlier. You do not need to shoulder it alone, my love. Then again, it is not just that, is it? You have become high on the decadence of everything – and now that need is consuming you. You are heading for a crash, you know it, and instead of slowing, you are putting your foot down on the pedal. Maybe in some ways you see that the crash is inevitable, and you only want to get there faster – but why, love? Because you cannot change, because the road you chose is what you deserve? I do not know your reasons, but

I have to watch your descent. That is why you are not queen, my love, and I'm afraid you never will be.

'And lastly, David, my little brother. What is there to really say that we haven't said already? I welcome you back into my home, I risk the sanctity of the Crown on this wretched thing called familial blood, and for the first time, I am forced to confront a dreadful mistake. You are that mistake, brother. Why do we have such a bond that I can allow what you have done to happen? I look at you and see everything that the monarchy should not be. And then the word comes – my little birds witter in my ear, that thing you have run from for so long. The truth. How it must keep you up at night, dear brother – how it must feel looking in a mirror – looking at what you've become. It's despicable, and we cannot do a thing about it. Is it better or worse, knowing that you will never face any consequence – better because you never have to truly face it, but worse because you will never feel atoned? A disgusting crime, encased in amber.

'This family is warped beyond repair by the pressures of the Crown. We are all something horrible, capped by the promise of full potential. And outside of these walls we would struggle to even survive. We are all attached to this thing called the monarchy with tubes and threads. We are on a kind of life support. And it does not let us think straight.

'This is why you don't really know what I'm going to say, not completely – because your intrinsic design does not allow you to. I do not mean to sound accusatory, even though I know that is undeniably how it is coming

344

across. For the old guard, we have not known anything different for so long that we cannot fathom something so drastic. For the young, you cannot fathom the true follies of everything we have experienced. For everyone outside of these walls, the British public, who grow weary of our excess, they cannot fathom the true price paid.

'What I announce today, I announce for not only us, or that public we serve so candidly, but for the generations to come, who do not need certain aspects of this world bearing down upon them. As I have said before, the world has grown beyond our bounds, and we are stuck in time, drinking our tea, and having our little meetings, and eating our buffet lunches, and turning a blind eye to the fact that we are all old and tired and we simply do not fit any more. We are an old puzzle piece, to a world that accepted us lost and has moved on to five more jigsaws since ours. But enough of the laborious metaphors. Maybe I am simply writing this, speaking this, to delay the inevitable. But we all know where I am bringing this from, we have all seen it, all felt it. We can deny it until the royal geese return for the summer, but we know.

'That is why I stand before you now – not only to announce my abdication as king. I am here to tell you that, at the soonest convenience, I will stand before the establishment and give my recommendation – the recommendation for the complete and absolute disassembly of the British monarchy. This ends, as all things do. Let us be descended from musty, fragile kings, but let us not be those kings ourselves – we do not deserve it, and the grand truth is that no one ever did. The world has moved on without us – maybe if we start walking now, we can try to catch up to it.

'I hope you all agree. But my resolve is as set as the foundations of this castle – the Royal Family is over.'

Jon stopped reading and realised he was shaking. He chanced a look up to the room, to see every face painted with the same shock and awe.

'He printed his name— Eric Windsor.'

LII
Kingmaker

Marjorie was the first to crawl out of the pit that the late king had cast them all into. 'Can he do that? Could he have done that? Dissolved the entire Royal Family?'

'No,' Miss Darcy said, 'the King of England could not have done that. But he would have tried his darnedest. And he would have created a fuss, and unrest, and somewhere, someone along the chain would have told someone else and it would have snowballed into something beyond anyone's control. He would have sowed his seeds of doubt throughout the entire family. One by one, you would have come around to his way of thinking.'

'Father was right,' Maud said. 'He was always right.'

'There is no way I would have signed off on such stupidity,' David said. 'The monarchy is sacred. It is what makes Britain Britain.'

'Well, you wouldn't get a vote anyway, Uncle!' Emeline snapped. 'In Britain, criminals can't vote. I say, we should dissolve the monarchy. Today is a great indication of the rot at the core of us.'

'Oh shut up, Emeline,' Marjorie said. 'We all know you don't mean that.'

'Grandfather,' Matthew muttered. 'He wasn't going to name me. He never was. He was going to save me. He was going to save us all.'

'It doesn't matter,' Marjorie said, 'because he couldn't do any of that. He was just a stupid old man, believing he had more power than he did.'

'He was the King of England,' Martin said.

'King is just a title, little one. The ones who put you on the throne have all the power.'

It was the most sensible thing Marjorie had said all day, and with the power of those words, Jon finally saw everything as it was – he wished he could go back, but he could not. And there it was, the thing he had read in the king's medical notes, under a heading marked 'Ailments'.

No allergies.

Dear God.

He spoke slowly and clearly, as though those words emanating from his mouth were his last. They very well could have been. 'Your Royal Highnesses, you are not seeing the great picture here. You are not seeing the centre of the puzzle box that we find ourselves in.' Jon turned to Miss Darcy and Tony Speck. He had known that they were acting strangely. Ever since they had entered the room, with all their pomposity, he had somehow known the truth he was about to speak. Tony Speck had attacked him out of anger for 'ruining everything'. 'Princess Maud did not kill the king. Nobody in the family did. The king had no allergies. You killed him. The government.'

'What a wild accusation, Jon,' Miss Darcy said, as though she were remarking about the weather.

'I poisoned the whisky though, Jon,' Maud said, her voice still hoarse. 'I killed him. I confessed.'

'No, Princess Maud, you didn't. You put wasp venom in the whisky. Wasp venom that would do nothing to anyone who wasn't allergic to it. And he wasn't.'

Miss Darcy said nothing, but Tony Speck betrayed her by almost looking proud. 'Maybe everyone should move over to the far end of the room, hmm?'

'What is Jon saying?' Maud asked, as Speck advanced towards everyone and they obeyed him, coming to join Jon on the other side of the fireplace.

Miss Darcy had to break her silence for this. 'Do you really think the king could be taken down by a silly little wasp? The allergy was fake. Sometimes a king needs a weakness to lure danger. Danger we can act upon. So we sowed a little seed, and waited for it to sprout. We told the king he had a little allergy. It was simple enough – he never actually reads his doctor's reports. We never knew it would spiral into this, though. It was the king himself who actually procured wasp venom – set about a plot to end himself by asking Matthew to kill him one day. We didn't know. We also didn't know Matthew, and subsequently Maud, was going to use this day to act.'

Maud, once believed to be unbreakable, broke a little more.

'Excuse me, but then how did the king fall?' David asked, shepherded to the back of the group. 'If he is not allergic to this polybius wasp thing, or whatever – how did he react to it? We all saw him drink the whisky and then die.'

Tony Speck, still practically vibrating with glee, stepped forward. 'It was never the whisky, you imbeciles. You've been chasing around, looking for the wrong clues, and the wrong information, and the wrong people. Jonathan Alleyne, you are quite simply awful at this.'

'No,' Jon said, 'no, I'm not. Because I think you still would have tried to cover this up if I wasn't here. If I was doing such a bad job, why did Miss Darcy have to return to the castle to fix your mess?' He backed up with the rest of the family.

Speck's smile flickered. He was right. 'OK then, Mr Detective. If it wasn't the whisky, what was it then?'

As if by chance, Jon's foot hit on something as he backed up, and he glanced down as the familiar soft tinkle of 'God Save the King' filled the room. Jon knew what it was, even before Speck bent down and retrieved it. The puzzle box – Interregnum, making its presence known once again.

Could it be . . .

'Garlic,' Jon said.

'The wheels are turning,' Speck said.

Oh no. It was that simple. He had devoted his day to the wrong weapon. It was in front of his face the entire time. 'The king said he smelled roast potatoes and garlic. Martin gave the king the present, but who procured it for Martin?'

'That's far enough,' Speck said to the family. They

had all shifted to the back of the room, by the fire. Emeline, Maud, Martin, Matthew, Marjorie and David. Jon was ahead of them, confronting Speck.

'You see,' Miss Darcy said, 'opportunities like this one don't come around very often. The king announced all by himself that he wanted all staff to leave him alone this Christmas. I suggested Balmoral after a quick look at the forecast. Totally remote. We could not have the king announce what he was going to announce. So I got to work. I suggested to Martin that he give the king a puzzle box for Christmas – I even offered to get it myself. It had the rather unique attraction that it sprayed a smell when one of the stages of the puzzle was completed. It was easy to drain the liquid out and replace it with a scent of our own. Arsene, the gas version of arsenic. Or at least our special version of it. You get someone to breath it in, and, well, it isn't pretty. It has the rather unique property of smelling exactly like garlic. I gave him a very slight dose – it would not have killed him quickly, but it would have made him feel so unwell that he would have had to instantly retire to his room. His speech unspoken. He would have died a few hours later. To all outward perception, it would have been quite peaceful. And most importantly, it would seem natural.

'But there was an unforeseen development. The whisky laced with a perfectly harmless venom, except for the fact that when it is mixed with our particular strain of arsine it acts as an accelerant. The king died as soon as he drank the whisky. Speck saw it on the cameras, at the security station in the watchtower, and instantly called me back to fix the mess you'd all made.'

'So, you see, in a roundabout way, the old codger killed himself,' Speck said. 'Silly bastard.'

'You watch your mouth, security man!' David spat.

'No,' Speck snarled, 'I think we have now progressed to the point where you should watch yours.'

'But Thomas Crockley,' Jon said, 'he exhibited signs of being poisoned too.'

'Close contact with the king would have produced nothing but a minor headache and some sniffles,' Speck barked. 'Sorry, Princess Maud, but I think your husband may have been a little soft.'

Miss Darcy ignored them. 'We had to course-correct somewhat, in an effort to regain some control of the narrative. It didn't work quite as well as we hoped. Jon was an awful pain, darting around the place all the time. At one point, the camera in this room malfunctioned, so we had to get manual eyes on it from outside. Martin just had to go and spot that someone outside, and we had to shut the power off to cause a distraction. A couple of falling dominoes later, that led to me having to go outside and reveal myself to Jon. I thought maybe it was for the best anyway – I was absolved from killing the king due to timing, and I could try to pass it off as a natural death.

'I could not have foreseen that young Matthew would go and do something as stupid as killing Thomas Crockley. Speck had to go and clean up after him, make it look like Crockley had killed himself. Of course, then murder was back in play.

'So here we are. Who would have thought that killing a king would be so much of a faff?'

'But why?' Matthew said. 'Grandfather is right, he was fundamentally and categorically right. The world has left us behind. Why is it such a bad thing to watch the monarchy wither and die like a forgotten houseplant? I don't understand.'

'Boy,' Speck chuckled, 'do you know how much money the Royal Family makes the British government a year? It's insane. Tourism, national pride, a real sense of history. That all evaporates if you aren't around, filling your bellies in grand castles.'

'This is all this is about – money?'

Miss Darcy decided to take this one. 'To an extent. It is also about the unity that royalism brings. Europe hates us, the rest of the world is going the same way after we fumbled with the pandemic – if we turn on each other, we will have nothing left. But, yes, mainly, the money.'

'You're sick,' Matthew seethed. 'This is sick. Now your secret is out, what makes you think we will not revolt, tell everyone of what the king intended, start telling people ourselves? You allowed Jon to read the speech – are you not concerned you just unleashed the jar of whispers yourselves?'

'I do not think anyone in this room will say a word for the rest of their lives. We have the security tapes from today – taped and sealed and ready to send away to wherever is worst for you. At some point in time, every single one of you has incriminated themselves in some way. We have the ammunition to take everyone down.

353

If anyone speaks up, we will use the correct information to frame them for the murder of Eric Windsor.'

'What about the death of Thomas?' Maud piped up.

Miss Darcy did not even miss a beat. 'I will tell you a little secret now that I have been biting my tongue on for years, Your Royal Highness. No one gives a shit about Thomas Crockley.'

Speck laughed. 'There is one issue here. And as always, it is Mr Jonathan Alleyne. What do we do with this little cretin? Such a bloody nuisance. Someone seize him.'

Now the murmur was one of confusion.

'What?' Matthew said.

Tony Speck looked to Miss Darcy and back, as though the royals were missing something incredibly obvious. 'Can someone please seize Jon Alleyne?'

Jon stepped forward. 'Nobody needs to seize me. I am not going anywhere.'

Speck scratched his moustache. 'I will never understand that stupid loyalty you have.' He picked up one of the high-backed bony chairs and placed it in front of the fire. 'Sit down.'

'Why?'

'Sit down or I will make you sit down.'

'Now, look here . . .' Surprisingly, this came from David.

'Martin, what are you doing?' Maud asked.

Martin flew at Speck again, much as he had in the corridor, but this time he was not aiming for his back. He was aiming at his outstretched hand with the gun in it.

Speck realised a little too late, pointing the gun at Martin but not able to pull the trigger. Martin collided with the gun and scrabbled for it. Both of them went sprawling on the floor. Martin was lighter and up on his feet again in no time. Jon felt utter relief as he saw Martin had the gun in his hand.

Speck was up too then, but Martin pointed the gun at him. 'I'll shoot.'

Speck howled with laughter. 'OK, little man. I believe you. Trillions wouldn't.'

'If I kill you, then it is all over,' Martin said shakily. He did not seem convinced of what he was doing, but he was doing it nonetheless. 'One way or the other.'

Speck made his way over to Miss Darcy, so that Jon and Martin were now the only ones in the centre of the room, as if they were the battle line. On one side, the establishment, and on the other – the Royal Family. Martin made the gun follow Speck, but with every inch, it seemed as though he were finding it harder to move, his resolve shaken.

'I suppose that is a solution,' Miss Darcy said softly. 'Kill us and chaos reigns. Or you may choose the right option, the quintessentially British choice. You can choose inaction. You can live your lives out as they have always been – royal. Matthew will inherit the Crown as his grandfather once intended. The rest of you will be doted upon. Emeline, you will be the new king's most trusted aunt, an icon. Anton can be by your side, we will allow that. Maud, any previous infractions will be forgotten. Marjorie, you will be given all the wine and cheese you like. And, David, you will not be exiled, and we will make all these little frivolous accusations simply disappear – thoughts of prison or New Zealand just a bad dream. Or you can go to New Zealand with a massive payout. We really don't care. Doesn't it sound like heaven?'

'It sounds like hell,' Matthew responded. 'I am a murderer, and I want to pay for it. I want to be locked away, put in shackles.'

'You never wanted to be king, young Matthew. Isn't the Crown shackle enough for you?'

Matthew went silent.

From Jon's vantage, he slowly saw the royals change. They fully understood their situation for the first time in a long time, maybe more than any royal ever had. They were stuck – well and truly. The only person who was not stuck was Martin, because he still held some kind of power.

Jon saw them all in turn. Emeline would not meet his eyes – she saw the power of the establishment. Maud apologised to Jon through glassy eyes – she knew that the only way to save her family was to bend the knee to those who decided the king. Matthew opened his mouth and closed it again, words failing. David was looking mightily confused, but also had a hint of opportunity in his eyes. Marjorie seemed the soberest she'd been in years, her gaze fixed on Miss Darcy. It was clear that she had lost and her younger opponent had won. Marjorie had tried, however misguidedly, to protect the family. It had not worked.

Martin saw his family too. And the resignation of them.

'No,' Martin said. 'No, we are not going to bow to you. We are the Royal Family.'

'You are the Royal Family because we, the commoners, said you were, child,' Miss Darcy spat, before signalling to Speck. 'It is time. I'm growing tired of this.'

Speck faltered for a second, then seemed to realise he did not really care and put two fingers in his mouth and wolf-whistled. For a moment, nothing happened. Then a great thundering of footsteps came down the hallway and the drawing room door opened. Two security men rushed in and took their places either side of Miss Darcy and Speck. They both had guns raised, but that was not the most notable thing about them. One of them was dressed in Jon's red coat. The other was dressed in a kilt.

'What the hell is this?' Marjorie squealed.

Martin was looking around with panic in his eyes, but to his credit, he did not lower his gun.

'Do you honestly think,' Miss Darcy said, 'that we would leave you all alone up here at Balmoral on Christmas Day? Jon, meet your spectres.'

'Thanks for the coat,' the one nearest Jon chipped.

The other seemed intent on justifying the kilt to everyone. 'It was supposed to be my day off.'

Jon's two ghosts.

'You see, you never really had a choice. Any of you,' Tony Speck continued, as if nothing had ever happened, still under the sight of the barrel of his own gun. 'But we will permit you one, Martin. You see, you don't have a motive either. We have nothing on you. And we have a problem there next to you. Jonathan Alleyne. Kill *him.*'

Jon could not believe what he was hearing. They really wanted Martin to kill him. He forced himself to look the boy in the eye – exude a united front between bone, muscle and brain. Inwardly, however, he was panicking – he did not think the boy would do it, but it would not be the first time he was wrong that day.

'Martin is not going to kill Jon,' Maud said to the establishment.

Martin, however, faltered. His eyes scanned the perimeter of silent armed foes – with all the power in his hands to turn them into allies.

'Do it, Martin,' Marjorie said. She didn't sound like she enjoyed the proposition as much as Jon thought she would have.

'Mummy, no!' Maud screamed.

'What – we are royal, we can't survive in the world, we can barely survive in here. My vote is do it, kill him. I'm not happy about it, but there it is. You want me to be the bad person, well, I've had plenty of years' experience.' She sniffed and reached for a glass of wine that wasn't there. To counteract the failed gesture, she just repeated, 'Shoot him.'

'Shoot him, child.' Of course, it was David.

'No, this is not what we will become,' Maud said.

'I'm afraid it is,' Miss Darcy said. 'Martin, kill the chef or we kill your family. We'll start with your mother, then go to your brother, then you can choose, I suppose. Who cares? But you'll be last. Then the Crown goes to your extended family. Those in the wings. I bet some of them are gagging for a chance at the Crown. It'll be bad – the Balmoral massacre, someone broke in on Christmas Day and killed the whole family – but we endure. Maybe we can call it a terrorist attack or something, further some other cause.

'But you kill Jon here, and we continue as if nothing happened. King Eric died peacefully in his bed. Thomas Crockley's body goes away – no one'll miss that bore anyway. You get to live your life in luxury. There is really no choice to be made here. We are offering you death or a life of adoration. Just kill the chef.'

Jon knew that the tide had turned at this, but he did not falter. He did not stand up, he did not run. Where would he run to? Martin seemed convinced and Jon's fate was sealed. Who would not do anything to protect their mother? This was not Martin's fault – being put in this position. Jon did not hold it against him. He shifted his gaze to Miss Darcy. 'You were meant to protect him. You were specifically tasked with protecting the king.' The tears were streaming down his face – it was all catching up to him.

'No, Jon, you never understood. You always say, "For the king and for the Crown", don't you? You fail to understand that sometimes it is: "For the king *or* for the Crown".'

Martin turned the gun on Jon. He whispered to Jon then, 'I am so sorry. It'll be all right. I hope.' And Martin's jacket opened slightly to reveal something in the waistband of his trousers. A yellow book that Jon had last seen in the pantry. *Fun Facts*.

Something Martin had said throughout the course of the day threatened to be remembered, but did not reveal itself. Jon ignored the thought, he didn't have time. He did not begrudge the boy's choice, but that did not mean he had to look at him when he did the deed. 'I did used to say "For the king and for the Crown". But I got it wrong. How about this, "For Eric Windsor".'

'Do it.'

'But . . .'

Jon nodded to Martin – *It's all right*.

'DO IT.'

The gun erupted and everything went black.

LIII

The Answer to the Riddle

Jon was somewhere else. This somewhere was incredibly peaceful; there was no sound, except waves lapping against a beach of shimmering sand. It was dark, yet not cold. A light breeze was playing on his face. Was this home – not Barbados, not Balmoral, but a real home? Did he have to die to finally see it? He would not see anything with his eyes closed.

His eyes flung open, as if he had just been having such a terrible nightmare that his body had activated him. The fiery pain in his stomach didn't relieve – it was not part of the nightmare.

He suddenly remembered where he was. The drawing room of Balmoral. He was lying on the floor in front of the fire – now extinguished. The room was dark.

Shot. Shot. Yes – he had been shot. That was the unbearable fire in his stomach. He tried to raise his head to look down at himself but could not. The pain threatened to send him back to his nightmares. He did not need to see to know. Blood, and lots of it. He could feel it leaving him. He did not quite know how he was alive. There were two searing pains: one in his gut and one in his lower back. The bullet must have gone straight through. Remarkably, it did not hit anything vital.

There was someone pacing around his field of vision. Two steel-toed boots were walking up and down, up and down . . .

'Are the Royal Family secure?' A familiar voice. Tony Speck. On the walkie. 'Yes, I'll get rid of the body.'

Jon stayed as still as possible. Martin had shot him. Martin knew where to shoot someone – isn't that what he'd said at dinner? Martin wanted him to survive. But how was he going to get past Speck?

'Wait,' Speck said, answering Jon's question, 'what do you mean, the rascal's gone? Shit . . .' Speck stopped. Jon was as still as he'd ever been, holding his breath. 'Jesus, OK. Well, Alleyne's not going anywhere. Think he's dead already. I'm on my way.' And with that, Speck flew out of the room.

Jon wasted no time. He reached up to the arm of the chaise and used it to pull himself up with half of his strength. The other half of his strength was used to keep the scream from rising up his throat. He had to stop once he was in a seated position to assess his wound. It was indeed a mess – he could barely see it through the scarlet stain on his shirt, but he could feel the hole the bullet had made.

How had he been shot? This was not how anything was meant to happen. By now, he was supposed to be in bed, after a happy if strenuous Christmas Day. As he watched, the scarlet stain grew bigger. He was dying. If he had to go, let him not die here in the drawing room.

Jon pushed himself up to a standing position. He'd thought that the tumour was what would kill him, but now he felt as though his life was in his hands every time he placed a leg down on the floor, and a fresh stab of pain thundered along his spine. But as he got to the door, a rumble of footsteps came from beyond it, as a group of people walked past. Jon braced himself, but they did not stop. The footsteps disappeared the other way, down the hall.

Balmoral was alive once again. But not in the way that anyone would have wished.

Jon waited until the footsteps had disappeared completely before he slipped out into the hall. Much like the drawing room, it was quiet and dark – the veins of the castle were indeed pumping bodies around, but none were here. That was good, because Jon did not wish to see anyone.

He made his way down the hall, passing the portrait of the king without even looking at it. He did not need to see it again, the image was already burned into his brain. The king in the portrait was not looking upon him fondly.

Jon wondered where the Royal Family had been taken, but then realised that they could not be his burden any more. He was dying, and they had killed him. Loyalty needed to have an end.

Jon made good ground. There is something to be said about the dying finding it in themselves to perform incredible feats before death. A surge of adrenaline. Jon's incredible feat was to return home. So he did.

He had to hold tight onto the bannister, as he descended the stairs down into the servants' quarters. He was going to his kitchen to die, and once he had finally completed his journey down the stairs and through the archway, he thought that death might want to hurry up a little.

The pain was so great he rested against the wall next to the archway, looking upon his magnificent kitchen. He had left Barbados all those years ago, looking for his place in the world. This was it, this kitchen, right here. He started to cry and when he finally knew it was over, his knees buckled and he slid down the wall until his bottom connected with the cold floor. Blood was pulsing through his shirt – he didn't know if it had sped up or slowed down, but it was still seeping.

It did not matter.

Jon wiped his eyes, and looked upon his kitchen without tears now. He looked at the cabinets that he had to fight to get installed, the ovens that each had their own quirks and follies, the fridge nearest to him where . . .

There was something slotted peeking out from the crack between the counter and the top of the fridge. A red envelope. Then Jon finally remembered . . . His Christmas card, from the king. He had never opened it. How odd – if he had never collapsed here, he might have forgotten about it completely.

Jon forced himself forward so that he could pluck the card from its slot. The red envelope he hadn't seen for what seemed like years. He had been so busy at the time. He opened it and was startled when a tightly folded bunch of papers, bound together by the folds, fell to the floor. They almost fell beyond his cognition, lost to the void, but stayed within reach.

Jon opened the card first. A simple white card with a cartoon smiling lion on it dressed as Santa Claus. The king's style. He opened it to see the king's familiar handwriting.

To Jon,

You know of that old fable I always tell. The common family going to the zoo to see the lions. The first time I heard that story was my first ever memory. My father was sat at my bedside and he told me the story and he asked me exactly what I always ask – which is the most important part of the story? He kept telling me the tale until I got it right. I did eventually. And I resolved to tell that story to my family.

The lions in the zoo, the common family, the glass in between them, separating them. I always ask my family which is the most important. They never understand, they name one or the other. The lions, the family. They couldn't see. Not one of them understood that I referenced three entities. The lions, the family and the glass in between. The glass in between, Jon.

Maybe it is time for that glass to break?

Happy Christmas, old friend. Don't ever let anyone tell you that you are not home.

Eric Windsor

Jon didn't quite understand until he retrieved the papers that had fallen onto the floor. He unfolded them. A copy of King Eric's speech, but this time the king had signed it. This was the evidence that Jon needed, but was it too late? He was over, done. Maybe this plot was too.

No.

Not today.

For Eric Windsor.

Jon heaved himself upwards, pushing with his legs and his back so that he thrust himself up the wall until he was on his feet again. As he stepped away, he noticed that he had left a red smear up the white wall. It hardly mattered. He was going. He took one last look at his kitchen and then was off, down the corridor.

He was glad to see that his red coat was still on its hook, having been replaced who knew how many times. He put it on with some difficulty, his stomach roaring at every movement of his arms. Finally, it was done, and he stuffed the speech into one of the pockets.

He braced himself. And opened the door to the outside.

It had stopped snowing and the sky had somewhat cleared, as if the snow were merely here to view the passing of a king and had left once it was done.

It was time for Jon to leave too.

Where was he going?

He didn't know. But he was going to make a stop first, if he got that far. He needed to visit the watchtower.

One Year Later . . .

Epilogue

Jerusalem

'Jerusalem' was playing on the radio on a perpetual loop. The costumiers would not stop circling him, but finally they seemed to be done. Matthew Windsor stepped down from his perch, away from the mirrors surrounding him. He did not like to look at himself any more. The room was full of his family and personnel, ready to shepherd them all to the Abbey. The coronation was set for three o'clock. The crown was heavier than it looked.

Matthew saw that, for the first time in a long time, nobody was looking at him. Quickly, he took off his red velvet cap with fluffy white trim. He placed the crown back on its cushion. He could do it now, and he would. There was an open window across the room, nobody in the way. He could get there before anyone realised, and then he would be out – whether he would be able to climb down, or whether he would just fall and be done, he did not really care. He took a step towards the window, but instantly felt a hand on his shoulder.

Maud clutched her son, giving him a hug and a small shake of the head. That was not the way. Matthew relented to her and went back to his plinth, as the costumiers returned, his chance gone.

Maud was worried about her boys, and she went to find her other. She found young Martin sitting in the corner of the busy room, on the floor, with his head on his knees. The boy had never been the same since he had to do what he did. Maud could not imagine the amount of strength it had taken him to do the deed required of him. She slid down the wall next to him, ignoring the squawks of the personnel muttering that she would ruin her dress. She touched Martin on the knee.

Martin got up and stormed away. He could not even look at her. He could not even look at any of them, most of all himself. He pushed his way through tens of samey-looking men and women, all with coils in their ears and all only here to keep them in their place. He was going so fast that he bumped into Anton Blake, who was hugging Emeline. Blake looked down at him and smiled, and Martin stalked off again.

Anton Blake knew he had picked the right ring when Emeline's eyes had lit up with that same fire he had seen in her before Christmas Day last year. She was getting it back slowly, but there were still glimpses of the utter sorrow that they all felt. Blake himself felt it too, although he knew that Emeline was not telling him everything of what had happened that Christmas Day.

As they ceased their embrace, Emeline searched Anton's eyes. That expectant glint was there – the problem was that she had no idea what was being asked of her. She had said yes to marrying him, hadn't she? What else was there? He had been all she wanted. Now he was just another man who she couldn't tell her secrets to. Anton went to kiss her, but she gestured towards the drinks table and made her way over to it. It wasn't that she did not love him any more, it was just that she was different now. She wished she could get therapy, but of course they would never allow that. It wasn't her fault she was changed. It was his fault he was not. Maybe that wasn't fair, but there it was.

At the drinks table, as Emeline obtained a glass of water, Marjorie ordered an aide to pour her two glasses of wine. Marjorie took the wine thankfully and immediately disposed of half of one of the glasses down her throat. She went back to her seat in the corner of the room and placed the full glass next to her, looking to her side. He wasn't there, he would never be again. David had decided to take the payout, signed an NDA willingly and buggered off – he'd run away from his family and gone back to New Zealand. She had been forgotten again. But at least she had an extra glass of wine and a seat. She was becoming an old woman and should be allowed a nice sit-down once in a while. She would have to do plenty of bloody standing up later on in the Abbey. She drank the rest of her wine, and her legs seemed to get a little better. She drank his glass in one and they got even stronger. And now she had no wine – she almost wished she'd gotten Eric one too. Suddenly, before she could cackle loudly, someone came and plucked her glass from her hand, and refilled it.

Miss Darcy left the bottle with Marjorie. It couldn't hurt – well, any more than it already had anyway. Things were going well, on such a grand day – almost too well. Tony Speck was by the door, talking into his earpiece. It seemed important, but he smiled at her anyway. Nothing to worry about. All royals were accounted for. Miss Darcy regarded them all. And saw, almost as a premonition, that the day would go swimmingly.

'Jerusalem' began again.

George Tippin had gotten into the office early that morning, even though the entire production company had been ordered to stay at home and watch the coronation with a notepad in their lap and a Dictaphone in their hand. Tippin somehow couldn't bring himself to care though. He used to be so driven, enthusiastic, brazen even. That drive had taken him to The Gentlemen that day years ago and had secured the company the biggest source of royal information that they had ever seen.

Something had happened in the last year though, since the king's death. Thomas Crockley had gone quiet, disappearing at the same time as the king and the chef. Since then, the Royal Family had been on lockdown – more secretive than Scotland Yard, less penetrable than the Tower of London. *The Monarch*'s ratings had soared as rabid royalists looked for their royal fix, but information was incredibly light. Tippin spent most of his days travelling the country, chasing whatever scraps of knowledge he could. And he was dealing with the fact that something didn't sit right with him – what had happened last Christmas up at Balmoral?

The official line was that the king had died peacefully in his sleep, the king's brother had actually decided to travel back to New Zealand after falling in love with the country, and Thomas Crockley had decided to withdraw from the public eye to focus on his business. That was all widely accepted. It was the chef that Tippin was confused about. It was not reported even slightly, but Jonathan Alleyne, the king's private chef, had been dismissed on Christmas Day 2022 as well.

Tippin had to search Alleyne's name in many different databases before he found the very odd and intriguing words: Wanted for questioning. After further exploration, he came up with nothing but dead-ends. He had to employ the services of a friend who worked over at *Crimewatch* to dig deeper. His friend came back to him white-faced and troubled. He told Tippin that Alleyne was being hunted down with the tenacity the government would hunt a terrorist. But even unlike a terrorist, there was a Protocol 219 order out on Alleyne. When Tippin said he'd never heard of 219, his friend had laughed. No one had, because it didn't exist outside of being attached to Alleyne's name. What was Protocol 219? That was comparatively easy to uncover – Protocol 219 was 'shoot to kill'.

Did Alleyne murder the king? And if so, why was the government not alerting the public to this dangerous individual? Why had Tippin needed to dig to even find Alleyne's name, let alone his status? What had really happened on 25 December 2022?

Tippin put some coffee on, switched on the television in his office and flipped over to the coronation build-up. He knew he should at least have it on in the background.

People were flooding into Westminster Abbey, while commentators were talking about the eagerly anticipated arrival of the new king. Tippin slid over the box his assistant had collected with three months' worth of post piled up.

He rifled through letters that didn't look at all important, until he happened upon a beefy padded envelope with a wobbly handwritten address in green felt tip, fastened closed with a single piece of dirty masking tape. If it wasn't so ramshackle, Tippin might have overlooked it, but as it was, he ripped it open and upended the contents onto his desk.

Five unlabelled CDs clattered off his desk and finally a small USB stick came to rest on the top of the pile. He shook the package and peered inside. Nothing else – no note, no explanation.

He took a sip of coffee and glanced down at the pile of post next to his desk. He should ignore this and go back to his boredom. His eyes rose to the television. He should watch the Royal Family arrive at least. He should do literally anything other than putting this no doubt virus-ridden USB stick into his computer.

He put the USB stick into his computer.

It was a 256GB stick, full to the brim with video files. Most files had timestamps and locations on them. They were all jumbled. West Corridor East View 09:00 to 10:00. Bedroom 37 13:00 to 14:00. East Courtyard South View 23:00 to 0:00. Et cetera. Et cetera. It just went on and on, but as Tippin scrolled down, he saw a video file labelled 'Play First'.

He clicked on it.

A close-up of a face filled his computer screen. Old. Defeated. Broken. The man on the screen was a shadow of what a man should be. His thick beard made him look almost unrecognisable.

'Hello,' the man rasped. It seemed that it pained the man to talk. 'My name is Jonathan Alleyne.' What — how could this be . . . But it was. Under all that greasy hair lay the former chef. Tippin's eyes flitted to his office door. He quickly dashed to it and closed it, before sitting back down and inching closer to the screen. 'I'm sure by this point you know that I am wanted, so maybe you won't listen to me. I used to be an optimist, but even optimists die, and I'll almost certainly be dead by the time you see this. I got shot, as you'll see. It's infected. And that's not even mentioning the tumour. That doesn't matter though.

'You have no reason to believe what I'm about to tell you. But I've come to you with evidence — evidence of what really happened. I've sent you every video file from every security camera, inside and out. Yes, inside Balmoral Castle — they had cameras everywhere.

'Everything I'm about to say will be backed up by the footage. I'm telling you simply in the interest of time, and because I was there. So are you ready to hear what really happened on 25 December 2022 at Balmoral Castle?'

'Holy shit . . .' Tippin whispered.

Alleyne took a break to splutter his way through a coughing fit. When his eyes raised to the camera again,

Tippin could see some of the spark of life that he'd seen in Alleyne's photos.

Alleyne did an odd thing then. It was almost imperceptible under his beard, but Tippin realised that he was seeing it reflected in the chef's eyes. Alleyne smiled, and said, 'First, I need to tell you a story – a story about a common family who went to London Zoo to see the lions . . .'

Acknowledgements

To my agent, Hannah Sheppard, and the team at DHH Literary Agency, my UK editor Francesca Pathak and Orion, and my US editor Mark Tavani and his team at G.P. Putnam. I really couldn't have asked for a better team behind me where everyone believed in this idea and worked to make it what it is today. Thank you all!

To The Northern Crime Syndicate – Trevor Wood, Judith O'Reilly, Fiona Erskine, Rob Scragg, Rob Parker, A.M. Peacock and Dan Stubbings. It's amazing to be a part of such a fantastic group of Northern writers, and I always feel like I have somewhere to turn if I need advice or just a good chat!

To the #SauvLife crew – Francesca Dorricott (or Francesca May as many know her), Jennifer Lewin and Lizzie Curle. These guys are always the first people I tell about exciting things, and I'm always so happy when I hear exciting things from them too!

To my mum and my sister for their constant support. And to my partner Aimy, who read *A Murder at the Castle* at a pivotal point when I was losing a little bit of hope with it, and gave me the reassurance to keep going. Also, to my animals, all the small ones, my cat Toony and my dogs Winnie and Roo. Roo hasn't chewed any copies of my book this time so that's good. There's still time though.

Lastly, to you, who have taken time to read this book (and even the acknowledgements). I'm grateful you chose to spend some of your time with me and I hope you found some enjoyment in these pages.

Credits

Chris McGeorge and Orion Fiction would like to thank everyone at Orion who worked on the publication of *A Murder at the Castle* in the UK.

Editorial
Francesca Pathak
Lucy Brem

Copy editor
Jo Gledhill

Proofreader
Jade Craddock

Audio
Paul Stark
Jake Alderson

Contracts
Anne Goddard
Dan Herron
Ellie Bowker

Design
Charlotte Abrams-Simpson
Joanna Ridley
Nick May

Editorial Management
Charlie Panayiotou
Jane Hughes
Bartley Shaw
Tamara Morriss

Finance
Jasdip Nandra
Nick Gibson
Sue Baker

Comms
Alainna Hadjigeorgiou

DON'T MISS A SINGLE NOVEL
FROM THE KING OF THE
LOCKED ROOM MYSTERY

ONE ROOM. FIVE SUSPECTS.
THREE HOURS TO FIND A KILLER.

GUESS WHO

'An impressive debut'
JAMES OSWALD

CHRIS McGEORGE

Six people went in.
Only one came out . . .

FROM THE AUTHOR OF
GUESS WHO

NOW YOU SEE ME

CHRIS McGEORGE

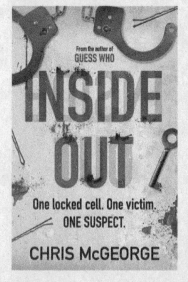

From the author of
GUESS WHO

INSIDE OUT

One locked cell. One victim.
ONE SUSPECT.

CHRIS McGEORGE

CHRIS McGEORGE

HALF PAST TOMORROW

She has twenty-four hours
to stop a murder . . .